MW01324829

The Sin Eater

The Sin Eater

Jacques S. Whitecloud

Writers Club Press
San Jose New York Lincoln Shanghai

The Sin Eater

Writers Club Press
an imprint of iUniverse.com, Inc.

For information address:
iUniverse.com, Inc.
5220 S 16th, Ste. 200
Lincoln, NE 68512
www.iuniverse.com

ISBN: 0-595-17522-8

Printed in the United States of America

Dedication

Thank you, Grandmother, Grandfather, and All My Relations; thank you, Tulane School of Medicine; Susan Barrett, for suffering drafts; Lee Deigaard, for suffering more drafts; Greg Brewster, who now has a medical school named after him; you, for reading. Yap if you like it and spread the word.

I

Henry would be $160,000 in debt by the time he finished Brewster Medical College in New Orleans. He doodled the figure on the corner of a box. He was unpacking.

"Human life means that much to me, I guess," he muttered to himself. If he owed that much money to the mob instead of the bank, he would be dead.

He kept his guns in a locked steamer trunk. He could explain his love for them no better than other men could their love for football or cars: it had always been there. He had grown up in New Orleans. An only child, his parents had moved to Tampa after he left for college. He was a little over six feet tall, and knew that he was more shy than he should be. In a week he would be 22.

His building stood on Bienville Street at the edge of the French Quarter, a few blocks from the medical school. Ferns squirted from between the bricks in the wall that faced the school. His was a walk-up, furnished apartment, with a fair-sized kitchen and bath, and a cavernous living room separated by a set of French doors from the bedroom. The living room had a long table and a folding chair against one wall, which he would use to study once school started. He had taped black garbage bags over the windows, because in college he had studied in a big closet that received no natural light, and he was superstitious about breaking the habit now. Studying in a closet was disorienting, especially in

California. He would go outside and it would be dark, but everybody on the street was tan.

Another set of French doors opened from the bedroom to the balcony. Mounted in the transom above one door was an insufficient air conditioner. He had forgotten what it was like to sweat all the time, and that the sweat was impossible to wipe away because any cloth or towel already felt damp. Even paper felt wet. He remembered a big rain purging the air every afternoon in August, but it hadn't happened since he had been back.

* * *

For a break from unpacking, he opened the trunk to handle the guns:

The AR-15. It looked just like an M16. This was the twin brother who had been missed by the draft–civilians could buy one. He could see himself kneeling in a rice paddy with this gun, wearing a dripping poncho and keeping sleepless eyes on the jungle.

The Mossberg 12-gauge pump with a magazine extension. Potbellied and able, the sheriff in mirrored sunglasses rests it on one hip.

The Glock 17 9mm. He had wanted an automatic handgun, but he didn't like this one much once he had shot it. With no external safeties, a plastic frame, and sixteen shots plus one POPPOPPOPPOPPOP. It was too easy. He was a gun lover, and he was surprised it was legal. When it was loaded he could feel it hum.

And a .38 blue-steel Smith and Wesson two-inch snub-nosed Detective Special revolver. This was the cheapest of the lot, with just a nip compared to the others' bites, but it was essential. Get out your Fedora and act black and white. Everybody in those old movies talks fast.

The AR-15 was the real prize. Bought before the assault weapons ban, it still had the bayonet lug and a barrel threaded to receive a flash suppressor or silencer. Only a police department or an army could legally buy or sell this gun now.

Ammunition and registration for each weapon were kept separately, in the old white wardrobe with the mirrors on the doors. He called the wardrobe an "armoire" because that sounded like "armory." He ran coated cables through the breeches of the rifle, Glock, and shotgun, and through the frame of the revolver. These cables were then locked to a heavy wheel he had bought at a junkyard, and the wheel sat at the bottom of the trunk. He would feel terrible if one of his guns got stolen and killed somebody. Within the chest, each gun was wrapped in its own rich towel to protect its finish.

His landlord told him that pirates had built the place in 1650. Unlikely, since the city wasn't there yet until 1804. But just because pirates hadn't built his place didn't mean it wasn't creepy. The wall in the stairway turned to dust when he rubbed hard on it with his thumb. The ceilings were high enough that an invisible, twin room hung up there. It was easy to think so at night, since the light from his bedside lamp couldn't reach the ceiling. As he went to sleep, he thought, if I die in here my ghost will move up to the ceiling and live in the empty space.

* * *

Brown and windowless, Brewster College of Medicine had been left by a glacier in what would later be downtown New Orleans, two blocks from Canal Street. A display case in the lobby contained lead balls removed by Brewster surgeons in the war between the states. There was a saw used to take off legs.

Orientation day began at 8:00 AM with the finest free breakfast he had ever seen, with little quiches, shrimp and redeye gravy, and grits. A table had an orientation folder for each of them with a typed tag clipped to it. His read *HI MY NAME IS Henry Marrier UC Berkeley*. He was glad for the tags because he was terrible at introductions. He recognized Iago Pachary, from high school; he hadn't seen him since. But he pretended not to know him. He hadn't liked high school, and wanted to erase it.

Each student received a cotton tote bag, a hardcover book of stories about doctors, free pens, vouchers to start cellular phone service, letter openers, and penlights. These were gifts from drug companies. Coupons were given by local businesses who couldn't afford gifts.

"We received sixteen thousand, four hundred applicants for this year's class. Those applicants represented the best that American universities had to offer; the one hundred sixteen students in this room represent the best of *that* best," said the dean in his opening remarks. Henry looked around the auditorium and thought they looked like students anywhere; still, he got chills.

After ID and class composite photos, they were appointed to groups of four with two upperclassmen advisers. Henry had two jokers with a routine. Both were from California, but said that they had medical school at Brewster figured out:

"Medical school isn't hard; it's just like drinking from a fire hydrant going full blast—" said the first.

"—and New Orleans has the highest per capita murder rate in the country," said the second.

Neither was the first to say so. They elaborated: don't try and learn everything you're told, or you won't sleep until Christmas; the note sets are more important than textbooks; don't walk anywhere in the city after dark; don't carry guns because a freshman a year earlier had dropped his in a crowded elevator.

Henry asked, "What kind of gun was it?"

Neither of them knew. They were taken on the same tour of the medical school that each of them had received on their admissions interview. The tour ended back in the auditorium with a video on hand-washing. Next they were herded single file into a conference room beneath baleful portraits from when doctors wore black. A nurse at the door told them to roll up a sleeve, and they were immunized against tetanus, measles, mumps, rubella, and hepatitis B. The shots hurt more than he had expected, and he wasn't the only one. He saw a lot of brimming eyes. They were given a shot receipt on the way out. The bottom of the sheet said in bold face that nothing could protect him from hepatitis C and HIV, and by becoming a health care provider he had just entered risk groups for both.

That night the upperclassmen had scheduled a cocktail party. Classes started the next day. He still felt flustered about having forgotten his jacket and tie for the class composite—he had borrowed—and didn't want to make another mistake tomorrow. He knew that they would begin with dissection of the back, so he read the pages in the lab dissector and ran over almost every word with a Highlighter.

New Orleans had opened a casino on Canal Street. It was a handsome building with a green copper roof; beneath its eaves was a line of taxicabs. He took a cab from there to the party.

The happy hour was held in a bar in the Warehouse District. The clean streets reminded him of San Francisco, but this was New Orleans. Forget jackets, avocados, and rocks, even gravel. Remember shorts, shrimp, and sea shells spread over parking lots and between railroad ties. The yankees showed up sweating, and they picked with trepidation at the boiled crawfish in washtubs on the floor.

He couldn't remember any names. He had suffered with terrible acne until he was twenty, and nights like this he could feel the ghosts of his pustules in plaques on his cheeks. He had gotten away with only a few scars and now had a forgettable face, which was fine with him.

Parties in college had reminded him of parties in high school; this med school party reminded him of junior high. Girls spoke to girls, boys to boys, and no one to him. At least he could get drunk legally. He drank more than he had planned and got another cab home. It wasn't late, but he got in bed, since tomorrow started with an 8:00 AM Gross Anatomy lecture.

He wished he weren't alone tonight. Catherine had been his girlfriend through most of college. In the dark she once had said, "I knew I loved you when we visited my family and you read to my little brother on the back steps."

Without thinking, he had said the truth: "I knew I loved you one night when you were brushing your teeth on the toilet."

She was a romantic and didn't like that at all. But now he remembered her talking around her toothbrush in the bathroom, and her knees, and he just ached.

He heard that Catherine had gone to graduate school in Michigan.

* * *

The head of the Gross Anatomy department was from Mississippi and talked like it. "This is primarily a laboratory course. These are the rules of the laboratory. Do not use the bone-saws without permission. They cost about a thousand bucks a piece, and your tuition is high enough without paying for broken saws. Do not pry out gold fillings; grave robbing will not be tolerated. Finally, all body parts will stay in their lab of origin. That means a penis from Lab A will not be found in Lab D. I only use that example because every year we have problems with a penis errant." This drew some titters from the class, and they were dismissed for lab.

The labs were on the third floor. The doors had smoked glass windows, and beneath them red plastic signs that said ANATOMY LABORATORY ABSOLUTELY NO ADMITTANCE WITHOUT PERMISSION. Old schools and LSU had all the cadavers laid out on tables in one room the size of a warehouse; the tables and cabinets could be rolled out of the way and the room hosed down. Brewster's Gross Anatomy department used smaller labs, with four cadavers to a room and four students to a cadaver. Each student had a numbered, secure lab cabinet and desk space already labeled with his or her name—as at the free breakfast, Henry felt pampered. The cadavers were held in rectangular tubs on wheels called tanks; doors closed them up at night. Closed, the cadaver tanks looked like stainless-steel food warmers laid flat, being brought to the restaurant hospital on stretchers. Oversized flourescent lights and swing-out lamps mounted on the tables minimized shadows.

His lab instructor was an iron, Southern woman who had been teaching Gross for twenty years, on cadavers that were bigger than she was. She had the students stand arranged in a semicircle in front of her.

"How many of y'all here have seen a cadaver before?"

All hands went up. They had been shown on the tour.

"How many people had trouble getting to sleep last night?" she asked with a smile.

Fewer hands went up, and there were some nervous chuckles. Henry didn't raise his hand; he was going to be a surgeon and knew that this would be his best class.

"Okay, what you will find is that cadavers don't even look like people anymore. A lot of the time you can't even tell if the person was black or white. They're just kind of beige now. Now if we were in a morgue, that would be a different story.

"You will also find that your Anatomy Atlases show nerves as being yellow, arteries as being red, and veins as blue. That's kind of like how Louisiana is green on a map. In a cadaver everything is brown or white. You will have to learn how to tell arteries from nerves, and the only way to do that is to come to lab. It's against Brewster policy to require attendance at anything, but it isn't against policy to bribe y'all. Ten percent of your final grade will come from me. So be here. These people gave their bodies for y'all to learn. I also help write the test, and I give lectures that can be very, very, very helpful.

"Clean up every day after yourselves. Nobody likes messy doctors." She pointed. "See this garbage can that says 'human remains only'? That means human remains only. Don't let me catch anyone throwing scalpel blades or gloves in there. Gloves go in the regular garbage. Scalpel blades go in the sharps bucket, there on the wall. See this thing that looks like a sink you can flush, this toilet sink? Don't let me catch you putting cadaver parts down the toilet sink. I better not see an arm in there, like I did one year. It shouldn't clog up. But it could.

"These are the same cadavers you will be tested on in the practical. That means that it pays to do good dissections and to take care of them. You have to keep your cadaver moist or it will dry up on you and make everything look even more alike than it already does. So at the end of the lab get a bottle of the cadaver cologne from there in the spigot jug and wet them down. It's just dilute formalin, so it won't do anything to you but make you stink. Maintenance is supposed to keep that full, but if not, water will do.

"About stinking: you are going to. There's no way to avoid it. You go to eat a sandwich for lunch and even though you wore gloves and washed up, your hands stink like cadaver. At night you can smell it in your hair. For you chemistry majors, it's the fomaldehyde that makes it stink and the phenol that makes it kind of greasy and hard to get off your skin. The best you can do sometimes is mask it. Washing your hands with alcohol and then with toothpaste works pretty well.

"I don't really care what you wear to lab, but I wouldn't wear anything nice in case you get squirted. I see some of you already have dissection gowns from the bookstore, those are fine. The gunners who are going for surgery all seem to wear scrubs. That's fine, but don't steal them from the hospital."

Henry only had a dissection gown—he had to get over to the hospital and steal some scrubs

"Lab safety." She turned to the table behind her and picked up some silver instruments. "This is a scalpel. Scalpels are sharp. They will cut your skin, muscle, and nerves just like they cut through your cadaver. To change a blade, use hemostats and pry it up on the bottom here, then slide it off *with the hemostats.* Grab the sharp part of the new blade *with the hemostats* and slide it on. Every year I give a demonstration, and every year we have an accident. Usually it's one of the boys in scrubs.

"Now the tanks. You see those handles at either end that look like shopping cart handles? Those are the levers you use to pull the cadaver up. Get one person on either end of the table and push down until they lock into place. *Don't let go until it's locked.* If the cadaver drops and swings that lever back up with your chin right there you're going to lose all your teeth. Another thing: don't stand on the handle. A couple years ago a student stood up on it to see a structure better and leaned over too far. Her cadaver weighed about two-fifty and she got catapulted in the air and landed on top of it. She wasn't wearing but shorts and a t-shirt and got it all over her."

The room was quiet, waiting to hear that she was a joking. She continued:

"No questions? Okay, the first thing you're going to do is take the bag off your cadaver and wash it down, then get all the hair off it. Every other year we had razors; this year somebody forgot. After that, get as far as you can on the back."

* * *

He had nicknames for his table mates within minutes. He would remember nicknames.

Eager wore her hair in a ponytail and was raring to go.

Earnest was sincere and from Broken Bow, Nebraska.

Chinese Guy was Chinese. He had gone to Yale.

They all wore the brown dissection kimonos and latex gloves sold in the bookstore. Their cadaver was a male in a clear, plastic bag tied at the top like a bag of garbage. Eager tried to pick the tie open, but it was sealed to itself. Henry could feel his heart beating. He took a pair of scissors and cut a slit in the bag from the gut to the feet, and Chinese Guy ripped the bag the rest of the way up. The same went on at the other tables. The room smelled like a burning tire thrown in a pool of old urine.

"Look how much his toenails grew since he died," said Eager.

The cadaver's toenails curled half an inch away from the ends of his toes.

"That's a myth," Henry said, "The soft tissue contracts, and the nails don't."

Their cadaver had been a tall man when he was alive. On a table he was just big, and hairy. They did their best to remove the hair with the scissors from their kits. But while the large scissors might work well on flesh, they weren't sharp enough for hair, and the little cuticle scissors were too small. So they ripped the hair out. Eager busied herself with the cuticle scissors on its head hair.

The other two guys winced and groaned and laughed as they ripped hair from the chest and armpits. Henry was proud that he only winced when ripping out the pubic hair. He had done a lot of lab work, some of it cruel. He had collected semen samples from bullfrogs. If he could grab a live bullfrog by the legs, whack its head on the lab bench, and draw semen from its cloaca with a syringe, he could deal with a dead body that didn't even look like it had ever been alive. The face was bloated like the bullfrogs' had been, and the scrotum big and blue like a dirty cartoon.

Earnest walked up with two stainless steel bowls of sudsy water and squares of cheesecloth. They washed it, silently. The gentle washing made Henry uneasy for some reason.

"How do we do the back?" Eager asked. "Do we turn him over? Are we allowed to do that?" She hurried to find the lab instructor.

When she returned, she said, "She's like, of course we're supposed to turn him over, how else are we going to do the dissection? I just wanted to be sure."

It took all four of them to turn him over. He was stiff, with only a little wobble to his legs. Henry had been to a Texas barbecue. The meat was between black grates with handles on either end, flipped by two men. The cadaver flipped the same way.

Everybody else was being coy about washing between the legs, so Henry went ahead and did that. Then he washed the right hand. It was cupped, with the palms back. And for no reason, this came to him as plain as words: my own hand would feel like this through the rubber glove. Cold, wet, and white.

He let the stiff thing go, washed up the arm, and under it. Despite himself, he returned to the hand. He still felt like he was shaking hands with himself. It made him queasy, and that was embarrassing. He hoped his face didn't show that.

Earnest wanted to cut first. So did Chinese Guy. So did Eager. The small town in Earnest won out. "Ladies first," he said, and stepped away.

"Women," she corrected.

Chinese guy said nothing.

The cadaver was prone, its face pressed into the table. Following a diagram in the dissector, Eager made a tentative slice from the inion to the twelth thoracic vertebra, then from T7 transversely to the right, then to the left. At first they all stood as if at a bedside, then without realizing pulled closer, closer, each working with two hands now. All except Henry. He couldn't forget the hand.

He volunteered to write down the identifying marks, as instructed by the dissector. No one paid him the slightest attention. If the three of them had wondered the night before if they had the stomach to hack Gross Anatomy, you couldn't tell now. Now they were ready to hack the cadaver to pieces to get at the greasy knowledge inside.

The lettering from a hospital or morgue band had bled backwards onto the man's ankle. Henry couldn't read what it said. He remembered that the cadaver's chest had been covered with moles that now felt like warts. He drew some warts on the chest of the figure in the dissector.

Lab was over two hours later. They hadn't gotten far. The latissimus dorsi were cleaned of fat and fascia, and contrary to what the instructor had said, looked exactly as the atlas showed—a set of red and silver wings beneath the skin. It was beautiful. I really am in medical school, he thought.

They soaked cheesecloth and paper towels in cadaver cologne and draped them over the muscles and closed the skin over it all. Dead legs and arms were spiraled in paper towel and cologne poured over them. Dissection kits were washed in the toilet sink, and instruments slid back into their loops in the kits. I didn't even use mine, Henry realized. From the tank he scooped up the scraps of yellow fat mixed with hair in his gloved hands. It didn't bother him like the hand; in fact, he wondered what it would feel like without the gloves. Maybe he was just more hung over than he had earlier thought. He dumped the mess in the human remains can. Where did it go after that?

In the hall bathroom he washed his hands for a long time. No one else was in there. He tried washing his hands as shown in the hand-washing orientation video: crank out the paper towel first; let it hang there. Then wet the hands, squirt some soap on them, scrub for at least fifteen seconds, paying special attention to the wrists and between the fingers. Then rip off the paper towel and pat the hands dry, and using the same towel turn off the faucet so as not to recontaminate yourself. He felt like a surgeon. I'm going to wash my hands this way for the rest of my life, he thought happily.

But in the afternoon Histology and Embryology lectures, he could still smell it.

After buying rubbing alcohol at the Woolworth's on Canal Street, he decided he should celebrate somehow before doing the reading for tomorrow. He remembered a place he used to go for muffalettas. The place was gone, replaced by a coffee shop manned by a sullen transvestite.

A daiquiri shop on Bourbon Street featured pizza in a display case. He asked for a slice, and the cashier put it in the microwave on a paper plate. She looked like she should be in high school. He sat at the counter and ate.

A black man was spraying out the shop with a gun nozzle on the end of a brown hose. Henry lifted his feet. The man pushed the water at the door with a squeegee. One whiff and Henry knew he was home. All of Bourbon Street smelled like the floor, sweet enough to twinge the jaw. Mardi Gras smelled like that.

Across the street a woman stood in a Southern belle's petticoats and red dress, fanning herself. The fan was a menu from the restaurant where she worked, she had a tattoo, and the dress was a petroleum product. Tourists wandered in and out of t-shirt shops with drinks in their hands; there were open container laws where they were from. The t-shirts shops sprayed the street with the sort of jazz that no one listens to anymore.

He smelled the cadaver as he brought the pizza to his mouth. The smell wasn't so bad that he lost his appetite, but he smelled it nonetheless. He thought of its hand in his.

It's what you smell like after you die, he thought. Everyone in heaven smells like burnt piss.

* * *

Back at North American Martyrs' High School of New Orleans, he had been taught that he was on earth for the greater glory of God. Implied was that if he lived a life devoted to church and school, he would make it to heaven. In those days he wore a scapula—if he died in an accident wearing it, he was automatically in. The Virgin Mary said so. He didn't like swimming because that meant taking it off, and if he drowned, he would die forever.

Then, in college Biology he learned that an individual's purpose in life was to reproduce. He traded the scapula around his neck for a condom in his wallet. But a condom would prevent reproduction, and his biological purpose was not to get laid, but to perpetuate his genome. Like a gull or a bee, all Henry was here to do was to keep his DNA on earth. Over the generations it would be washed away, but a few generations is better than one lifetime.

He believed Biology, because without DNA there would be no people, and with no people, no church. He also believed that the only afterlife was to have kids or to donate organs. His driver's license authorized the harvest of his corneas, heart, lungs, and kidneys. In case of accident, he would go on.

The cadaver wasn't going anywhere. Regardless of whether the dead man had children, he was still dead in a tank. That was not debatable. He smelled the proof on his hands.

2

There were no more free breakfasts. After three days, all that school had to give him was work. He was sitting on his balcony, so exhausted that he felt like he was vibrating. The balcony was held up by metal braces stuck into the wall; he worried it might collapse. He tried to imagine the breeze into more than it was. It came off the river with the smell of brown water under calliope music. One of the paddle wheels for river tours still had a steam calliope on deck.

No lectures were scheduled on Friday afternoon. Ronaldo was coming to pick him up.

Ronaldo was his best friend from high school. They were the same age, but Ronaldo had the experience on him. While Henry had his nose stuck in books all these years, Ronaldo had been a student, a lawn mower, a jukebox delivery man, a bingo caller, and a drug dealer. Henry hadn't seen him in three years, because Henry had gone to Tampa for the holidays after his parents moved. They hadn't even talked much on the phone, because Ronaldo thought his phone was tapped. Maybe it had been, because he got busted. But Ronaldo had gotten off because his dad was a policeman.

Someone Ronaldo had met through dealing had gotten him a mortician's apprenticeship, which would lead to a respectable job. Now Ronaldo had a job for Henry: he would get paid a hundred bucks just to study.

"The only catch," Ronaldo had said over the phone, "is that somebody's got to have a funeral."

Ronaldo had said that he would pick him up and take him to meet their boss. He was late. Henry leaned over the railing again to look for a car. On the corner across the street was an auto shop with an open parking lot, and a sagging fence around a small storage yard. Tires leaned in a pile against the fence, gathering rainwater to hatch mosquitoes to spread yellow fever. A black man, woman, and small boy walked toward it. The boy saw Henry watching. Henry waved, and the boy waved back. The woman looked up, saw Henry, then said something to the man. He did not look up. The man hopped the fence. He threw over four tires. He carried two, the woman one, and the boy tried to roll along the last. They stole them, just like that.

A hearse came up Bienville. It wasn't a proper hearse, but a Bronco painted silver, with no windows in the back and a metal integral sign where a window should have been. The top was upholstered with tough, gray vinyl. It looked like a car with hydrocephalus. An advanced hydrocephalic's skull sat in the trophy case at school, taking the space of two shelves. The bone was solid from teeth to eye sockets. From there it spread thinner than an eggshell. After the shell, only scalp had held the brain and water in. That skull was big enough to hold two volleyballs.

Henry went inside, and found himself running down the stairs. Quit smiling, he thought.

Ronaldo had left the hearse running at the curb with the hazard lights blinking. The last time they had seen each other, each had just begun to shave.

Even in high school, Henry had never seen Ronaldo wearing a T-shirt. Now he was wearing black triple-pleated pants, black boots, and a white shirt with starched cuffs. His black tie sucked light. He looked more shrewd. Ronaldo's grandfather had also been a New Orleans police officer, and until he got busted, Ronaldo was also going to join the force. Now his father wouldn't stand for it. Henry doubted Ronaldo would've been able to stand the uniforms.

"Look how big you got on me!" Ronaldo said. Henry had grown four inches in college.

Henry's fingers shoved the new skin on Ronaldo's forehead. "Shit, Ronaldo, you're going bald." It was no use–he couldn't keep the smile off.

Ronaldo yanked on Henry's bangs. "Shut up with your California ass!"

They stood there with nothing to say. Henry felt like hugging; Ronaldo felt like it and did it. The slapped each other's backs twice, and got in the hearse. White curtains could be drawn across the back, but they were open now. A plywood slab with Astroturf nailed to it lay back there. The coffins slid on top. There was no radio. A cellular phone was plugged into the lighter. Ronaldo drove them toward the interstate. "How's school? Hard?" Ronaldo asked.

"It's not hard, really. There's a lot of it," Henry said. He was already feeling guilty about not studying. "I think the key is just not to stress out too much."

"Let me get this straight," Ronaldo said, "you spent the summer after your graduation beating off frogs?"

* * *

They got off the interstate in a blank subdivision in Metairie. At least the yards were big. Ronaldo pulled down an unpaved back alley and into somebody's covered car port and killed the engine. On the other side of the alley was a small trailer park. Henry wondered where the funeral home was.

Henry figured Ronaldo was pulling a joke, but he climbed out.

"This is it?" Henry said.

"Chicken shit, isn't it?" Ronaldo said, "The funeral home I run is going to have columns on the front." Ronaldo had a strong New Orleans accent—a Brooklyn one, slowed by heat, and with "y'all". It should be called a Metairie accent now, because everyone who talked that way moved to the suburbs out of fear and distrust of the blacks in Orleans Parish.

Ronaldo unlocked the heavy door that opened from the car port. A small ramp ran up to the door. Henry had been expecting columns, and a line of hunchbacked, black hearses—real hearses. This funeral home had been somebody's house, and a small one. But it had real, blue painted wood, not siding or fake brick like the houses on either side.

Henry followed him down a hallway; he could see the spots in the paint where picture hooks had been. The doors had been replaced with heavy, institutional ones with locks in the knobs. They took a left and were in the front office. It had been the dining room. A picture window faced the street. Ronaldo stopped in the doorway.

"Mr. Landry isn't here," Ronaldo said. "He said he would be here." He walked around the desk and sat in the burgundy chair, picked up the phone, and began dialing.

Henry walked to the window and looked out at the lawns. Was it legal to embalm in a neighborhood like this? The house had a small, shaded porch, and hanging from the underside was a painted sign, too small to be seen from the street:

PALACE SPRINGS
FUNERAL HOME

All the other funeral homes in town had triple proper names, like law firms.

Ronaldo hung up, dialed another number, waited, and hung up again. "Fuck him," he said, "I'll tell you about the job. I told you how somebody's got to die, right?"

Two armless chairs stood in front of the desk. There was a couch against the wall. Henry sat in one of the chairs. It was uncomfortable and needed arms. It wouldn't be pleasant to sit in one of these chairs and talk money. Next to the desk blotter was a large box of tissue.

"Here's what I meant," Ronaldo said, "We're cut rate. We get people that fucked up their funeral plans somehow, or else they don't give a shit about who died. We specialize in broke and unprepared people. That's really old deceased and young deceased.

"Now here's where you come in. If you want to rob a house, what do you do?"

"I break into it," Henry said.

"And you don't want nobody there, right? Well, how are you guaranteed that no one will be home?" Ronaldo enjoyed stretching out the presentation like this. "You check the obituaries. You got first and last name, and when the funeral is going to be held. Get a phone book, find the address, and you're guaranteed at least 45 clear minutes to rob somebody blind. Longer, if there's a wake."

"You got to be kidding me, Ronaldo," Henry said.

Ronaldo laughed. "Welcome home. People who know their loved one's going to die, they ask for a friend of the family to watch the house. But for a lot of young people, everyone they know goes to the funeral. The funeral's like a wedding. And these old people have no one left that can watch over their place."

"What about the young people's neighbors?" Henry asked, "If I died in high school, we could have gotten the old lady next door."

"We had one kid who died in a three-wheeler accident in Harvey. His parents asked the neighbors, who were this illiterate trailer trash from the River Parishes. They got back from the funeral and the white trash asshole and his friends had stole the damn refrigerator. Not only that, but the house was a double, and they smashed through the wall into the other half. No one from the street could see. They ripped off all the stuff that belonged to the lady in the other half. Her refrigerator. They didn't just steal, either, they put more holes in the walls, for no reason. The neighbors were watching from outside and thought the family must be moving after the death."

"So you want me to watch the houses," Henry said.

"Mr. Landry will pay a hundred bucks to anybody who can housesit for these people while we bury their stiff. I suggested you. Who isn't going to trust a medical student. Y'all are ethical as shit. All you got to do is answer the phone and the doorbell. Other than that, you can bring your books and notebooks and whatever and study."

"The house of some dead stranger doesn't sound like a good place to study," Henry said.

Ronaldo leaned back and put his fingertips together, taking on the airs of a boss. "It's all a sad comment on the human condition, I know," he said. He sighed, "But who am I to talk about the human condition. I got a jar full of gold fillings, back there in the cold room where we keep the meat. Gonna take those fillings to Adler's and get a ring made and make some lucky girl very happy."

"I got bad eyes," Henry said, "If you find any contacts, can I have them?"

At this they both smiled. It was like no time passed in all. Ugly jokes were their specialty. Ronaldo was the only person that had ever made Henry feel witty.

Ronaldo said, "Want the job or not?"

"I'll have to think about it."

"Don't think too long. I need you tomorrow."

"*Tomorrow*?"

"It would help me out tons, Hank," Ronaldo said, "Otherwise I got to drive him to the funeral and then hustle back and watch their house, then get back here."

"Who was it?" Henry said, "Did you embalm him?"

"I helped," Ronaldo said, "I'm getting to be pretty okay at it."

"That doesn't bother you?" Henry said.

"It's just like you and the cadavers at school," Ronaldo said.

Henry hadn't touched the cadaver after the first day. He didn't say so.

"What we do is actually harder than what y'all do, because all y'all do is cut. We have to be combination hairdresser, makeup artist, and plastic surgeon. And businessman." Ronaldo reached into a desk drawer and came out with a white binder with gilt edges. The cover could have said *Our Wedding*. "Check this out. These are coffins we sell." He pushed the book at Henry and turned it around.

There were bad photographs of caskets, taken in the room where they now sat. All the caskets were made of metal.

Ronaldo leaned across the desk, over the book. "You see how there's no prices? We put one cheap one here in front. They ask and we tell them: eight hundred. Then these next four pages are high, like in the thousands. About now they start to ask, how much? We tell them. They look unhappy. Then Mr. Landry turns the page and says, 'Now here's a handsome one that won't break your budget.' Look."

Henry looked. He flipped back to the first page. "This is the same one as the first one." It was even the same photograph.

Ronaldo laughed. "Yeah, but now it's eleven-hundred. Why else would it be hanging in the middle of the thousands, right?"

"Nobody else has noticed that?" Henry asked, "It's pretty obvious."

"To you. But you're not fucking delirious from lack of sleep. Nobody you know is dead," Ronaldo said, "We do get some cheap, heartless shits who might have noticed. They're burying some in-law. But most people don't want to seem cheap dealing with this stuff."

Henry handed the book back. "You get a lot of black clients?" he asked. He was thinking about what Ronaldo had said about "broke."

"Nope. I'll say this for them," Ronaldo said, "they bury their own."

"So who is this that died? The one whose house you want me for," Henry said, "Tomorrow's my birthday, by the way."

"Twenty two? Really? Happy birthday," Ronaldo said. "Some dead kid. I spackled up the bullet hole in his head."

"He shot himself, then?" Henry asked. White kids shot themselves; they didn't get shot.

"He did," Ronaldo said, "So you going to do it? You going to help me out?"

He could use the money. Moving had cost more than he had expected, and the first loan disbursement was weeks away. "Yeah, I'll help you out."

"Great!" Ronaldo said. "Here's the rules. Dress professional, but not too nice. You don't want to show the family up. Dress like me."

Henry looked at Ronaldo's boots, poking from beneath the desk. "You dress like a hit man."

"That's professional. And be sympathetic. Be on time."

"I don't have a car."

"You don't have a car?" Ronaldo was incredulous. Maybe he wouldn't need Henry after all. "Why didn't you say so?" He slumped in a chair. "Oh well. I'll pick you up. And one more thing—no guns, Hank."

* * *

Mr. Landry never called, or even showed up. Ronaldo had to leave to get an air filter for his mother's car. Ronaldo lived with his mom. Henry remembered her as a blonde who liked to smoke, sleep, and talk on the phone. And to flirt. Sometimes with him. She lived off two alimonies and some family money.

Ronaldo dropped him off at the medical school. Ronaldo's goodbye: "After the funeral, me and you will get fucked up."

He would go to the histology lab and do penance for wasting the afternoon by studying all night. A group of his classmates was standing outside, and they stopped talking to watch him get out of the hearse. He felt more infamous than embarrassed.

3

He woke up at 11:00 and paid attention to whether or not he felt older. His dad had offered to buy him another gun. He wasn't sure that he needed another.

He was in his underwear eating noodles when the doorbell rang. He pulled on some sweat pants and a t-shirt, ran downstairs, and found Ronaldo at the door.

"You're not even dressed!" Ronaldo said. Again, he was dressed well.

"You're early," Henry said.

"I'm late! Get dressed, I'm in somebody's driveway," Ronaldo said. He followed Henry upstairs.

Ronaldo said, "This place is gloomy. We ought to move the fucking funeral home here." He sat at the desk and glanced at all the papers there. He wasn't interested. He nodded at the French doors, with their windows covered with black plastic. "I've never seen garbage bag curtains. Why don't you cover the walls in toilet paper."

Henry grabbed his book bag and went into the bedroom. Ronaldo couldn't see him. He dropped the .38 revolver and six bullets into his bag and got dressed.

"Hurry up, Hank," Ronaldo said, "The kid in the truck's got to be in front the altar in a half hour."

Henry came out with the bag hanging from one hand, tucking in his shirt with the other. "He's going to be late for his own funeral," he said.

"And it would be so like him," Ronaldo returned.

He had figured Ronaldo had been joking upstairs. He wasn't. The hydrocephalic hearse was parked across the street, in a driveway, and the curtain was drawn across the back. Once inside, Henry pulled the curtain back. Looking back at him: a green metal coffin, like a square American car from the 1970's, and big enough for more people.

"I don't believe you," Henry said. He thought that Ronaldo would drive his own car.

"What?" Ronaldo said. He started the engine. "No jig walking by is going to fuck with a hearse. I can park this anywhere. They're afraid of ghosts."

"That's not what I meant," Henry said. He let the curtain fall back into place. He had his microscope in its plastic box between his knees.

The hearse didn't handle all stately like it carried a dead body. Ronaldo gave a loud honk to a person waiting for the green arrow to turn onto Canal Street, then cut around him. On the highway, other drivers yielded for them, and when passed, they looked away. Two high school guys in a jeep tried to see into the back.

"They act like we're cops," Henry said.

"That's cause I got the headlights on," Ronaldo said.

They got off the Interstate near City Park. Ronaldo pulled over near an arched bridge over a canal held in by a steep levee. Ronaldo got out of the hearse and said, "Come on."

Henry followed him up the levee. The canal was high with inky, smooth water. The sky was perfect in it.

"This is the address," Ronaldo said. From his pocket he pulled a slip of paper, crumpled like a gum wrapper. "I passed by yesterday. It's the first street on the other side of the canal. We can't see it because of the levee. The house is right about there." He pointed at an angle into the water.

He smoothed open the paper. "And the deceased's name is—was—Paul Oh Hines""

"What?" Henry said, "Let me see." Ronaldo showed him the paper.

"Not 'paul oh'," Henry said with a smile, "Paolo. It's a Latino name."

Ronaldo gave Henry the paper. He said, "What's with those clothes, dude?"

"These are professional clothes," Henry said. The pants made him sweat like they were made of garbage bags like his curtains.

Ronaldo looked at them in horror. "My God, Hank. Are those Dickies? Those are like our old uniforms. And those are our old uniform shoes." He looked to Henry's face for an explanation.

"Cheap," Henry said.

Ronaldo shook his head, turned, and walked down the levee.

"What am I supposed to do, Ronaldo? Don't leave me here," Henry called after him.

Ronaldo turned and said, "I got to get to the funeral. You just walk over there to the house and explain who you are. They expect you at 12:30. I'll pick you up when it's over."

"Why don't you just drop me off?"

"Think about it. Do they want to see that?" Ronaldo pointed at the hearse.

"I have forty minutes until then."

"Kill some time," Ronaldo called over his shoulder.

* * *

Before pulling off, Ronaldo remembered Henry's microscope and bag, and let him retrieve them. Henry walked over the bridge. He stopped to look into the canal. When he looked up, drivers were staring at him. He was thankful for the clouds; it was hot enough without sun beating down as well. He stopped in a Circle K to look at magazines, his bag and microscope close to him. He flipped through *Gun World*, then went outside and looked at the sky. More shapeless clouds had gathered. Maybe it would rain. The family would feel the funeral was more authentic.

In the Winn-Dixie supermarket next door he looked at the corn dogs and the tripe and a high school girl bagging groceries. She was pretty hot. The high school boy at the register saw him staring. The boy turned back to the conveyor belt, shaking his head slowly. Not in judgement, or disbelief. Like he was sad about something.

"Fuck you, peach fuzz," Henry muttered, "I'm a med student." He was blushing. But to leave now would admit defeat, so he went back to the magazine rack and picked up a teenage girls' magazine. There was a page which chronicled readers' embarrassing moments:

"I went to a dance. He brought me flowers, and everything. Then the DJ farted. No one else heard it, but I was so embarrassed for the guy that I made my date take me home!"

He let out a stage laugh, so that the kid at the register would hear.

If he took more time walking, he would only be a little early. The neighborhood was in the corner formed by an Interstate overpass and the canal. Oak trees canopied the streets, but this wasn't Uptown. The one-story houses were dressed with either yellow or red fake brick. This was like a suburb that had been cut off from its body. Toys bleached on a lawn.

At 12:20 he reached the house, which had red brick, an orange roof, and a concrete walk running between two squares of grass that needed mowing. Maybe that had been Paolo's job. An old American station wagon that looked like a frog was parked at the curb. He took a breath, rang the bell, and prepared himself to make small talk with a pained, understanding smile.

The man who answered the door said, "We don't have time."

Henry didn't know what to say. A suicide's father should be a bald businessman, or a pudgy lawyer. The man looked wrong, as did this house. It should have had a lot of glass to it, and a big yard; the tragedy was when a boy with so much going for him did it.

The man before Henry had the right exhausted eyes, but he was handsome and short like movie stars are in real life. He wore a black double-breasted suit, a short ponytail, and alloy glasses. He could be a carpenter, but the suit and glasses were too nice. He made a movement with his mouth and started to close the door.

"I'm from the funeral parlor," Henry said. He hadn't wanted to say "funeral."

The man looked him up and down. "I thought you were a Mormon," he said. He smiled and opened the door, looking curiously at the microscope case.

"I don't have a bike," Henry said as he stepped in.

"What?" the man said.

"I'd need a bike to be a Mormon."

The man looked at him politely.

"Don't worry about it," Henry said.

To the left of the front door was an empty table with four high-backed chairs around it. A white, plastic accordion-curtain was pulled across the room to the right. It swayed when the door closed.

A slight woman in a blue dress peeked from a hallway and came forward. She looked younger than the man, but her hair was silver. She let it hang over her shoulders. Henry wanted to stare, she was so beautiful. A tiny, gold SCUBA diver hung on a gold chain around her neck.

"You're early," she said.

From the corner of his eye Henry could see the man staring at him. Taking his measure as a guard of their house, he guessed. "I thought he was a Mormon," said the dad.

"It's this shirt and tie, I'm afraid," Henry said.

She reached a hand towards him and said, "Oh!" and laughed. The man smiled with his hands in his pockets. Henry laughed, but by then they had stopped. They started again so he wouldn't feel alone, but then all three of them saw it was just pointless.

"Why don't I show you the house," she said, emptily, "That goes to the bedroom and the bath." The man moved down the dark hallway she indicated. "The living room is there. And the kitchen is here."

They were standing in the kitchen. She opened the refrigerator, full to the top with Tupperware and plates covered in aluminum foil. These were gifts from the neighbors, no doubt, so that the family could worry only about grieving and not about preparing meals.

"We have lots of food," she confessed.

She shut the food away and moved quickly to show him where the dishes were. She didn't sound like she was from New Orleans, or even like a mother. She had the slow, sure voice of a professor, with an accent he couldn't place. "We only ask that you rinse your plate and put it in the dishwasher. Not too much to ask, I hope."

"No, ma'am," Henry said.

"Don't call me ma'am," she chided, "That makes me feel even older."

"Sure," Henry said.

"So you're a medical student," she said.

"Yes. Just starting."

"I've always thought that being a doctor took as much dedication as the clergy."

"Well, people are generally happier to see us standing over them," Henry said.

It was supposed to be a joke. But he shouldn't joke about *that* now. Not about dying. That part of her that could smile fell away. He saw the haggard, betrayed face of her insides.

His hand moved toward her shoulder, but he stopped it. It looked like he was waving at her from one foot away. She excused herself and went down the hall.

She came back with her daughter. She was about fourteen, and distracted by her good looks in her short black dress and polished combat boots. He would never act on it, but Henry had a dirty thing for girls like this, whose faces weren't developed yet so that they looked like monkeys. He knew this was because he had never had a girlfriend in high school, when he also looked like a monkey with acne. He looked at the teen magazines for pictures of girls like this one.

Her combat boots meant this: from this day on, the girl would wear whatever she wanted. She would stay out later and sleep with boys in the house, because her parents would think, what have we got to lose. Maybe they had been too strict with her brother. Maybe they could be more strict, and be sorry again, when she killed herself or ran away. She would accuse her parents of not caring as much about her. Henry could see her tiny ribs heave under the dress, wisps of calcium like a minnow's.

Henry followed the three into the foyer.

"This might be the best place for you to study," the mother said. She was facing the dining room table. Without realizing it, Henry had left his bag and microscope just inside the door when he came in. He shouldn't be so sloppy with a gun.

The father still stared at him–blazed at him. "Watch my house?" he said.

The girl chewed on the inside of her cheek.

"I'll take care of things here," Henry said.

He watched the door close and heard the dead bolt slide into place.

* * *

He thought of a mnemonic for the family name. Paolo was Latino, like South American; Hines was German. Pretend they were descendants of Nazi ex-pats.

His note binder was on the table before him. He could still hear it sliding out of his bag. He had never been in a house so quiet.

He would worry about Anatomy later. He would worry a lot about Anatomy, since he hadn't seen but flashes of the cadaver for the last week when the other three stepped back and held up some cut nerve, or pointed out a muscle. Right now he was more scared of Histology. He had never liked using microscopes. They hurt his neck and gave him a headache.

No one can point in Histology and ask if he's correctly identified a structure, since a finger would black out the whole field. The right eyepiece contained a wire arrow that projected down onto the field; but even when he maneuvered the field so that the arrow pointed to an arteriole or the collagen he was supposed to find, he would then find that the picture in his atlas was quite different. Ask the lab instructor for help and you get this:

"Use your imagination."

This was medical school? "Imagination?"

So today he would sit down with his lab guide, his own class notes, and microscope and pull everything together. Then tonight he would catch up on his Embryology reading, sitting with his Anatomy atlas open so he could better understand how all the mesenchyme matured. Then tomorrow he would do the Anatomy reading for the next week, and study the Atlas for the relevant structures covered—uncovered, rather—in the last week.

Happy birthday.

He plugged the microscope into a wall outlet, but the cord wasn't long enough, so he had to move the table. Remember to move it back, he thought. He began with a review of the slides covered in this week's labs.

Someone could easily sneak up on him while he had his eyes occupied. That's what he thought, instead of thinking of collagen.

He put the slides aside and studied his class notes with his hands on his forehead. Again, this blocked his vision. He leaned back and held the page at his waist. He listened to the silence.

He just went ahead and said it aloud: "Someone died in this house."

The chair opposite him didn't answer.

He unzipped his pencil pocket and drew out the revolver. An automatic with these clothes would be simply too Secret Service. With the blue steel .38 snub thrown on the table as carelessly as another paper, he was just a private dick getting his work done.

In a house where a kid shot himself.

He looked at the notes he had taken this last week; he could barely read them, and even if he could, they would make no sense. The professors just went too fast.

Behind the white accordion curtain across the hall was a room. He leaned back and regarded the curtain. The top half was in shadow. It was only about a quarter before one, but all the houses in this neighborhood had to be dark, under the clouds and overpass, and surrounded by the levee and trees. He had the light on over the table.

If I stare at that curtain long enough, he thought, I'll convince myself that it hides something awful.

He shook his head and smiled. Get to work.

Only three months ago he had studied for exams. Four months before that he had studied for exams. Now he was studying for an exam. A week from now he would be studying for an exam. "P equals MD," one of the jokers had said in orientation; it meant that even if you barely passed, you would still be a doctor. A doctor, but not a surgeon. If you weren't in the top ten percent of your class, you might as well just be a pediatrician. Chinese Guy and

Earnest also wanted surgery. And there were two more at every other table.

He opened the revolver and spun the cylinder. It spun as quietly as the house sat.

Did the curtain move?

Maybe a vent had come on, but he hadn't heard it. He was cold. Did it move, or not?

He looked at it. It didn't move.

He pushed the cylinder back into the frame and stood up with the gun in his right hand. Maybe someone was back there. He really doubted it, but he would go crazy if he didn't find out.

He took careful, quiet steps toward the curtain, and when he saw his left hand reaching to throw it open, and his right hand holding a steady gun, he smiled because he was in a movie.

He threw the plastic curtain aside.

Annoyed, he flicked on the light with the gun barrel. It was just a workroom. He guessed that the father worked in here and shut himself off from the rest of the house.

Along the walls were spools of naked wire and wooden bins containing circuit boards stacked as neatly as files. With a fax machine and a screwdriver this guy could assemble and sell computers, or something else that was useful. Instead he had a soldering iron and assembled earrings. He was an artist. On the wall hung a bulbous chrome hubcap with wavy sun rays cut from circuit board glued around the edge. A title tag was tacked next to it, just like in a museum: *Cyber Sun $600.*

Though he had never seen anything like it, he thought after seeing the title, That's not very original.

In the center of the room was a heavy table, like a chopping block, and on it lay a fine-toothed jigsaw and templates for circuit-board animals, smiley faces, skulls. The skulls, like the hubcap sun, were male things, and that's how he could tell it was the father that worked in here. He stuck on silver trim and a safety pin, and sold the skulls and animals as corny badges. Probably for too much money, too.

He did like the resistor necklace, hanging from the lamp over the work table. Colored bands that would encode Ohmage in a circuit made the resistors painted, even beads when strung end to end. He had never seen them as other than electronics.

Under the table was a box for sixteen small fire extinguishers, but seven were gone.

The phone rang. His skin prickled. He ran to the kitchen and answered the phone hanging by the refrigerator.

"Hello?"

The other end hung up.

He went back to the work room, gun in hand. He liked his bowed reflection in the hubcap. It felt good to play with a gun again. He hadn't played with them since he had gone away to school, since the laws on getting them into California were so strict.

Back in the dining room, he put the revolver away in his bag, and decided to quit fooling around and get some work done. He moved the microscope back to the edge of the table and put a slide on the stage. Outside the picture window to his right was a short concrete wall, holding back the levee, which held back tons of rain water.

* * *

He couldn't concentrate.

That phone call—someone had called to see if the house was empty. He should feel safer because he had answered, and that would deter a robbery. He got up and closed the blinds on the levee. Once he was standing, he realized he needed a study break. He hadn't seen the news in a week.

The living room was off of the kitchen. The television seemed too ancient for parents as young as these. Its cabinet had been manufactured of stained press board with artificial drawers to make it look like an antique. It was an antique. Come to think of it, the parents' chronology was also off. They seemed too young to have teenage children. The mother's hair was prematurely gray.

In front of the television was a sofa and a coffee table; on the table, an Asics shoe box. This house reminded him of a hotel. The pictures might have been bolted to the walls, if there were any pictures.

They had cable. He picked up the remote from the top of the cable box and sat on the sofa. On TV the old man was telling Scott Baio, "*You're in big trouble, Charles–*"

"—in charge," Henry said, just above a whisper. He didn't want to disturb the house.

Behind the sofa was room enough for someone to sneak up and stand over him, and a doorway to the bedroom hallway.

He changed the channel to MTV, to see the girls in the zit ads. At the bottom of his vision he kept seeing the Asics shoe box. He wanted to respect their privacy...well, it was their own fault for leaving it on the table like this. And he had already violated their privacy by going in the workroom.

There were photographs in the box, still in the developers' envelopes. When he saw them, he got chills.

The family had been in Berkeley. In one picture he could see the corner of his old building on the corner of University and Telegraph; he had probably been upstairs studying in the closet at the time, since the sun was shining. There by the stoplight was the boy who was being buried right now. Paolo Hines, about age fourteen. He posed with a skateboard between two police women in riot gear. The cops looked patient. There was usually at least one riot a semester in Berkeley.

The boy smiled, brown hair hanging over one eye. Henry used to be so jealous of good looking kids like that.

There was a whole roll taken of a day at the beach. It looked like Santa Cruz. There were individual shots of each family member in profile at sunset. Corny. The father was wearing white linen pants and carrying black tassel loafers. Henry had read that some cocaine king had died with his loafers in one hand, a gun in the other.

Paolo wore an old "Possessed to Skate" Suicidal Tendencies shirt. Then a shot of the daughter, younger and very monkey-looking, hugging her parents. Paolo had taken this picture, and Henry was seeing with his dead eye through the viewfinder.

Now he really felt like there was someone behind him. He was afraid to look, so he got up and walked over to the television and sat with his back against the screen. He used to do the same when he was little and their television was so big it needed floor space. His father had told him the electromagnetic field was going to mess up his brain.

The screen gave him more light, so he didn't need to squint. He hadn't thought to turn on the light when he came in. Pictures of old people and the children; pictures of the parents when younger, taken on a wooden deck. They stood with beers in their hands, looking barely older than Henry. Men and women in t-shirts talked in the background. A red-bearded man pointed at something in the trees and smiled. The father with hair hanging down his back dropped sliced tomatoes in a pot. The kids were out of the picture a lot of the time.

Family pictures must be in an album on a closet shelf in the master bedroom, Henry thought.

Paolo had been good-looking and happy in California. The state did it to you. When he had been at school there, Henry had sometimes felt good-looking and happy himself. Further down in the box the boy got younger, but the whole time Henry could tell that he smoked a lot of dope. From the backgrounds he gathered that the family had lived around Northern California. There were no pictures of New Orleans, since they were refugees from California. That would explain the family's preternatural beauty, and the father's jewelry making. They hadn't gotten fat yet. He better find another job, Henry thought; not enough people here have money to blow on his sort of art.

Paolo couldn't take the meanness of kids down here, or sweating all the time. That's what happens when you leave the Bay Area for a real place. You kill yourself.

He put the pictures away and decided to take a look around the kitchen; maybe he would eat something. He felt he was being watched, maybe sniffed at. He tried to ignore it.

He opened the cabinets. Two health food cookbooks. None of the pages were stained. An older book of home remedies. None of the pages were stained. Maybe the family had just moved, and the rest of their stuff hadn't arrived yet. There were four glasses, four plates, and four bowls. One set for mom, one for dad, one for daughter, and one now for Henry.

There was about half a cooked cow in the refrigerator, and boiled crawfish in a garbage bag. The neighbors had been generous. He stood at the open refrigerator door with a plate in his hand. He saw the Tupperware and thought, it's stacked as tall as Paolo. I'll take out a square and his eyes will be peeking out at me.

"I'm out of here," he said aloud.

He had said it as a joke, but the house had made him uneasy from the moment they had locked him in. Now it was making him anxious, especially after seeing the pictures. He would go in the yard for a few minutes.

The back door wouldn't open.

He laughed to let it be known that he had a sense of humor, then tried again. It wouldn't open.

He looked at the bolt again. It wasn't locked. The door should have opened for him.

He jerked on the knob. He kicked the door. He could feel the refrigerator behind him, and was cursing rather loudly when he saw that there was another lock in the knob. He turned it and the door opened.

He stumbled into the plain, empty yard. The neighbors on all sides had grown dark green hedges. No one could see him, unless they hid in the hedges. He needed a cigarette. He didn't smoke, but it seemed the right thing to do in a situation like this.

The back door was open. The last, loudest word he had yelled while beating the door was "Please." He was talking to Paolo, whose ghost was in the refrigerator. In all the meat left by the neighbors in Paolo's stead.

He had always loved guns and always feared ghosts; he didn't like to talk about either, because people would think he was a nut. He thought this job would help him get over it; it wasn't working. When he was five, he had told his mother that ghosts were in his room when she wasn't there. She had too many shirts and dresses for her closet, and stored the overflow in his room. She thought that her clothes, hanging there on a rack, looked to him like people when the lights were out. She had turned on the light and run a hand over the dresses and shirts with a harmless smile.

She could be so dense. He *knew* that they were clothes. The ghosts were in the fabric. The ghosts were in toys left out on the floor.

Ghosts weren't dead people until he got older and learned that. The pressure he felt from an empty chair—and he had felt pressure from the chair opposite him in the family's dining room—that pressure was an invisible dead person, by nature of its ghostliness, jealous and evil.

Here he was, twenty-two, with a Molecular Biology degree and a spot in med school, and still he had run out of the house.

Ashamed of himself, he went back inside and locked the door again. He looked through the big window behind the television. Outside was the yard where he had just been. He might as well look in Paolo's room. That would show this house who was boss.

There were three doors down the dark hallway. One door was plain—the parents' room, he guessed. On the next door hung a collage of "You mean he LIKES me?" lines cut from teen magazines, mixed in with pictures of skinny models hugging each other—the girl's room. At the end of the hall, by the bathroom, was a door with a Grateful Dead poster. The one with the skeleton in a red, white, and blue top hat sitting on a hill, holding its knees and looking down at the Golden Gate Bridge.

He opened the Grateful Dead door. There were two rectangular windows high on one wall, as if the room were in a basement. Sun would get in here for only about an hour a day. He turned on the light. Beneath the light switch was a dresser. There was no bookshelf. Against the wall beneath the windows was a mattress on a box spring, the sheets twisted onto the floor. Black ivy drawn in permanent marker crept up the wall, toward the sunlight. Paolo's artist father had allowed him to draw on the walls.

I wonder if he shot himself in here, Henry thought. It gave him goose bumps, and he looked for blood and hair. None. For no reason at all, he imagined that Paolo slept in his clothes a lot.

For flowers the ivy had peace signs, a pentagram binding a goat's head, and a right hand giving the finger. As an artist, Paolo had sucked. The peace sign was lopsided, the goat looked like a dog, and the hand like Mickey Mouse's. But he hadn't been bad at roses; he had given up on the harder fruit for them. Henry imagined a never-to-be snapshot for the shoe box on the living room table: Paolo shirtless on the bed, his tongue stuck out of the corner of his mouth. He is frozen copying the rose from the cover of *American Beauty.*

There was no closet door. Paolo had been partial to sturdy, pastel surfer clothes. The shirts in particular had ghosts in them. But the most haunted was the motorcycle jacket. From the pictures, Henry guessed that it had been way too big for him. But when Paolo saw himself in the mirror, he had filled it. Henry knew, because he still had the motorcycle jacket his dad had given him in high school. It hadn't fit him until he was twenty, and he hadn't worn it much then because around Berkeley they were everywhere. But when he was 16 and wore it, he wanted for nothing. Paolo's parents had done a terrible thing by letting his jacket hang here. If they knew their son at all, they would have buried him in it.

On the closet floor were plastic crates of t-shirts, black Converse Hi-tops; the year's edition of Air Jordans, very clean; and red Doc Martens. It was strange that his sister had only combat boots; they were nowhere near as cool as Docs, and she had an older brother who would have let her know. That gold diver around her mother's neck was odd, too.

As was this, at the bottom of the closet: another crate with a red bandanna spread over the contents. But the contents were only more bandannas, in every pattern Henry had ever seen, and then camouflage ones, then plain black, plain red...he quit looking. The crate was filled half to the top.

At the foot of the bed sat a small stereo and a box of tapes with no cases. Paolo had given his skateboard to a friend before the family moved, Henry decided. Traded it for a few joints, though he had cared enough for the guy just to give it to him; he just didn't want to seem sentimental. Henry knew how a life-long Californian would think: New Orleans would be a backward place, ultimately friendly but xenophobic at first. Black people in white t-shirts could walk only on one side of the street. Storefront porches, old polyester white men playing washboards and accordions. Paolo had decided he needed a more mellow persona so as not to upset the natives, but one still different enough to fascinate them. So he quit being a skater and became a Deadhead.

And Henry could just see it: he would have shown up at McMain Magnet in a purple shirt and leather jacket. At lunch in the first week, a zitty skater in cut-offs had shoved him: "Fuckin' California purple shirt wearing *faggot*!"

The skater in Paolo never died. That was a skater's pentagram on the wall, a skater's Slayer tapes mixed in with the newer Dead. But in New Orleans, it was too late to switch back to what he had been before.

But where were his stroke mags? You can't stop beating off just because you're a Deadhead.

He checked under the mattress. He checked under the box spring. It was impossible that this kid had nothing to hide.

"Ah," Henry said, "You were just shy."

There was something heavy inside the hollows of the box spring. Paolo had hidden his dirty pics inside the bed instead of under—talk about paranoid. They bulged against the cobweb-cloth stapled to the frame.

Henry pulled the bed away from the wall and felt for a slit in the side of the box spring. He lay across the bed and grabbed what was inside.

It wasn't dirty magazines. It was a giant Zip-Lock bag of cash. Henry fell on his back and held the money up to the light, but he knew what it was.

"You dumb asshole," he said.

There was only one way a kid got a ton of small bills that had to be hidden away: selling drugs. Henry knew that because Ronaldo had stashed bags like this one under his own bed in high school. And Henry had a stash of his own in Berkeley, when he got in on it.

Henry would send Ronaldo sheets of acid. Out in Berkeley he could get a hundred tabs for fifty bucks; Ronaldo could sell each tab for five or more in New Orleans. Then Henry would receive an envelope—no return address, twice the postage—containing half the profits. Ronaldo said New Orleans didn't see much California acid, and he was a good salesman. Henry sometimes got six hundred dollars in new twenties at the end of the month. Since Ronaldo was over eighteen then, he could walk into a bank or store, say he was a waiter, and wanted twenties for the ones he got in tips. That wouldn't have worked in high school.

Catherine, Henry's girl, didn't see anything really wrong with what Henry was doing; it wasn't like he was selling cocaine. And she was a libertarian. And the money was good. But Henry enjoyed the thrill more than the money. Wearing latex gloves pilfered from lab, he would seal the sheets in a legal-sized envelope—a sheet was only a little bigger than a dollar. Then he would strip off the gloves, scoop up the drug envelope with his phone bill, and sandwich another envelope on top of it. If he had no letter to go on top, he used an empty envelope. This prevented fingerprints on the drug envelope. Then he would walk out to the mailbox outside the University Center and drop all of it in the slot. Every time, he had felt like a spy.

He sat on the bed with the bag of money in his hands. He had called Paolo a dumb asshole because he had ended up at the other bad end of the drug business, besides jail—dead. Maybe he had been murdered. This was New Orleans, after all, not San Francisco. If so, Henry didn't like being here with the money—

An alarm bell rang. He leaped into a corner and held the bag of money pointed at the door. His gun was out in the dining room, in his backpack.

The bell rang again. It was the doorbell. "Oh shit. Oh," he said.

He put the money back into the box spring, then pushed the bed back against the wall. Whoever was at the door rang again. He hurried into the dining room.

He paused, looking at his backpack on the table. He unzipped the pencil pocket and dug around for the bullets.

"Just a minute!" he called to the doorbell. His fingers were shaking as he dropped the shells into the cylinder. You're loading a goddamn gun, he thought, You're going to kill somebody.

He didn't want to. But what if this was someone sent to collect Paolo's debt? Or, checking to see if the place was empty? This was New Orleans, not San Francisco. He adjusted his grip on the gun and placed the barrel, silently, against the inside of the front door. It wasn't a heavy door. Whoever was out there wouldn't see the gun, and if he had to, he could shoot whoever it was right through the wood. He hoped.

He threw back the bolt, and left the chain on.With his left hand he turned the knob, and with his left foot he stopped the door at the bottom after opening it a crack. He peered out.

"Domino's!"

It was some stringy white guy, holding a square, red mitten for pizza boxes. He looked amused. Why would he be amused? What joke was Henry missing?

Behind the door, Henry cocked the hammer. It wasn't fair. It wasn't fair that this should happen to him.

"I didn't order any pizza," Henry said.

The man looked at his face, still looking as though he were about to laugh. He opened one end of the mitten and peeked inside. "My mistake," he said. He turned and started to walk away.

"Wait," Henry said, "Wait a minute."

The man looked back over his shoulder. He turned around and faced Henry with his feet neatly together. He didn't know there was a gun pointed at him.

"Let me see the pizza," Henry said.

"You didn't order it. Order if you want a pizza to look at." He started to walk away again.

"If you work for Domino's," Henry said, "where's your uniform?"

The man looked at his clothes. He was wearing denim shorts and a golf shirt. He smiled, and said, "Uniform's dirty."

"Where's your car. I don't see any Domino's cars out there," Henry said.

The man put the pizza mitten under his arm, light and easy like it was a book. There were no pizzas in there. It was a prop. He still smiled. "Guess the car's dirty, too," he said.

He turned, and without looking back walked slowly toward a white van with a busted tail light, parked across and down the street. He opened the door and threw the prop pizzas in like a frisbee.

Henry locked the door. He pointed the gun at the floor, turned his face away, and eased the hammer down. His eyelids fluttered. He hated the damn things when they were loaded. He was very afraid of them.

Well, that fucker definitely was here for something untoward.

He stood over his book bag and opened the cylinder to unload the gun. All this time, while he was looking at the pictures and in Paolo's room, the slides and notes had been waiting for him. How much time had he wasted, time better spent studying? It made no sense, but he thought that if he had not brought the gun, the robber wouldn't have been summoned.

The gun was still loaded, but harmless with the cylinder open. If he held it up, he could see his microscope through the frame. Loaded gun or microscope, which did he hate more?

He gently pushed the cylinder back into the frame.

He stuck it in the front of his pants and pulled his shirt out over the butt. He opened the front door and scanned the street outside.

No sign of the van. He didn't really know what he was doing, but it was more fun than being stuck at the eyeballs to a six hundred dollar anxiety machine, learning to tell vein from venule.

He walked across the narrow street, and pushed himself up onto the concrete wall, then climbed the steep, short levee. If the rainwater broke through, this neighborhood would drown.

The sun had broken through the clouds; they would have no rain at their funeral, after all. Paolo's room would get its light soon. Henry's books were waiting for him on the dining room table. They were always waiting; so it would be, for years. In the canal was still a backwards, green, upside-down sky. Looking at it, he felt more desperate than he had in a long while.

* * *

Back inside the house, he unloaded the gun and zipped the bullets back in the pencil pocket, then buried the gun at the bottom of the bag.

There was one sure way to tell if Paolo had been murdered: find out what he sold. He had already been through the room. So he went to the kitchen and looked in the freezer, paying no mind to all the food stacked up in the closed refrigerator. Inside the freezer were some lumps in white paper—more meat—empty ice cube trays, and an open box of corn dogs. The open end of the box was shoved against the wall of the freezer.

He picked up the box, and there inside was a flat foil package, just like he had kept in his freezer back in Berkeley between mailings. He smiled. Though he wasn't glad it had happened, it was comforting to know that Paolo had killed himself after all, as he had believed before the pizza guy arrived. White kids kill themselves, and acid dealers didn't get murdered.

Inside the foil were two hundred and thirty tabs, in sheets, each stamped with a black spade with a skull inside it.

"Motorhead acid!" Henry said, "Kids these days...."

He felt like he had second sight to find it here. He felt giddy.

Fuck it, he thought, I'm going to sell this shit. His parents will never know.

And before he could change his mind, he was back in Paolo's room, digging the money out of the bed. With the bag and acid in one hand, he went into the daughter's room. This was the only room he felt wrong to be in, like a voyeur. None of the other ones bothered him. They deserve it for inviting me in, he decided.

On the daughter's floor was a purple backpack, very much like Henry's own. She had a high bed, with a warm, down comforter spread over it, like she was still in Northern Cali. He imagined that she got by with little guidance from her brother or parents. She had drawn a rainbow on the wall. Paolo had made fun of it, Henry was sure; he had only spoken to her to make fun. On her dresser was a pile of teen magazines. He didn't touch them.

The parents' room had a double bed, a night stand on each side, and a dresser. Henry was so sure that the top drawer contained a bag of weed and rolling papers stashed in a cigar box that he didn't even look. The room was anonymous, except for the two boxes stacked in the corner. The one on top was the size of a shoe box for one shoe. It was half-full of Zippo lighters, fine ones. Some were etched with men fishing in a stream. The bottom box was full of cognac in bottles made of smoked, green glass. There were no photo albums in the closet.

He went back to his books, and threw the money and the drugs on the table. Did he really want to sell it? Ronaldo would be in jail now if it weren't for his dad. Henry's dad worked in insurance.

He pulled a sheet of blank paper from his binder. Since high school, he had never had a problem which couldn't be solved on paper. Used to drive Catherine up the wall, especially because it worked. But when he showed her a work sheet, she said that it was sort of a found poem; it certainly was very Henry.

At the top of the left margin he wrote *ASSOCIATIONS Re: Med School*

Then he let his brain work:

$160,000

cadaver piss smelling (urea group on formaldehyde?)

boring class mates/ not friends

smug people? Yes. Full of themselves

Some of the other future surgeons walked the halls as if braziers waved the way with sweet smoke.

buy yr own microscope

lots of work\not interesting\not HARD

Another old saw: med school isn't hard, there's just a lot of it. It wasn't science—there was nothing to understand. The other day they were reciting the branches of the brachial plexus over and over, like a bunch of grade school kids learning the days of the week.

!!SURGEON!!

Beside it he drew a smiley face.

Another four years

ASSOCIATION Re:drug dealer

SLEEP LATE

Poss. prison

but no death w/LSD

Unless you kill yourself like Paolo.

money

but not much w/LSD

He thought and turned the pen end to end on the desk. Then he wrote

COOL

w/o getting anyone addicted

Henry had always wanted to be cool and never achieved it, due to his studies and his acne. He had done worksheets on coolness. He had reflected then that the only reason he had the time alone for worksheets was that he was not cool.

His findings:

Lesser cool: the capacity to like and be liked, by more than one person. This is the one that eluded him. "Henry's all right—he's cool." He couldn't imagine anyone saying that.

Greater cool: the feeling of a gun. The state of total competence. He couldn't really put it in words, but he didn't play with guns because he wanted to kill someone, or because they made his dick feel big. With a gun in his hand he simply could handle anything. Not just violence, anything—love, natural disasters. Fatherhood.

Surgery took greater cool. Split an abdomen, take out the bullets, then undo the damage—what greater competence?

solitary

Ronaldo had said that after his bust he realized that he had no friends. He was dealing all kinds of stuff, even a little cocaine—Henry hadn't approved of that, but didn't say so. It had become difficult for Ronaldo to differentiate customers from friends, so he just treated everyone as customer and as customer-to-be. And when a business goes under, as Ronaldo's had, the customers take their business elsewhere.

Outlaw
clever
young

Being alone, a dealer can't be bothered with lesser coolness. Henry was already a loner. And since he can't rely on the law, a dealer has to have greater coolness about him. His dealer in Berkeley had been a black man with dredlocks, even in his beard. He would sit in a Telegraph Avenue cafe. They would chat about school, and the dealer would refer to "my thesis" without ever really answering what he was writing a thesis on. Then he would hand Henry a book from the ever-changing stack on the table and tell him a chapter. He would open the book, and there was the acid. Henry would take it, close the money in on the same page, and that was it. Cool. Like spies. They did it this way because the Telegraph Avenue Cafe had signs on the wall reading NO DEALING.

Henry had wished the dealer *was* writing a thesis, or at least reading the books. When it came down to it, all he really seemed interested in was Henry's money. Henry wanted him to care about more because he liked him. In his experience, greater cool was always followed by lesser cool—or at least by the respect a surgeon gets.

Resolved: dealing as extracurricular.

Now he had done it. He hadn't gotten into med school by going back on his convictions.

* * *

Paolo's family came home and found Henry studying at the dining room table, his backpack sitting closed on the chair to his left. They had brought home with them an enormous, red man. Henry recognized him from the pictures in the shoebox, where he had had an orange beard and pointed at something in the trees.

"Normally I'm a vegetarian," the red man said. He went into the kitchen, and Henry heard the refrigerator open and Tupperware being plopped on the counter. "MOO MOO MOO," the red man said.

Henry looked at the mother, father, and girl. The girl chewed the inside of her cheek. She had felt ashamed of her clothes at the funeral. She wanted to go to her room but was scared to be alone right now. The mother and father were smiling at the red man for Henry's sake. Their eyes were very red, but they weren't done crying. The red man embarrassed them to make them smile. After Henry left he would be even sillier, but the mother and father would start really blaming themselves tonight.

Henry held his binder under his arm and slung his backpack to the opposite shoulder. He had already packed up his microscope into the case and grabbed its handle.

His backpack felt obscenely bloated. His binder wasn't even in it. They had to wonder why; the money took up too much room. He backed toward the front door.

"You're not hungry?" the father asked. "Eat with us."

"I'm stuffed," Henry said. He felt behind him for the knob.

"We have plenty of food," Hines said. That's how Henry thought of him—just Hines. Too broken now for "mister."

"No, really. My ride's coming," Henry said.

Hines's lips were parted. He moved toward him. "It would be no trouble...."

"No." Henry opened the door and backed out. "My ride is coming."

He waited at the corner for the hearse, looking back twice at the Hines's house. He hadn't waited long before it rolled up. Ronaldo leaned over and opened the door before stopping. He was singing, badly:

"Teen Paolo, can you hear me?

"Teen Paolo, can you see me?

"Are you somewhere up above

"With that bullet hole I spackled up?"

Ronaldo held out two fifty-dollar bills. Henry took them without laughing. At that, Ronaldo looked concerned.

Henry rode with the backpack on his lap, and wondered why he had filled it with a gun, stolen drugs and stolen cash. It wasn't like him to act impulsively, and it worried him. But then again, it wasn't impulsive. He had added it up on paper.

After some minutes, Ronaldo said, "You okay?"

"Sure," he answered.

"I can do this myself if it freaks you out," Ronaldo said, "More money for me."

"It doesn't," Henry said.

They had to drop off the hearse at Palace Springs. Henry still hadn't said much. Mr. Landry still wasn't around. Maybe Ronaldo really ran the place, while Mr. Landy only did the embalming, his real passion. Henry imagined a black top hat. Ronaldo talked at him and sat behind Mr. Landry's desk. Ronaldo asked what the hell was wrong with him?

Henry took a deep breath. Then he placed the acid and the cash on the desk in front of Ronaldo. Ronaldo glanced at it, then gave Henry a pleading look. He looked as pale as Henry felt.

"How would you like to go back into business?" Henry said.

4

Ronaldo jumped up like the money and acid had snapped at him. "Jesus, Hank, what did you do?" he shrieked. He walked over to the window and closed the curtains.

"The money was in the kid's room, and the acid was in the freezer," Henry said. Why that was supposed to justify his taking it, he didn't know.

"You weren't supposed to do that, Hank!" Ronaldo said, clutching his head. He stared at the curtains, squeezing his head like that.

Ronaldo turned back to the desk. "All right, how much is it?" he said.

Henry dumped the money out on the desk. Ronaldo's hands moved as fast as if he were typing and broke the money up by denomination. He finished and grabbed some of Henry's pile.

Ronaldo said, "Five sixty-three."

"Two hundred six," Henry answered.

Ronaldo stood up again. "I need cigarettes. I don't smoke any-more, and I need a cigarette," he said. He turned to the curtain again. It was like he imagined a scene being played out on the other side. Henry sat there, waiting.

"Okay," Ronaldo said, turning back to the desk. "The money was in the kid's room—where?"

"In the bed," Henry said.

"And the acid was in the freezer."

"Right," Henry said. "Should we worry about the foot that was in there?"

Ronaldo wasn't in the mood. "Shut up," he said, "Get that shit off the desk, and I'll take you home." And he left him sitting there. He walked out, toward the back.

The office had been the dining room. The light fixture had been replaced by fluorescent tubes. Under them, Henry felt like he had been left in an empty classroom, and he had been kept after school. Ronaldo had left him alone like the principal, so he could think about the wrong he had done. Since when did he get so righteous, Henry thought. He counted the money into halves and prepared his defense.

Ronaldo was locking a door in the hall.

"Let's walk and get some cigarettes," Henry said.

"I don't smoke," Ronaldo said. He had calmed down.

"Liar."

"What do you mean, 'walk'?" Ronaldo said.

Ronaldo drove a silver Escort that had belonged to his mother. It was dying. Only Ronaldo could get it started now. But the air conditioner worked, and plugged into the lighter's socket was a cellular phone, worth more than the car. They drove to a Circle K on Transcontinental Drive.

"I want you to know that I haven't smoked in almost four months now," Ronaldo said as they parked.

"I'll treat you," Henry said.

"Oh yeah," Ronaldo said, disgusted, "A thief like you can afford it."

Henry had rolled the money into cylinders as big around as coffee cups; he had snapped rubber bands from the desk around them. He peeled off some ones and dropped the roll back into his backpack. He saw his notes, which reminded him that he had no time for this.

Inside the store he grabbed a twelve-pack of Budweiser bottles from the cooler. At the counter he asked for a pack of Marlboro reds. That's what Ronaldo smoked.

"Soft or hard?" the clerk asked.

"What's that mean?" Henry said.

"Well," the clerk said, puffing on his own cigarette, "One is soft. The other one's hard."

"Hard," Henry said. The clerk gave him a box of cigarettes. He didn't ask for ID for the beer; in California he would have.

Ronaldo stood by the car and watched him get into the passenger seat and hold the beer in his lap. Then he got in and said, "What are you doing?"

"I am handing you a beer," Henry said. He had taken one out and opened it.

"It's three in the afternoon," Ronaldo said.

"This is New Orleans."

"You're not a little bit worried about what you just did? You're not a little worried that if a cop pulled up right now and decided to look in your bag, both of us could go to jail?"

"Not at all," he said. A lie, but he wasn't going to show it. He was thinking not of cops, but of phony pizza delivery men. And now that he could review what he had done, and what could have happened, he would make no mention of the man he might have shot. He unwrapped the cigarettes and tried to shake one out for Ronaldo, but they were packed too tightly.

"Give me that," Ronaldo snapped, and snatched the pack from his hands. A cigarette jumped into his hand. He unplugged the phone and replaced the lighter. Once he had lit up, he said "I don't want to stink up my car," and got out. Henry put the beer on the floor and got out also.

Ronaldo was smoking with his arms by his sides. This was the Ronaldo Henry remembered. Without a cigarette, Ronaldo had seemed like he had lost a finger. He glared at Henry and shook his head.

"What's the problem?" Henry said.

"My problem is that I put you in a client's house," Ronaldo said, then lowered his voice, "to keep the jigaboos from robbing it, and then what do you do? You rob it!"

Henry shrugged. He still didn't know why he had taken the stuff. The money wasn't worth the risks.

"And you can forget this, 'Let's go back into business,' shit," Ronaldo said. "I been there. It's not worth it." He grimaced at his cigarette. "Why didn't you get lights? I haven't smoked these since high school."

"I'll throw them away then," Henry said, and Ronaldo threw him the pack. He put it in his shirt pocket. His shirt stuck to the sweat running down his back. The beer would get warm if they didn't drink faster. He picked up the bottle from the seat and drank from it.

"Will you keep that bottle down?" Ronaldo said, "You want to get busted for open container? That's just the excuse they need."

He finished it and threw it on the floor. He hadn't had a beer since orientation, and it felt like too long. It occurred to him that he had been drunk every night for the two weeks before orientation. Every lab worker he knew drank a lot. "It wasn't really stealing," he said, "I'll grant you that morally, it was stealing. But it wasn't really stealing."

Ronaldo gave him a guarded look.

"Think about it. The money and acid belonged to the kid. He's dead. How are they going to know it's gone?"

Ronaldo looked untrusting and untrustworthy. "All right, Berkeley grad. The money was his," he said, "Now prove to me with the Pythagorean theorem that the acid didn't belong to the dad? Or the mom?"

They got back in, Ronaldo pulled out, and after opening another beer, Henry answered. "Who cares if it belonged to the parents? They can't tell the cops that their drugs were stolen."

"You know what, Henry? I don't care," Ronaldo said, "I don't care because I just realized that it's your problem." He didn't look away from the road.

"Don't take me home," Henry said, "Take me to Lakeside."

"What do you need from Lakeside?"

"We need to hang out in the parking lot. Today's my birthday and I want to hang out in the mall parking lot," Henry said. He turned the tuning knob on the radio, but could find nothing like an anthem playing.

Ronaldo looked at him. "Is it really your birthday?" he asked.

"I told you yesterday."

"Happy birthday. I'm not taking you to the mall," Ronaldo said, "I have things to do. I'm supposed to go to jail with you? Sorry. It's called growing up."

"If you take me to Lakeside Mall," Henry said, "I'll give you half of the money."

After not much deliberation at all, Ronaldo did a U-turn. "Pass me one of those beers," he said.

* * *

Lakeside Mall is not, in fact, on the lake, but within walking distance of a drainage canal. Before either could drive, he and Ronaldo used to wear open flannel shirts and sit here in the parking lot on weekend nights. Ronaldo would smoke; Henry didn't, because it was bad for him. They brought skateboards to sit on. Once Henry had gotten his license and his motorcycle jacket, his dad set him up with a yellow van whose key had been broken off in the ignition. You started it with a knife. They used to drive to the Lakeside lot and make fun of the kids hanging out there with their skateboards. Ronaldo sold them weed.

Ronaldo parked in the shade by the Red Lobster. He left the motor on for the air conditioner. Outside, some boys in clothes baggy enough for fat adults kicked around their skateboards when they messed up. The skateboards had a tail on each end now.

"Happy birthday," Ronaldo said. He touched his bottle to Henry's.

Henry reached into his bag for one of the rolls of cash, and tossed it into Ronaldo's lap.

"I can't take this, dude," Ronaldo said. But already he had snapped off the rubber band to count it again. "Keep that beer down, damn it."

Henry saw how his hands enjoyed the money. "So how we going to sell it," he said.

"If I were you I would go in the mall there and flush those sheets down the toilet," Ronaldo said.

"See," Henry said, "we need your expertise."

"You still haven't proven to me why the sheets don't belong to the dad."

Henry had thought about it more on the ride over. "How many people you know who would have that much acid around for personal consumption? Their kids would have had two heads apiece. Paolo would have had to shoot himself twice."

"How do you know they weren't selling it."

"How many kids would buy from an adult guy like that? They'd think he was a cop," Henry said, "And how did the money get in Paolo's room like that, if it was the dad's."

"Maybe the parents put up the front money and the kid sold it for them."

"You know I'm right about this," Henry said. He wondered how long it would take to run out of gas if they just ran the air conditioner like this. Ronaldo had picked up the habit from his cop father, who used to sit for hours in parking lots in his cruiser.

"You're not right," Ronaldo said.

"Okay," Henry said. He put out his hand. "Give me back the money then, if you think I have anything to worry about."

The money had disappeared; he didn't know where Ronaldo had stashed it. "That's just gas money, as far as I'm concerned. I don't know where you got it, or why you gave me so much. I don't know anything."

Henry was uncapping another beer. Ronaldo reached for it. Henry uncapped another for himself. "Fine," he said.

Neither of them said anything. Outside, a skateboard barked against the curb, and the boy riding it fell on his elbow so hard you could see it spit stars. He tried not to cry in front of his friends.

"There's something else you should be worried about, then," Ronaldo said, "They say suicides can't get into heaven because they killed someone, but they can't go to hell because they didn't kill someone else. So they roam the earth."

Henry belched. It sounded like a bark. "Who said that?"

"They."

"It sounds like you just made it up."

"I did," Ronaldo said, "That doesn't mean it's not true. You better wear a crucifix when you go to sleep tonight."

"That's for vampires," Henry said.

* * *

Six beers left. Ronaldo drove them to another island of shade. Henry was growing happier by the moment that he wasn't studying. He hoped Ronaldo had nowhere to go.

"Thanks for doing this," he said.

Ronaldo grunted. From here they could see the skaters better.

"Look at them," Ronaldo said, "Sometimes I feel pretty terrible about selling to kids like that."

"The stuff I used to send you?" Henry asked.

"I mean before that. When we used to come out here."

Henry thought about it. "Kids can't molest kids," he said.

"What's that supposed to mean?" Ronaldo asked.

"I mean if a little kid is playing doctor with another kid, no one calls that child molestation," Henry said, "You were just a kid when you sold to those kids."

Ronaldo said, "That's a rationalization."

Henry was glum. "I know," he sighed, "I knew then that it was wrong."

"I mean, what if the kid is thirteen and fools around with an eight year old? That's molestation," Ronaldo said, "Can you give me one good reason why you want to sell those tabs, while we're on the subject?"

"I'm going to be $160,000 dollars in debt when I finish school."

"They let you borrow that much?" Ronaldo said, incredulous.

"They know they'll get it back from doctors," Henry said.

Ronaldo scowled, then let out a stage laugh. "I love it. Berkeley mad science graduate knows how to jack off a frog, but still doesn't know enough to stay away from easy money," he said. He hit Henry on the arm with the back of his hand. "How much money will you make off those tabs? Twenty-five hundred, tops? That's if people still fall for that double-dip con, too."

"What's that?"

"Give it up, Hank," Ronaldo said. "That's when you tell them there's twice as much liquid per tab. There's not. You just charge twice as much. Do you have any idea how hard it is to sell that much, anyway?"

"That's why I need your help," Henry said, "Your expertise. Like I said."

"Any more of my expertise and I'm going to prison," Ronaldo said. "I don't like tattoos and I don't like lifting weights and I don't like men."

"You're no fun anymore, Ronaldo."

"I have a job now, Hank," Ronaldo said, "I can't be going around every night to the Quarter and Uptown anymore. Selling that much–you might as well work instead. I only made any real money when I got big enough to sell sheets at a time. Unless you get in with the Tulane fraternities, and then you're always getting undersold by these rich prick tennis brats."

"It's true," Henry said, "Acid lasts too long." He thought, and realized that soon, he would need a bathroom. "A dose will get someone off for, what, twelve hours? And after that, all but the pumpkinheads are going to need recovery time. The pumpkinheads and their patchouli. While they recover, you're not making money off them.

"Now crack, that's a dealer's drug—twenty minutes later and they want another rock. Some enterprising soul needs to turn every acid eater into a pumpkinhead with a psychedelic crack. I mean a real short acting, intense psychedelic. It already exists. I got the synthesis protocol off a web page. It's called DMT. They smoke like three drops of it, and before the smoke even clears they're in the future. One guy wrote that every time he did it the elves came to turn the wheels of the death machine for a hundred years; forty five minutes later he was fine. And another thing I thought of was this: what if somebody mixed DMT with that pepper spray the cops use? Can you imagine that? They spray you, you can't see, you can't breathe, and to you it seems to go on for a century?"

Ronaldo said, "So how do you plan to sell these tabs you stole, Henry."

Henry put down his beer very carefully. "I'm going to go to the bathroom," Henry said, "And when I come back I'll have a plan that won't involve you."

As he walked to the mall entrance, he saw by the shadows that it was later than he had realized. A skateboarder gave him a bored look. The mall had been renovated with archways since he had last been here. Girls were shopping for school clothes, some of them with their mothers, and he felt blasphemous for being here drunk. It took some time to find the bathroom.

Standing at the urinal, it occurred to him that he might go back outside and find Ronaldo had left him there.

* * *

Ronaldo hadn't left. Henry got back into the car, moving slowly, like his muscles were sore.

"Look at you," Ronaldo said, a new beer in his hand "You're rat-assed. That's what they say in England when people are drunk. 'Rat-assed'."

"When did you go to England?"

"I never did," Ronaldo said, "Why couldn't we go to a bar? Why do we have to sit here in a parking lot."

"This makes it more old times' sake," Henry said, "You got money for gas now."

"I get my gas free," Ronaldo said, "Don't worry about how." He pointed at the cigarette pack in Henry's pocket. He gave him one, and Ronaldo lit up. He no longer cared about smelling up the car. "If I were still selling, I could get you a date. I could get us both dates. That was the only time in my life I felt like a male model."

"Is anyone we used to know dead?" Henry said.

"Where the hell did that come from? Yeah." Ronaldo asked. "Weren't you dating some girl?"

"She wants to write poetry for a living," Henry said. Henry leaned forward and flapped his shirt against his back to cool off. Then he settled in. "Who," he said.

"Remember Dwayne? Demon Dwayne? He's dead," Ronaldo said.

That really isn't surprising, Henry thought. Dwayne: voted Most Likely to Sell His Immortal Soul. He used to sacrifice cats to the devil. He hadn't done it for attention; he had done it because he was really crazy. "What happened to him?" Henry asked.

"He was passed out in the front seat and his girlfriend ran into a bridge post," Ronaldo said. "She was drunk too. She lived, though. Air bag."

Henry said, "Dwayne had a girlfriend."

"I didn't go to the funeral," Ronaldo said, "I feel kind of bad now about it. I didn't go because I don't like the funeral home that did it. They're snobs."

"Anybody else?"

"Yes, you sick bastard," Ronaldo said, "Pierre died. He was drunk and tried to rappel face first off his fraternity at LSU."

"Pierre was in a fraternity?" Henry asked, "Did you go to the funeral?"

"I had to work," Ronaldo said, "That was when I was delivering those damn video poker machines. Vending machines, too."

Ronaldo named someone else. "I don't even remember who that was," Henry said.

"You been away a long time, haven't you?" Ronaldo said. "Like earlier, you said we should walk. Nobody walks anymore. Too many assholes got guns."

Henry thought of the revolver in his bag; he turned to the window so Ronaldo wouldn't see him smile. "Don't you think it's a bad sign that two of the people we used to eat lunch with every day are dead?" Henry asked.

"No," Ronaldo said, "Look who they were. I have to take you home now. I hope you've enjoyed your birthday."

"Where do you have to go?" Henry asked. Now he was in the mood for a bar. It had clouded over again and the sun was going down.

Ronaldo didn't look at him. "I have this thing," he yawned, "for work. You know."

Henry took a voice like a documentary for kids: "Embalming may sound like fun, but it takes all the dedication of the clergy."

Ronaldo smiled. "Exactly," he said.

"Seriously," Henry said, "What are you doing?"

Ronaldo shrugged. "You still haven't told me your master plan. You said you would figure it out in the toilet." He pulled out into the heavy traffic on Veterans.

"Pull into this gas station up here," Henry said, "After that, I'll tell you my plan."

Ronaldo pulled in. He watched Henry go in and come out with a case of beer.

"Christ, don't study too hard," Ronaldo said, "I really want you for my doctor someday. You'll puke in the patient."

"It's my birthday," Henry said, "Fuck off. I'm going to drink one of these bastards for every year."

"All right," Ronaldo said, "Let's hear it." He pulled into traffic, more aggressively than made Henry comfortable.

"I'm not going to sell it on the street," Henry said, "There are a lot of people at school who went to Tulane and LSU for undergrad. They know people who are still there who trip." Henry in fact knew of only one long-haired guy in his class who looked like a total druggie. He had never spoken to the guy.

"All those Tulane Phish heads will buy it up in no time. They trip there like students at other schools drink. They drink like students at other schools study. The mean on one of their organic tests was a twelve. I won't even need a car. I'll get their addresses and mail it to them when I get a check."

"A check?" Ronaldo asked.

"They're college students."

"They never gave me checks," Ronaldo said.

"Did you ever ask?" Henry said, "I still have my notes from undergrad. For some reason I thought that they'd be useful now. I'll photocopy them and send them along too. That way I can just say I'm selling notes. Not that the cops are going to check the mail. You and I know that from experience."

Ronaldo took a sip from his bottle, keeping it low. The guy in the car ahead was drinking too, but made no attempt to hide it. "They'll just write you bad checks."

"Ronaldo, you don't understand college students," Henry said, "They'll bounce a check for rent, but not for drugs. That would be this real uncool faux-pas. And I can just wait until it clears before I send it." He had never actually heard of anyone using a check for drugs. And now he didn't see why they couldn't just send cash, as Ronaldo had to him. But he wasn't willing to change the plan. It was pretty good, for having been made up on the spot. He pulled beer through his teeth like it was whiskey. "So, you want in, or what?"

"What do you need me for?" Ronaldo snapped.

"You can do the mailing for *me* now," Henry said.

Ronaldo cut off a truck and pulled across the left lane, into a Daiquiri's parking lot. He parked in a handicapped spot, and reached down into his socks, and pulled out the cash. He threw it with both hands at Henry, so it scattered like a bag of leaves hit by a car. A pile of ones had fallen by the park brake, and he threw it at Henry's face. Henry was trying to pick the cash from the dashboard so no one would see it.

"You think I like getting thrown on the fucking floor with a gun in my face?" Ronaldo said. "You think you're going to outsmart that?"

He hadn't heard the details of Ronaldo's bust. He didn't know it had involved guns.

Ronaldo had turned red above the collar. "My dad made me watch the video of my bust, with the little time counter in the corner and everything. If I ever go to his house, he makes me watch it again."

Henry spent a couple of minutes picking up the money. He pretended that it took all of his concentration. Then he said, "I'll send the photocopies of the notes. A little before, or a little after, they get another envelope with the acid. Any relationship between the two events is purely circumstantial."

"So you're a lawyer now, too," Ronaldo said. He meant it as a jab, but it sounded like surrender. If Ronaldo had thought of a mail order LSD service for students, he wouldn't have been caught.

"They pulled a gun on you for acid?" Henry said.

"It was ecstasy at the time, and it was my dad," Ronaldo said.

Henry looked at him. "Your own dad pointed a gun at your face? You got busted by your own father? Was he in disguise?"

"Don't be a moron, Hank. They got somebody else for that part."

Henry looked out at the NO PARKING sign. "Was it loaded?" he asked.

"Shit, Henry, it's the thought that counts." Ronaldo got the car started again and pulled out. As upset as he was, he seemed like he had needed to tell someone. The car lurched backward. Back on Veterans, Henry held out the stack of bills. Ronaldo didn't take the money.

"Just take it. I don't care," Henry said, "You know me. I wasn't in it for the money."

Ronaldo looked at the money with one eye, and said, "Put it in the glove compartment. That's my consultation fee."

"I don't care about that either," Henry said, "Let's go get fucked up."

"I told you, I got things to do. Plans," Ronaldo said.

Back on the interstate again; then back off. Afternoon sun was perfect for drinking, and he was going to get dropped off. Ronaldo whipped the car down the narrow streets of the lower Quarter. Henry was lost, and he lived down there. A right turn, and they were in front of his building.

He could feel the books left behind in his apartment gloating—now they had him. He wobbled out of the car with the microscope dangling from one hand, the bag with the empties in the other, his backpack over his shoulder, and his arms full of beer.

When he stood up, he thought, I am drunk.

Keys. The door needed a key. He swivelled around for it. But his pocket moved too.

Ronaldo got out of the car to help him. He snatched the bag of empty bottles. "Throw them away, Hank!"

Henry made noise about recycling.

"You're not in California anymore. Look at you. I thought you had all this work."

"It's only been a week," Henry said.

Ronaldo got back in the car, and left before Henry had the apartment door shut, which Henry didn't appreciate. He had no light in the stairway, and had forgotten to leave the kitchen light on. Remember to ask the landlord for a light in the stairway. He could feel the walls squeeze the air in the dark, like a hollowed out hill. He found himself ducking his head on the way up.

Being drunk around these high ceilings will take some getting used to, he thought. He could feel the space above him; he was glad to get the desk lamp on, and then the radio, loud. He spun the dial for something not at all gloomy. He put the beer in the refrigerator, the acid in the freezer, but then he worried the moisture might bleed the drug out of the blotting paper. He needed a plastic bag. He dug through his backpack for the bag the cash had been in, and used that.

He placed the revolver on the kitchen table. It made the place feel less empty. From the proper angles, the little gun looked like heavy machinery. A bulldozer part.

Back in his bedroom, he put the bullets away in the armoire. What pleases me right now, he thought, are the acid and the revolver. These are both new and scientific. What frightened him was this apartment, and the money, which like this building was the work of someone dead.

Maybe I shouldn't have taken that stuff, he thought.

He couldn't put it in his bedroom; he'd never sleep. And it couldn't be stashed in his study, because then he wouldn't be able to study. Paolo might as well have had his portrait on the bills. So for now, at least, he threw it in the freezer. Tomorrow he would figure out what to do with it. While he was there he grabbed another beer. And he found an open one on the counter. He finished that one.

He took the pack of Marlboros from his pocket, put one in his mouth, felt his pocket for matches, then went to the stove. The stove was broken until he realized he was looking at the wrong burner. Happy birthday. While lighting the cigarette on the stove he heard a crinkling and smelled a roach caught in the toaster.

I don't own a toaster. My hair is getting singed. Remember to get a haircut.

He had experimented with nicotine in college. Fighting the coughs was worth it. Now he felt really gone, and school felt far behind.

* * *

Now, the memory of this was really embarrassing the next day, when he was hung over:

In front of the bathroom mirror in his motorcycle jacket he'd pretended to be Scarface. He'd gotten his rifle out of the chest and pointed it from the waist at the mirror.

"SAY HELLO TO MY LIL' FRIEN'!" with spit flying everywhere.

The real AR-15 launched a pretend grenade.

5

His landlord had emphasized that the bathroom had been completely renovated. The rest of his apartment was dark and empty; the bathroom was cramped and yellow plastic. His shower was hollow. Knock anywhere on the tub or the shower walls, and empty space answered.

Henry got on his knees in the bathtub and worked with a steak knife at the caulking where the front wall of the shower met the bathtub, beneath the faucets. The money was on the floor in front of the toilet, in its plastic bag. He had wrapped the acid in a sandwich bag and hid it in a Tater Tots box in the freezer. The thought of hiding the money in his bedroom, like Paolo had, unnerved him. He was going to hide the money in the wall of the tub.

The landlord had been cheap with the caulking. It was just a step up from gum, and already turning green. Once he had the wall open, it bent and broke away from the other wall, enough to allow his hand.

He put a brown paper bag over Paolo's money, wrapped it, and pushed it gingerly into the space he couldn't see, up to his elbow. Though he knew there was only about ten inches of hollowness to the side of the tub, he imagined it much larger because the first floor of the building was empty. It had been a cobbler's shop, now out of business. Now it was just dark, sealed air. No rats or even cockroaches. The tub was like a row boat, floating with the dead space under it.

The brown bag really wasn't necessary. Certainly it would do no good against moisture. But he had felt that the money should go covered, in Paolo's memory. He would have used nice cloth, if he owned any.

*　　　*　　　*

Henry had learned their real names. Eager was named Amanda. Chinese guy was named Eric. Earnest really was named Earnest. Through a complicated series of jokes, which weren't clear to Henry, the cadaver was now named Mr. The Cadaver.

Henry had stolen some scrubs from the hospital, but still he wouldn't touch the cadaver. His job was to read the dissector aloud for the two boys. Amanda usually was brushed aside, so she just stood there and tried to see what they found. In the long stretches when he wasn't reading, Henry wandered from lab to lab to see if other instructors were giving any test hints, or if any table had a really good structure. Through these visits, he got a feel for what made for a good cadaver, and for how cadavers were made.

All of their throats and some of their groins had been slit, the groins along the femoral artery, the throats along the jugular. He thought at first that they must have been hung up by the feet to drain the blood out, but that would probably be too messy. Some guy would have to come in with a hose and spray the heads clean. And there was no sign of rope burn on the ankles. More likely, the blood vessels did the work: hook up a clear tube to the proximal jugular, a drain tube to the caudal, and run cadaver cologne through until the line goes from red to pink to clear. Repeat on the arteries. Then the whole body was fixed in a tank of formalin for up to ten years. When fished out, what had been corpse was now cadaver.

Only sometimes the blood didn't drain well; maybe a cadaver tech had been in a hurry. So during the dissection of the deep lower back, the cadaver starts to bleed. The lab group is reminded that this person was once alive like them. And it can rot: Henry walked into lab F and retched. The ripe cadaver at fault got to smelling so bad that the department sent it back for a new one, after cutting off the head. That lucky table would have two heads to work on for the dreaded middle block exam, Head and Neck.

An over-preserved cadaver presented its own perils. The poor slobs of table 1, Lab A found out that everything inside had turned black. Henry's cadaver wasn't that bad, but it was close. Tissues withered and browned until they couldn't tell vessel from tendon from nerve. When they got into the complicated stuff like the hand, they would be in trouble. The answer was liberal use of cadaver cologne, which made it smell even worse. When the other members of his group threw open the table, they had to turn away a moment and then dive in, and breathe through their mouths until they got acclimated. The cadaver now smelled like rancid chewing tobacco.

But it was weight that left one lab group cursing, and another wondering how anyone could find Gross hard. The last thing you want to see when you swing open that table the first day is a tiny, old woman still wearing nail polish. Sure, one person can turn it over, and the big structures are easy to find, but the fine stuff in the neck can require a magnifying glass.

Fat was worse. There was the danger of being catapulted, as the instructor had told them on the first day. More distressing: everything under the skin bubbles with yellow fat, and it can't be peeled off in sheets. It must be picked off in clumps, and that wastes time.

In the different labs he had heard students joke that as they left school, they evaluated people in other cars and at crosswalks as potential cadavers. Every so often you saw a good one, and compulsively began to name the muscles and nerves working under the stranger's skin.

They were bluffing, Henry thought. No one could really be that enthusiastic about Gross. He didn't picture strangers skinless, just the people he knew. He wouldn't make a bad cadaver. His skin would be easy to get off, and his muscles would be defined because he was in shape, but he might be too tall. The tall ones were harder to turn over. Ronaldo would make a good cadaver. He was stocky.

Today they were cracking the vertebral column. They were not to use the autopsy saws. The saw was designed to vibrate through bone and only wiggle soft tissue, so unless they wasted a lot of time picking the backbone clean, they wouldn't get a decent cut anyway. And the instructor wanted them to really appreciate how tough it was. And she didn't like the sound of the saw. It reminded her of the dentist.

So they were issued yellow, plastic-headed ball-peen hammers and chisels. They were warned to look away, because chips would fly. One of the other labs was allowed to use saws, and with that whine and all the banging metal and shouting a visitor might think they were making chairs instead of breaking backs.

Or trying to break backs. Earnest had given up on the chisel and was trying the bone snips. They looked like a rattling set of long pruning shears with metal handles, with jaws instead of blades. He had the snips' jaws around the spinous process of a vertebra, at about L3.

"Ready?" he said. They looked away.

Earnest's feet were spread wide. He squeezed the handles together and twisted, but the snips slipped off the bone, and he caught himself with an elbow on the cadaver's buttock. Its butt was flat from lying on the table so long. When they flipped it back over, its face would be flat, looking back at them like a live person's would look pressed against plate glass.

He was embarrassed. "Here, you're taller than me," he said to Henry, "You can get better leverage." He shoved the snips at him.

"I don't want to do any work," he said, "You know that."

Eric wanted a chance—it showed in his face. But Henry was taller than him too. Amanda looked exasperated. Eric and Earnest had made it clear to her that this was a man's work.

He didn't want to, but now all three of them were waiting. Breathing through his mouth, he approached the table. He could taste the smell now. He opened the snips and with the jaws scraped away some meat and aspic. He wanted it to look as much like the Netter Atlas as possible, and not like human bone. Netter plates were done in water colors like Army recruiting posters from 1940.

He got a bite on the spinous process. He leaned into the handles a little bit to see what it would take: a slow, steady crunch or a sharp crack. The table rolled away from him. Amanda grabbed the tank before either of the guys and stabilized it. She folded her arms, waiting.

Henry decided on the sharp crack. "Look away," he said. They did.

His face was cold with sweat. He should sit down for a minute to feel better; but better to get this over with. He jerked the jaws closed and pried. The bone ripped off with a sound like an ice cube crushed between raw molars. It made his stomach hurt.

"All right!" Amanda said, "Go, Henry!"

Earnest looked at her. He and Eric both looked studiously unimpressed. "Now we know who's doing orthopedics," Eric said.

There was a slit now where the spinous process had been. Eric shoved the chisel in there and tried to break it more. Evolution won: not only was the spinal canal hard to crack, but once cracked, only chips would come away.

He stabbed a mark with the chisel. "Cut it here," he said to Henry.

"Can I try?" Amanda said.

"Don't y'all ever think about what the fuck we're doing here?" Henry said. By their faces, he knew that he must look as bad as he felt. "Jesus, this thing fucking reeks." He threw an elbow over his nose. The bone snips hung from his hand, mindlessly holding in their jaws a piece of Mr. The Cadaver.

Amanda watched him carefully.

Earnest looked smug.

"I'll do it," Eric said soothingly, and took the snips from Henry's hand.

The next table was watching now too. And Henry knew why: no one in med school cursed. No one except Henry. There would be gossip.

He calmed himself and said, "Never ask me to do anything ever again."

* * *

"You got problems," Ronaldo said over the phone. He hadn't even said hello.

Henry was at his table. He was thinking that the developing babies looked like trilobites. There they were in his embryology book. "What problems?"

"Ian wants to talk to you."

"Ian who."

"Ian Hines."

Henry swallowed. "Who's Ian Hines," he said. But he already knew.

Ronaldo sounded like he was talking around a hard peppermint. He took a while to answer. There was a TV in the background. "The family whose house where you were. Ian Hines is the father of that family."

Henry said, "What's he want?" But he knew.

"He wants to talk to you tomorrow. I'm going to pick you up at lunch. We have to do something first."

"I have class," Henry said.

"Why is this even on the air?" Ronaldo sobbed. "Who would make this awful show?!"

He wondered if Ronaldo was playing with him—revenge for stealing the acid. He wouldn't give him the satisfaction. "What are you watching?" he said. He tried to sound bored.

"Wait. What time am I getting you?" Ronaldo laughed. "Oh yeah. Lunch. So...be at home."

"Ronaldo," Henry said, "What time is lunch."

"One!" Ronaldo laughed. He hung up.

At one o'clock he was supposed to be in his first Medical Ethics lecture. But he had to face Hines. To do otherwise would be to admit guilt. He skipped ethics, showered, and wondered what he was going to say. Paolo's money irradiated his legs through the wall of the tub. He could feel it there. He ran through the possibilities in his head.

The money and acid belonged to Paolo; Ian Hines didn't know about it; he wanted to talk to Henry because he had tracked mud through the house or something. Or noticed fingerprints on the pictures. Or wanted to sell him some bad art. All of the above, unlikely.

The money belonged to Paolo, and the acid to Hines. Unlikely. It would explain why the money was in Paolo's room. But there was no way an adult could sell that much acid. Kids would think he was a narc.

The acid belonged to Paolo, and the money to Hines. Paolo would have been able to sell it. Hines stashed cash around the house. Maybe he was scared of the IRS. Or didn't trust banks. Or something. Plausible.

He got out of the shower and dried off. He admitted the truth to his reflection.

It didn't matter. For whatever reason, Hines wanted one or the other or both back. And you don't go to the police for things like this. He shaved again. The shaving cream made his teeth yellow by contrast.

In any case, the life he had imagined for Paolo was wrong, and he felt like Paolo had lied to him. That irked him. He had hidden the money away because it seemed wrong to have Paolo's work spread out to nothing in cash registers around the city. What if the money wasn't even his? The money was half-gone anyway, since Ronaldo had no doubt blown his share, on who knows what. Clothes.

What do I give a shit about this dead stranger, he thought. An answer didn't come.

Ronaldo was half an hour late. In the extra time he thought up this:

Hines is a bad Bay Area artist with good skin. He's short. I'll just deny everything. What could he do?

To make sure Hines wouldn't do anything, Henry brought along the miniature tape recorder that his mother had bought for him. It was hidden in his backpack. She had assumed he would tape lectures in med school. He would tape Hines incriminating himself.

There was the possibility of violence. He would deny everything in a public place. He would not bring a gun. There was no way he would risk his future over something that could be talked out. He wore his funeral home clothes; they made him feel like he had an employer behind him. I still haven't even met Mr. Landry, he thought.

Ronaldo pulled up in his rotten car. When he saw how Ronaldo was dressed, he knew something was wrong.

6

Ronaldo was wearing grey sweat pants and a t-shirt that said THE MORE I FIND OUT ABOUT WOMEN THE BETTER I LIKE MOTORCYCLES. He was wet-eyed and breathing through his mouth.

Henry got into the car. He threw the backpack containing the tape recorder at his feet. He said, "You look like shit, Ronaldo."

Ronaldo pulled away; he would not meet Henry's eye. They were waiting for the right turn arrow on Rampart and Canal before Ronaldo said anything. "Why do you do that?" he said.

"Do what?" Henry said.

"As long as I've known you, you've said stuff when people don't need to hear it. You told me one time you can't help it," Ronaldo said, "But I wonder."

Henry said, "I really can't help it. I'm sorry." He meant it.

"You smell like formaldehyde, too. I hate that smell."

"I showered. It might be my bag."

Ronaldo didn't look interested. "I got fucked up last night," he said, without looking away from the street, "I got fucked up on a bottle of Montezuma Tequila."

Henry shuddered. "Tequila's supposed to be from Mexico," he said, "Montezuma is from Michigan."

Ronaldo didn't laugh. "I also ate two tabs I had left in the freezer."

Henry's heart skipped. Acid heads made him nervous; anyone who would do that to their brain would do anything. "I didn't think you did that," he said.

"I don't. But last night was an exception. Last night I had no choice."

They were heading into Mid-City. Neither the funeral home or the Hines house was there. "Why?" Henry asked.

"See? That's a perfect example, Henry," Ronaldo said, "What kind of a shitty doctor are you going to be? What are you going to say—' Congratulations, Mr. Gerring, your name's going to be in all the medical books?'"

He didn't want to say the wrong thing again, so he kept quiet.

"What?" Ronaldo swatted him with the back of his hand. There was no humor in it. "Where's the asshole comment? HA HA HA. You smell like piss and you're going to be shitty doctor. HA HA HA."

He felt like hitting Ronaldo back. "Gehrig," he said, "Lou Gehrig's disease. Amyotrophic lateral sclerosis. I helped work on a rat model of it."

"Well, we buried somebody with it," Ronaldo snapped.

* * *

They entered City Park from the back. Ronaldo hadn't talked. On the right was the old, deserted, goofy golf course. For a while it was run by possums. These monkey rats lived in the cat's claw that covered the fence, and they never touched the ground. Sometimes they fell in the water trap and drowned and their babies would float out of the mother's pouch and drown too. When they were in tenth grade he and Ronaldo had broken in there. Ronaldo had destroyed the mini-windmill, and Henry had spray painted pentagrams and "666" on the blue walls of what had been the equipment shack. He doubted now that they had scared anybody. The place was now a Sheriff substation. At Halloween, low-risk parish prisoners used the place for a haunted house.

"What we're about to do is slightly illegal," Ronaldo said.

"How slightly," he said. He felt he was being punished for skipping his lecture. "What's this got to do with Ian Hines?" They went down a white-shell service road. Though they were only doing twelve, he clenched the park brake and the door.

"That's later," Ronaldo said.

He pulled into the shade under some magnolia trees near the back of City Park Stadium. Magnolias as big as plates sometimes fell to the ground onto the dead leaves. It's strange to hear a flower make such noise. The stadium had a high fence with square bars. Such a fence would cost too much today. The Beatles played here. Someone had somehow bent some bars apart long ago. Rust had eaten, was eating, where the black paint had cracked. Ronaldo walked toward the opening.

"So did you get into motorcycles while I was away?" Henry asked.

"Hell no! Do I look to you like someone who wants to *die?*" Ronaldo said over his shoulder. He climbed through the fence. "Some loser traded me this shirt right off his back for a joint. I was drunk."

Inside the outer fence was a new chain link fence, with new razor ribbon twisting along the top. But the gates were locked with only a sagging chain and padlock. Ronaldo pushed on the gates and they squeezed under the chain. They walked toward the stadium, across a concrete apron where buses might park. The stadium was made from the same concrete, four stories high. Henry felt like someone up there was spying on them.

He asked, "Is Hines here?"

Ronaldo's laugh was mean.

They went through the closest arch. Above were I-beam buttresses painted gray. At regular intervals, ramps ran up narrow chutes that opened to the stands. Through one chute Henry saw the football field, a red track, and the stands at the far side of the stadium. Maybe it was a trick of the light, but they looked as flat as three bands in a painting. Ronaldo walked past several green doors and opened one. There was a lock over the knob, but no one had bothered with it. Henry's eyes squinted to see in the dark. It was a storeroom. Inside was one push broom, dirty cinder blocks, and a washtub full of golf balls.

Henry picked up a ball—PROPERTY OF CITY PARK, it read. He slipped it into his pocket. Ronaldo picked up a cinder block in each hand and walked out of the door. Henry said, "Do we need more?"

Ronaldo grunted—Ronaldo was too hungover and fried for his stupidity today. Henry picked up two blocks and followed him.

Ronaldo left his bricks by the chain link gates. He passed Henry on the way back.

"Are we making a bookshelf?" Henry asked, trying to joke.

Ronaldo looked straight at Henry's face from a foot away. "Tell me," Ronaldo said, "what I need a bookshelf for." He walked back toward the stadium.

Henry was tiring of him as well. "Books," he shouted at Ronaldo's back. He followed him into the storeroom. Ronaldo was picking up two more bricks. In this light, he looked even more haggard.

"It's not a bookshelf," Ronaldo muttered.

Henry followed with two more blocks. By the fence, Ronaldo put his bricks down on their square ends, and sat on the end of one. The other stood there empty, like someone sitting there had gotten up and left. Ronaldo sat with his head between his knees.

Henry walked his blocks over, put them down, and sat on the one next to Ronaldo.

"Ronaldo, they sell these, you know," Henry said.

"These are free," Ronaldo said. He hadn't looked up.

Henry waited. In this heat, his half-cotton, half-polyester clothes felt like his old high school uniform. This was the most sun he had gotten since school started. Light meters tied onto med students in one study received about twelve minutes of sunlight a day —the time spent going to and from school. The meters clocked sixteen hours of fluorescent tubes and desk lamps.

Now it was clouding over. A wind spun magnolia leaves against the fence. He didn't want to go to lab tomorrow or ever.

Ronaldo got up. They each brought back two more bricks. "That's it," Ronaldo said.

Henry looked back at the stadium. The concrete looked too skinny to hold itself up—opposite, like a plaster cast of a coal mine. He didn't want to leave yet, especially if it was just to face Hines. "Let's check out the stadium," he said.

He thought Ronaldo would say no, but he shrugged. "You got time," he said.

They walked up one of the ramps. Clouds had wiped the sun from the stands and field. The track remained bright red and might have been floating an inch off the ground. It took Ronaldo some effort to get up the will to speak. Every action made him ache: he pointed at the track, and it hurt him. "They put that in for Olympic trials, a few summers ago. The city made a big fucking deal about this track. There's only three in the world and it cost six million bucks and now it just sits here for nothing."

"How come it's so easy to break in here, then?"

"City did a half-ass job, as usual. Nothing ever works out," Ronaldo said, "Soon as I can, I'm getting the hell out of this nigger trap. Want to see from the top?" Steps ran up on either side of the chute they had just exited. The fence they had come through rang in the wind, sounding too far away.

Henry took the steps four at a time and passed Ronaldo, who was plodding up with his hands on his knees. Ronaldo stopped to lie down on one of the aluminum bleachers with his hands over his eyes.

Henry skipped back down. "You all right?" he asked.

"What's this hard-on you have for *walking,*" Ronaldo said. He sat up. "How do you have the energy."

"I had to walk everywhere for the last four years," Henry said. The air tasted silver with the rain coming. He wanted to get to the top. "You're out of shape because you have a car."

"You can't walk around here because there's too many niggers. Take a walk in Orleans Parish and next thing you know you're getting cut up by med students like you."

"That's not true. They don't just take them from the morgue anymore. Ninety percent of the cadavers are donated now," Henry said. Their lab instructor had said so.

"That's what you think," Ronaldo said, "I heard there was this rice-nigger lab–"

"What's a 'rice-nigger', Ronaldo?"

"A chink."

"When did you get so racist?" Henry said, "You didn't used to be this bad."

"I'm not racist," Ronaldo said.

Henry rolled his eyes and started back up.

He heard Ronaldo behind him: "You just haven't been back long enough."

"Anyway, what about this lab?" Henry said.

"I heard there was this Vietnamese lab in the Quarter where they take people and steal their organs. I heard this guy disappeared from a bar on Iberville and a couple days later, the bartender found the same guy sitting up in a booth with both his eyes open. There were stitched up incisions on his back from where they had taken out his kidneys."

Henry said, "You can't live with no kidneys."

"He was dead. Why do you think he was sitting there with his eyes open like an asshole?" Ronaldo said.

"If they weren't trying to keep him alive, why'd they stitch him up? Why not just take everything from him and dump the rest?" Henry said.

"I don't know," Ronaldo said.

"Why'd they bring him back to the same bar?" Henry said.

"Just shut up, Henry. That's what I meant in the car. You never know when to shut up."

They were at the top now. A fence ran around it, with the top of it slanting in to keep drunken fans from falling to their deaths. Ronaldo sat down. They regarded the green roof of the park—magnolias along the sidewalks, oaks set further back. It made it easy to think they were in the Yucatan, where there was no windowless medical school with students inside getting old. The gray smudge of a storm was coming in off the lake. A thread of lightning looked to Henry like a vein—but it was white. A nerve.

Beyond the park they saw the roofs of houses. A family living down there would never know its roof like Henry and Ronaldo did now. Automatic transmissions drove cars around. Henry saw the levee by Paolo's house. Paolo and Ian Hines's. He wondered if he could hit that pole from up here with his AR-15. He took the golf ball from his pocket and dropped it. It took seconds to fall, bounced twice and rolled under the fence and the leaves.

He heard Ronaldo behind him: "You should have thrown it."

He turned to Ronaldo and the wind threw his tie into his face. He threw it over his shoulder. "So," he said, "So what do you think I should do about this Ian Hines situation."

Ronaldo took a deep breath. "You see how you feel right now?" Ronaldo said, "I told you. I told you how it was. But the brainiac med student didn't want to listen."

"I don't know what you're getting at," Henry said. It was a lie.

"I told you what it was like to get busted. Look at all this room I got." Ronaldo swung an arm over the park. "You have this much room." He pinched an inch of air and squinted at Henry through it. "That's what you feel right now. And it's going to get smaller."

"So you're saying I should just give it back."

"I don't see what you're trying to prove," Ronaldo said, "What? You've already proven you're smart in school, and now you have to prove how dumb you are? It's only Hines this time. Give it back."

"The money and the acid?" Henry said

"That wasn't his money," Ronaldo said, "I'd keep the money."

"How do you know?" he said.

"It's not his because it's not. You don't hide drug money where your kid can find it. You hide it where you can spend it. Otherwise, what's the point."

"It seems like your kid's bed would be the best place to hide it. Nobody would think to look there," Henry said. He thought of the hiding place in his shower wall. It was a safe place.

"Not everyone is as smart as you, Henry," Ronaldo said, "Some of us are just stupid. And they would look there, believe me."

They had to go back and load up the bricks, because Ronaldo's car might not start if it got wet. They rolled off with the bricks sinking the back end. A light rain started. The windshield wiper on Henry's side cut into the glass. He wished Ronaldo would turn on the radio to cover the grating sound; but if he asked, Ronaldo would think that he was insulting his car.

They left the park and listened to the windshield getting sliced. Ronaldo said, "I wouldn't wipe my ass with this car."

Henry looked at him, then looked at the road. Then he looked back at Ronaldo. He looked ready to cry.

He wiped his eyes with the back of his hand. "Every time I trip," he said, "Every time, I get emotional after. This is why I don't do it."

Henry dug for the right words. "So why'd you do it this time," he said.

"It's your fault," Ronaldo said, "I've been so nervous about this thing you did to Hines that last night I just had to get whacked out."

But Henry didn't feel guilty. Even if he had, it wouldn't have convinced him to give in to Hines.

They were at the end of Canal Boulevard, stopped at a red light. Banks and businesses line one end of Canal; cemeteries line the other. Henry and Ronaldo were surrounded by cemeteries. Civil War dead, yellow fever dead, car accident, cancer, old broken hip that can't crawl to the phone. An enemy had left a crow's head on one tomb. The rain beat the maggots from its trachea. Crepe paper streamers turned to pink water on a friend's grave, and an open, full can of beer had been left at the tomb's door. Deep down, even the enemy wants a reply. There's no shame in this.

You get buried above ground in New Orleans or you'll float away. From the intersection he could only see the first row of tombs through the fence. A copper statue of a kind woman carried a lantern to a door. Under the eaves there was a hornets' nest. The hornets were drunk on rain.

"Are these bricks for Hines?" Henry asked.

"These bricks are for Mr. Bordelon."

"Wait," Henry said, "Who's that?"

"You don't know anything," Ronaldo laughed—a real laugh, for the first time that day. "Mr. Bordelon died yesterday and you're about to help me get rid of him."

7

They pulled into the alley behind the funeral home. The Bronco hearse was under the car port. Ronaldo cursed at it. "Wait here," he said. He got out of the car, backed the hearse out, then drove it a little ways up the alley. He backed the car in to where it had been.

Ronaldo said, "Nobody's here yet. I want to get this done quick."

They got out, and Ronaldo unlocked the back door of the funeral home. A ramp for rolling caskets ran down from it. They lined the bricks Fup in the hall, beside the door to the cold room. Ronaldo pulled out a key chain and plucked out a key marked with dirty white tape. He put the key in the knob.

"Wait," Henry said, "What's going to be in here–this Bordelon guy? Give me a warning." He remembered what his lab instructor had said about the difference between anatomy lab and a morgue–a morgue was a different story. They still looked like people. A funeral home was the next stop after the morgue.

Ronaldo looked at him, then he turned the key and threw open the door.

"Oh my God!" Ronaldo shrieked at what he saw.

* * *

Henry looked. There wasn't anything horrible in there. His heart was still in his throat.

Ronaldo laughed. For the first time today it didn't sound mean. "Shit, Hank, you should have seen your face!" he said, "Change your pants."

The cold room had once been bedrooms for the children. The wall between them had been knocked out, and one of the doors boarded over. There were pieces of plywood where the windows had been, studded with two air conditioners each. None were turned on. Four-inch thick sheets of fiberglass insulation were nailed to the walls. Pink fur showed where the paper had been nicked. It was hot in the cold room. A radio on the window sill played "Rock Me Gently."

In the corner was a cabinet, and beneath it a desk top, not unlike those in the lab at school. A stainless steel table on wheels held two spigotted plastic barrels containing cadaver cologne, and some gray stuff that smelled even worse. On a lower shelf was a rusting pump-machine with needle gauges and two black hoses snaked around it. A plug ran from it to the wall. At about the same level, a faucet stuck through another pink hole in the fiberglass. Screwed to it was a twenty-five foot garden hose with a gun nozzle. The floor was covered in layers of clear plastic that ran up the walls. In the center of the room was a drain. Henry doubted it ran into a tank—just straight into the ground.

This place isn't a funeral home, he thought. Not a real one.

Over the drain stood a stainless steel table with a lip around the edge, and a gentle grade down to a hole at one end. This was the embalming table. Against the back wall was a table with the stretching, bending, rolling legs of a paramedic's stretcher, but instead of a patient on top there was a dull, copper coffin. The lid was open. It looked like it was lined with white prom dresses.

Ronaldo was still giggling at his own joke. He carried in two cinder blocks and dropped them into the coffin. It tried to roll away, but he caught its edge and hit a wheel lock with his toe.

"Well?" he said.

Henry shrugged, carried over two blocks, and dropped them in. Maybe this was a snipe-hunt joke played on new Palace Springs employees. He'd be a good sport and play along.

But Ronaldo kept bringing the blocks. Henry followed suit. Ronaldo straightened the bricks. He looked anxious, and hurried.

"Where's this Bordelon?" Henry said.

Despite himself, Ronaldo smirked. "Who's that?"

"I assume that we're faking a heavy coffin for a phony funeral," Henry said, "He's alive somewhere?"

"What's a death?" Ronaldo said. He looked deadpan idiot—the same face he had used to deny everything in high school; the priests had hated it. Henry started laughing. Ronaldo did too.

"Shut up!" Ronaldo sputtered, "This is serious!"

"Right," Henry said.

Ronaldo lifted one end of the coffin. "It's not heavy enough," he said, worried.

"We haven't got all of them in yet. We could break up some of the leftovers and put the pieces in the holes of the other ones," Henry said. He wiped the sweat off his mouth with the back of his hand.

"That might work," Ronaldo said. He turned around and ran out of the cold room. Henry swatted gray dust from the bricks off his tie. He remembered that he should be studying. He wondered if Hines really did want to talk to him. Ronaldo had been high when he called, he now knew.

Ronaldo came back with a sledge hammer. He whacked at a cinder block. "You're going to rip the floor cover," Henry said. He picked up the pieces and worked them into the space left in the other blocks.

Once the blocks were all shattered and tucked in, Ronaldo again picked up the end of the coffin. "It's still not heavy enough! I have an idea," he said. "Wait here." He ran out again.

Henry looked at his watch. Embryology. The word kept coming to him. Embryology exam.

This time Ronaldo came back with a five gallon bucket of dirt and shells and weeds from the alley. Sweat ran from his chin. “Help me spread this in there,” he said.

They each took hold of the handle, and Henry tipped the bucket from the bottom. Ronaldo used his other hand to spread the dirt out. Then Ronaldo uncoiled the garden hose from the floor and turned the faucet. He shot a beam of water onto the dirt; the mud would weigh more. Henry jumped back to avoid being splattered. It was only when he saw the coffin’s white lining ruined by the mud that he believed this was for real.

His head went light. All at once, he didn’t feel guilty for not studying. It had been too long since he and Ronaldo had worked on a scheme.

Ronaldo dropped the hose and lifted the end of the coffin. He looked relieved. “What time is it,” he said as he closed the lid.

Henry looked at his watch. Ronaldo wheeled the coffin past him. “Three after three,” Henry said.

“We dicked around at the stadium too long,” he said. “They’re going to be here soon.” Ronaldo had to open the office door and wheel the coffin in part way to make the turn down the hallway—a real funeral home would be better designed. He sent Henry with the hearse keys to back it in.

Henry started the hearse. In the mirror he saw Ronaldo’s car pulling out. The gas pedal and steering were squishy, and he made it lurch in reverse. He giggled. Without being drunk, I’m giggling; medical school has made me serious before my time, he thought.

Ronaldo was standing beside the coffin under the car port. He saw them in the rear-view mirror; he pressed the brake, and the brake lights turned the whole scene red like death in a video game.

Henry parked and got out. He said, "You look like you're in a vampire movie."

"I was supposed to buy real bricks for this," Ronaldo said, already opening the Bronco's back doors. Pushing with one practiced hand, he slid the coffin onto the green slab. He brushed by Henry and got behind the wheel of the hearse.

"Ronnie?" someone called from behind the funeral home's closed door. It was a man's voice.

Ronaldo turned sharply to the voice and went gray. His color had been on the way up while they loaded the coffin.

The door opened. A gray-haired, gray-mustached man stepped out, wearing a darker gray suit too tight on him. He was thin and gave the impression of being tall, but Henry could see over him.

Looking at Henry, he said, "Is this Henry? I'm Ed Landry." He offered his hand and Henry shook it. "You're going to be a doctor, am I correct?" He was native New Orleans, by the way he talked; he looked like he had an ulcer and not much money.

"I hope so," Henry said.

Ronaldo looked at them with his hands tight on the wheel.

Mr. Landry put both hands on the small of his back. "I've had two lumbar fusions," he moaned, "My back rejected the first one. So now they tell me to put a heating pad on it, or ice. Aren't those opposites?"

Henry had no idea, but this man gave him attention like no adult ever had. "It depends on whether the pain is from inflammation or cramping," he guessed.

"Oh," Mr. Landry said, "I guess that makes sense. I had a knee replaced too." He touched his right leg. "What's funny is that the knee is artificial, but my body took that, and they took bone from my hip here for the fusions, and my body rejected my own bone. It never fused right." He smiled and put up his hands. "I give up."

He wasn't a Texan, but like a Texan, Mr. Landry kept his mustache long so he could tuck away his mouth behind the hair when flummoxed. He looked like he did it often, and he did it when he looked into the back of the hearse. "Is that Bordelon?" he said, "Get that out, Ronnie."

Ronnie? Henry thought. And did Mr. Landry know what was in the coffin?

"You know the rules, Ronnie," Mr. Landry said. Ronaldo was already out of the hearse, walking toward the back. He didn't look at Henry.

"Come with me, please, Henry?" Mr. Landry went back inside.

Henry followed, then stopped. "Am I meeting with Mr. Hines?" he said, "Can I get my bag from Ronaldo's car?" He wanted the tape recorder.

Mr. Landry looked befuddled. "This won't take a minute," he said.

Ronaldo had opened the back of the hearse, and there was the casket again, listening to them. "I'll bring it in for you, Henry. Go in," he said. He shooed him away with his hand. He was hurrying the stretcher back in place with a clatter.

Henry followed Mr. Landry down the hall. He had no idea what was going to happen, but for some reason Mr. Landry disappointed him. Over his shoulder, he said to Henry, "You know, after the first fusion failed, they told me that the bone they took from my hip wasn't no—wasn't any good, and they should have used donated bone. Well, I said, 'Doc, you should have told me that before. In my line of work I can get my hands on plenty.'"

Henry didn't laugh because they were outside the office door, and Hines would be inside. Mr. Landry chuckled nervously. He opened the office door and stood with an arm out to guide Henry without touching him. The motion was the only graceful thing about him.

He first saw what appeared to be a high school football coach. Only a coach would wear blue Bike nylon shorts like that. The coach, solid and slit-mouthed, was sitting with his arms folded on a chair just inside the door. He sneered a little at Henry— to make *his* team Henry would have to eat a loaf of white bread a day and get some meat on him.

Mr. Landry indicated the coach, "This is Mike," he said.

The coach's face didn't change. He offered a hand with sausage digits, without taking the other from his armpit. Henry shook it.

Ian Hines sat in the other chair, in front of Mr. Landry's desk. He wasn't wearing glasses and looked like he would be happier elsewhere. He looked at Henry with his mouth a little open, then closed it.

"Maybe you remember Mr. Hines," Mr. Landry said, without a hint of accusation.

Henry walked up and offered his hand. Hines stood and shook. He was taller than Henry remembered. His suit was shiny like lead shavings. For a bad artist, Hines dressed exceedingly well.

"Henry Marrier," Henry said, "Good to meet you. Again."

Hines grinned sheepishly. Henry hadn't expected that, and it made him angry.

Mr. Landry stood there like he wanted to pull the three of them together in a hug. "Chairs," he said. He looked around like he had just lost a couple of them. "We need another chair."

"Right here, right here," Coach said, bringing his chair forward, "I'll stand." He put the chair down behind Henry, then went back and leaned on the wall by the door. Mr. Landry walked around his desk and sat down. He had drawn the curtains.

Hines and Henry sat. Henry tried to find the way he had held his hands and legs in his medical school interviews. From the corner of his eye, he saw that Hines had found it: legs crossed one over the other, with hands stashed on his knee. A suit like Hines' just tells the limbs where to settle. If Henry sat that way now, he'd look insincere. He was liking Hines less.

Mr. Landry rocked twice in his chair, pouting behind his mustache. He put his elbows on the desk and laced his fingers. He wore no jewelry, not even a watch.

"Well," he said, "I've already apologized to Mr. Hines for you, Henry."

Henry felt his face get hot.

"It was real awkward for me. I told him," he said, waving a hand at Hines. Henry didn't take his eyes from Mr. Landry's face. "I never even laid eyes on you before today. I could be a better businessman and meet the people I hire, I know."

A polite chuckle from Hines.

Henry couldn't manage a smile.

Mr. Landry laughed, "I mean, let's face it. If I was a good businessman I wouldn't be running a fucking funeral parlor out a three bedroom." Wimps like Mr. Landry shouldn't curse any more than a kid should. It didn't sound genuine.

Hines laughed. Henry wondered if Hines remembered that his son had been bled and pickled across the hall. Did he even bury a son? Or a coffin full of bricks?

"But joking aside, I want to get serious. Henry. I don't feel like my job is to make money. It's to help people through tragedy. It's disaster relief, like the government. I say again and again to clients, if I was helping out with the sandbags in a flood, I wouldn't want a lot of money," Mr. Landry said.

Henry thought of the rigged coffin catalog in the desk drawer.

Mr. Landry's voice went tender. "It does my heart good to hear Ian laughing now, after his tragedy." He cracked a sweet smile, then that faded. He sighed. "Obviously I'm just talking around this now. I've refunded Mr. Hines for your services that evening. For a business like ours, Henry, that's hard. I'm laying down crumbs month-to-month. Now, he's been good enough not to seek any kind of legal action. We couldn't afford that. No way, no how."

Hines raised a gracious hand and lowered it. Henry didn't care about Hines's tragedy—he did until Hines had called this meeting— but he was sorry that Mr. Landry had been dragged in. He was just an old man who thought that since he was lonely and poor, his work must be holy. Not too holy for the occasional rip off, but a man's got to live–he imagined him saying just that, and meaning it. If Mr. Landry was afraid of "legal action" then there was no way he knew what had been taken.

"So I suggested that we just settle this like neighbors. There's not enough of that in this world. I hope I wasn't out of line, Henry, but I told Mr. Hines that you would go with him now and replace the property involved. And, Henry, I hope you can afford it out your own pocket," Mr. Landry said. Looking anxious, he added "I hope it wasn't out of line, but I said that you would buy him *four* boxes of corn dogs."

Hines tittered. Henry laughed. "Corn dogs?" he said, "You worried he was going to sue over corn dogs?"

Mr. Landry looked dire. "I can't really afford to feed you at a job, Henry, I know. But still, I hope in the future you can control yourself better."

Henry said, "I think I can swing four boxes of corn dogs."

"Ian's laughing now because he's embarrassed," Mr. Landry said, "He feels silly for even bringing this up. But he was upset after his tragedy, and I said I wouldn't feel right until this got settled like neighbors. I figured four boxes would, you know, compensate."

Henry hadn't eaten any corn dogs. Hines must have said he had, knowing that Henry would get the message. He couldn't think of a way out. "I should have been more considerate," he said. He looked at Hines, who looked back deadpan—he was playing along too. "I'm sorry. I'll buy whatever microwaveable snack food you want. Pigs-in-blankets, even."

Mr. Landry said, "I also said, 'Ian, I won't feel right unless you go right from here and Henry buys them for you.' I know you don't have a car, but Ronnie can drive you home after you get back. Y'all two go in Ian's car."

From behind them, Coach Mike said, "Ronnie just left."

Henry turned all the way around in his chair and said, "He didn't leave a backpack, did he?" Coach shook his head. Coach saw the worry on his brow; Hines and Mr. Landry didn't. Now he had no tape recorder. Henry looked at his watch—not for the time, but for a little time to think. Classes were over by now. "I have a class. I really can't do it now," he said.

"How long could it possibly take?" Mr. Landry whined, "There's a Schwegmann's four blocks up. I can give you a ride back. Your only other choice is a cab, and you'll miss your class for sure then."

He felt like his chair was sinking into the floor, until Hines had a foot on him. "Sounds good to me," he said.

8

Mr. Landry dismissed them after shaking their hands. Coach was smiling now, like Henry might make the bench after all, and he slapped his back as he and Hines walked out of the front door. Across the street a little boy bounded down the sidewalk on a giant, green, plastic worm. When Henry was that age he imagined that when you got to heaven, you would be shown separate vats containing all you had ever eaten, peed, or pooped. A translucent angel stood there to commend your translucent soul on a job well done: the vats were very full.

Hines drove that blue, frog-looking station wagon. It was parked at the curb, and Hines unlocked the passenger door without saying anything. Henry got in.

Once Hines sat down behind the wheel, Henry said, "Well, let's get some snack foods."

Hines didn't go for it. "I thought we could go get a bite to eat and talk," he said.

"I don't think I understand," Henry said. He tried his best to look innocent.

"Will you reach in the glove compartment there and hand me the map?" Hines said.

Henry opened the compartment. Inside were several maps. Sticking from beneath them was the butt of an automatic pistol. His mouth went dry. "You want this New Orleans one?" he said. He saw from the corner of his eye that Hines was watching his face.

Hines sounded pleading. "I just want to talk this out," he said.

Henry offered directions, but Hines declined and pored over the map. He left the glove compartment open. Henry wondered if he really had needed the map–the gun was looking back at him. He could take it up and kill Hines. Hines folded the map without difficulty and asked him to put it away. He closed the gun away with the map.

Once they were on their way, Henry had time to think. He had no doubt the gun was loaded. He had no doubt that Hines meant to intimidate him with it. It worked. He was afraid.

He needed nerve to do anything about it. He thought of the work he should be doing and about Hines's bad art, and these made him angry enough.

At the stoplight on Causeway and Veterans, he reached in and took out the gun. By the time Hines had realized it, he had stripped out the magazine and checked the chamber—empty. Hines liked to keep it muzzled like Henry liked to keep his Glock. He locked the slide open and put the gun away and put the magazine—loaded—into his pocket.

Not bad for an unfamiliar gun. He had to suppress a grin; he felt like he had just jumped from roof-to-roof between two buildings. He had been afraid and did it anyway. Not bad at all.

"I don't like them loaded," he said.

He saw Hines's throat move when he swallowed. He looked sick.

On the interstate, Henry said, "Are you not from here?"

"You know I'm not from here," Hines said.

"I just wondered because of the map," Henry said, keeping it conversational.

Hines didn't sound mean, more like he needed several nights' sleep. "Let's drop the charade, can we, Henry?" he said, "I know you went through our pictures."

They got off I-10 on Carollton. Traffic was terrible. A black high school kid was getting laughs from his friends at the bus stop by pretending to have cerebral palsy and staggering spastically into traffic. Hines was the only driver to slow down.

"Where are we going?" Henry said.

"There's a place on Magazine Street," Hines said.

"There's a lot quicker way to get there, too."

Hines looked at him and said, "You know, you're making it really hard for me to feel good about myself."

That made him feel too guilty to answer. Hines drove without saying anything, and took the long way, down Carrollton to River Bend to St. Charles. The traffic was so slow that even the jogging Tulane students passed them.

Hines parked and walked them toward a cafe with walls mirrored above waist level, so each of them could watch the place like a fly. The floor was tiled in white hexagons, like fly eyes.

Henry remembered that he hadn't eaten lunch. He looked in the case, but all he saw was ice cream. Hines had not asked for his bullets back; he saw Hines's leg from the corner of his eye and wondered if he had another holster on his calf. The guy behind the counter was Henry's age, but instead of being in medical school he had a crew cut and a silver bone through his nose. At a corner table, some boys in Martyrs' uniforms sat hunched over milk shakes like they were beers.

Hines got a milkshake that took two hands to get over to a table. It looked good. Henry got the same and it set him back $4.97. For that much, he could have gotten a real lunch at the Popeye's across the street.

When he sat down, Hines said, "These are great. There's espresso in them, so you get the sugar rush, and then a buzz from the coffee. In this heat, I'm hooked on them."

"They cost enough," Henry said.

Hines looked at him and scowled. He sniffed. He reached into his jacket—

Henry stiffened in his chair. *Fuck he's got another gun and he's going to shoot me for insulting his milkshake—*

—And pulled out a tape recorder, the same size as the one left in Henry's bag, which was in Ronaldo's car. He had tried not to show alarm, but his face must have betrayed him, because Hines had a stupid smirk on his face.

He put the recorder on the table between them and pressed RECORD. "I just want to talk." Hines sucked on his straw. He looked like a handsome mosquito.

"Shoot," Henry said. He wished he had chosen a different word.

"Where are my corn dogs, Henry?" Hines spoke loudly for the recorder.

Who was going to hear this tape? Lawyers? Well, if Hines was going to talk in code, he would break it. "I told you that I would buy four boxes, Mr. Hines," he said, speaking loud, too, "That's what we decided with Mr. Landry. I don't think I understand how you expect to get back something I ate. I almost think that you aren't talking about corn dogs. Is this some kind of code for drugs?"

Hines's hand shot out and stopped the recorder. He glared, but through it he looked helpless. All he had was the tape recorder, Henry guessed; that was his plan. Hines left his hand on it and stared at him like he would wish him away, if only he had will enough.

Hines stared. Henry stared back. The Martyrs' boys got up and left. Henry lost the staring contest and smiled. "Damn it, this isn't a game," Hines said.

Henry guessed that he could take the tape as easily as he had the bullets, and he would feel the same wondrous joy at what he could make his hands do. Surgery would be like that. But taking the tape would be cruel. Still smiling, he said, "What is it, then?"

Each of them knew that threats would come next, and they were quiet again. Henry drank his milkshake and wiped off the mustache it left. Hines had turned sideways in his chair and was staring at the cash register. He put his fingers to his temple and closed his eyes, pouting, waiting for a new plan for getting his acid back. Sitting there quietly, he seemed older for the first time that day. Henry looked at people of Hines's age and dress and assumed they were competent enough to run the world. But here I am, 22 years old, and pushing him around, he thought. Hines wasn't doing his job. He didn't deserve to get his acid back. Henry waited to swat away the next attack.

And waited. Hines sat there, rubbing his temple. He wasn't waiting for a plan to come; he was waiting for an awful feeling to leave. He was growing older by the minute. Henry no longer doubted that his son was really in that coffin.

Hines took a deep breath and turned back to the table and his milkshake. He felt no better, and did not seem to expect otherwise. It was not an act. Henry felt he shouldn't stare, but stared.

Hines picked up the tape recorder and dropped it into his jacket pocket. He didn't press any buttons. "So you're in medical school."

"Yes."

"I was going to be a vet when I started college," Hines said, "But I couldn't stand the chemistry. Or more importantly, I couldn't get the grades." He forced a chuckle.

Henry said, "Are you kidding? It's so not hard. Chemistry's nothing but factor-label."

"Another problem I had was college in general," Hines said, "I came here for school in the early '70's—I'm not from the States—and believe me, it was a lot harder to be eighteen then. Anything you wanted to do, you did it, and there was somebody there going, 'Right on.' And I hadn't been prepared for that at all. I wonder now if I had been five years younger or older, things would have been more calm and I might have actually gotten some education."

"Where are you from?" Henry said.

"I grew up in Brazil."

"You don't have an accent at all."

Hines said, "Thank you. I've worked on it." He looked up from the table and said, "Just remember, once you're a doctor: money isn't everything. Take it from me."

Jesus, Henry thought, I already took your acid from you. He covered his mouth so Hines wouldn't see him smile.

"What's so funny?" Hines said.

"Nothing," Henry said, dropping his hand, "How old are you?"

Hines looked embarassed. "Forty-two."

Henry couldn't believe it. Hines had more hair than he did. "You don't seem that old."

"That's cause I don't worry about nothing," Hines said, and of this he seemed proud. "I don't even have a job." He smiled at that. He beamed. He sat up in the chair and faced Henry. You would think a stage hand had crept out of the wall and replaced the bulb in Hines that had blown out.

It made Henry uneasy, so uneasy that he didn't think to play dumb. "I thought you were an artist," he said.

"Now Henry," Hines said, "How would you know that if you had just stayed in the dining room at my house like you were supposed to? That's my wife's art."

Henry felt the heat in his face. "So what do you do?" he said.

Hines had been waiting for this. "I'm a gangster," he said. His smile said that he had won—hand over the acid.

Henry said, "You're a gangster."

Hines said, "Yes, I am a gangster. I'm a Brazilian gangster."

"Like not a Crip-Blood-Crack gangsta," Henry said, "Like a Chicago gangster."

"Yeah, but from Brazil," Hines said, "Like Scarface."

Henry couldn't imagine Hines beating anybody with a sawed-off baseball bat over an unpaid shy. But what did he know about gangsters, in real life? Maybe Hines was telling the truth, and he should give in. But one more question:

"Mr. Hines," Henry said, "How did the pall bearers carry your son's casket?"

Hines was stunned, but then his eyes went shiny. He knew this one. "Six guys, carrying it on their shoulders without using their hands."

"You mean like the picture every paper in the country ran when that witness in the Gotti trial got whacked. That's how you got that idea," Henry said, "And Scarface was from Cuba."

"Not in the original version."

"No. In the original he's Italian."

"You know, Henry," Hines said. These were prepared lines. "You're a smart ass. Notice I didn't say 'wiseass.' Someone who is wise knows better than to take what doesn't belong to him."

Henry looked dumbfounded. "I really don't get what you're talking about, Mr. Hines. I'm sorry."

"Henry," Hines said, "Do you know what a 'money drop' is? There's no reason you should."

"Sure. It works like this: the don gives some kid who wants to be in the Family an envelope of money—say, a thousand dollars. The don says, 'Drop off this eight hundred for me.' Whether the kid returns the extra money or takes advantage determines if he's trustworthy."

"It might also determine if he's dead or not," Hines said. "Where are my corndogs?"

Henry put his hand out to his glass and noticed it was shaking. To steady it, he remembered that he had Hines's bullets. "What kind of gun is that in the car?"

"A SIG-Sauer nine. It's the best in the world. The British special forces carry them."

"I've never seen a SIG before."

"They're hard to find. They get scooped right up," Hines said. After the perfect pause, he said, "Unless you go through special channels."

Henry was expected to ask about the special channels, but didn't. "How's it shoot?" he said, taking a swallow of milkshake.

"Actually, I just put some cheap stuff through it the other day, and it didn't feed right. That shouldn't happen in a special forces gun. I might take it to my gunsmith."

Henry reached in his pocket and took out the magazine. He held it low so the cashier couldn't see. "You know, you shouldn't keep it loaded up all the time like this. That might be why."

He hadn't taken it out to give advice. He had taken it out to remind Hines who was in charge.

Hines looked at it. He wanted it back.

Henry put it back in his pocket. That was the coolest thing I have ever done, he thought.

"Everybody knows that," Hines said, primly, "It just shouldn't be an issue with a SIG."

"I own four guns," Henry said.

Hines said, "I've always believed, beware of the man with just one gun. He's going to be good with it."

"I'd worry more about the man with four," Henry said.

That scared them quiet again. They looked everywhere except at each other. Hines got up for a cup of coffee. Ronaldo had been right in the car earlier: Henry often said the wrong thing. But not today. He couldn't believe the things he had said today. He couldn't believe he was still winning.

"'Epitome of a rat who lies'," Hines said.

"Excuse me?" Henry said.

"'Epitome of a rat who lies'," Hines said, with a relish like he repeated it to himself often, just for the sound. "Who was that."

"I have no idea."

"Sammy 'The Liar' Gravano. He was a witness in the Gotti trial."

"Oh right," Henry said, "They made little flyers with a picture of a rat body and his face on it. That was in the papers too."

Hines shut up. He looked like he was getting depressed again.

"That was something, huh?" Henry said, "The crowd outside the courthouse turned over cars."

"You know who the worst mob in New York is?" Hines said.

Henry had read that the Russians had taken over Brighton beach, and would pry out gold fillings after a hit. He had read that the Haitians were the most feared, since being so poor they were absolutely fearless. But he gave the classic answer: "Irish."

Hines looked crestfallen. "Right," he said, "Most people guess Italian."

"Too many movies," Henry said.

"Yep, they're by far the worst. They don't back down, they don't negotiate. Just put a round in your head, and then they drop the body facing east so you know it was the Irish they offended," Hines said.

Henry watched him take a sip. He had the feeling that if he showed any fear, Hines would now say, oh yeah, I'm in the Irish mob too.

"I thought it was facing west," Henry said, "I thought the Irish ran the East Side."

"It's east. They face the dead guy to where they are—it means, he stood up to the Irish, and looked what happened to him."

"I thought they faced him west, and put the bullet in east. That's why they're so ruthless, because they always got people from the back of the head, by surprise."

Hines's brow furrowed. "Wait," he said, "So you're facing west. If the bullet's going east, that's the front of the head."

"No. It's the back."

"No. Look." Hines said. He pulled out a Mont Blanc pen and began drawing on a napkin.

Henry then realized he might be wrong, but before Hines could prove it to him, he said, "Mr. Hines, can we get to the grocery and get this settled?"

"So you know what a money drop is," Hines said, folding the napkin into a square and putting his pen away, "Well that day at my house you failed one. The day you took advantage of my tragedy you failed one. Don't make me say more."

So he did know about the money in Paolo's room? Or was this more intimidation bullshit? "I don't get it," Henry said.

"You weren't supposed to take that stuff from my freezer. I'll leave it at that. You failed your trial," Hines said. He looked anxious. He's running out of lies, Henry thought.

"Mr. Hines, don't take this the wrong way," Henry said, "Did you do a lot of drugs in those college days?"

"I did."

"Do you still use them? I've sat here now for over an hour, and I have no idea what you're talking about. I feel like you shouldn't have a gun. I feel like I should possibly call the police, for your own safety," Henry said, "You've been through a lot recently." Maybe Hines was going to kill himself, too. He felt like a doctor for thinking it.

"Call the cops," Hines said, "You'll see."

Again he backed down, and again they were quiet. Henry thought that if this was thrilling earlier, it wasn't anymore. When he was calm again, Hines said, "You're right. I have been through too much recently. Henry—please give them back. This is the only way I know how to ask. It's the last time."

He thought that Hines would stare him down again. Instead, he looked at the table and closed his eyes for a moment.

"Is something going to happen to you if you don't have them?" Henry asked.

"No," Hines said.

Henry thought about it. He felt bad for Hines—but he thought of how ordinary he would feel with no secret. Hours and hours of nothing but paper... notes, books, atlases. Medical school would squeeze the juice out of him. He said, "I can't give them back."

Hines sneered out a chuckle, more at himself than at Henry. Henry had popped him with a nail, and he was deflating in his seat.

Back when Henry used to go to his Introduction to Clinical Medicine class, he had learned the questions to ask in a depression screening. The doctor needn't worry about offending the patient or making him feel worse. Often, depressed people are relieved to talk.

"How have you been feeling recently?" Henry asked.

"Worthless," Hines said.

"Do you ever feel like hurting yourself?"

"Are you checking if I'm depressed, Henry?"

The lecturer hadn't said the patient might be wise to the doctor. He was flustered. "Yes," he said.

Hines gave him a pained smile. "Even when I'm feeling good doctors ask me that. I must send out rays. They usually screen for mania, too, but I guess I'm obviously pretty fucking far removed from that now. I appreciate the concern," he said, "I'll save us some time: I am depressed. My son just killed himself."

They hadn't covered "mania" in lecture. It didn't sound good.

"Now you will ask if I've thought of killing myself and how I would do it," Hines said. He pulled out another napkin from the table dispenser and began wiping his hands, though they appeared clean. "Oh, I guess if I wanted to kill myself I would steal some drugs from someone in the mafia. Then I'd be dead soon enough." Hines smiled. If he had fangs, he would be showing them.

So they couldn't avoid it any longer. The threats were starting. Henry decided to leave.

When he stood up, Hines said, "Do you know what a two-in-one is, Henry?"

Henry knew. "I'm sorry you feel bad," he said, "I'll get a cab."

"A two-in-one is an Irish mob trick. They bury two guys in one coffin. It gets rid of a body that way. The Italians have them both dead. The Irish leave the guy on the bottom alive, tied up. He lies in there, and he can hear the funeral going on. He cries with the gag in his mouth and then they bury him alive," Hines said, "He can hear the dirt falling. I'm going to get Mr. Landry to do a two-in-one on you."

Hines was out of his mind. Out of that rinky-dink funeral home, Mr. Landry was lucky to get a one-in-one.

"Fuck you," Henry said.

Hines got up and grabbed him by the arm. In the mirror they could see the cashier watching them, alarmed. Hines said, "I want my corndogs back. I'll put eight grenades in your bastard mouth and watch your head blow up."

Henry jerked his arm away. His mouth said it without a thought from Henry. "I'll kill you," Henry said, "I got four guns. I got your bullets."

Hines let go of his arm and sat down. He had never threatened to shoot anybody before. Hines drove him to it, and judging by his face, he hadn't expected it to come to this either.

They looked at each other. After threats came fulfillment. Neither of them wanted that.

"I'll get a cab," Henry said. He walked out, and looked back for his bag. He remembered he hadn't brought it. Hines sat still, looking now his own age plus Henry's.

Once he was outside, the spit in his mouth went thick. Adrenalin, hitting him now after the argument was over like it hits after you've swerved the car. He thought of adrenalin hitting dead bodies in a smashed car. They hadn't swerved. Some Martyrs' boys at the bus stop stepped aside to let him by. He watched his reflection lumber by in a TV repair shop window. It reminded him of Bigfoot film footage he'd seen on a show about the paranormal.

By the time he got to the Circle K three blocks down he felt more powerful than monstrous. I just pulled that off, he thought. That wasn't multiple choice. That was my guts and my brains.

He withdrew cash from the ATM in the store and called a cab. While waiting he read *Seventeen,* but there were no monkey-girls in this issue. And he was distracted by the front window. He didn't feel comfortable standing by it. He remembered that he had to get his backpack from Ronaldo's car at some point. That was inconsiderate of him to leave with it like that.

In the backseat of the cab, he had two realizations: the Irish ran the West Side. They were called the Westies. So he and Hines were both wrong. And he realized that it wasn't that he didn't feel comfortable. He didn't feel safe. He thought, if Hines does his hand grenade thing I won't have a head. That will make it hard for me to kill him back.

But Hines couldn't get eight hand grenades. Hines couldn't even get his acid back. Hines couldn't keep his son alive. He had no doubt that Hines was still sitting at that table. Where did he go when his eyes went blank and he stared? Not far enough, because he came back as miserable as before.

The only thing that made him perk up was when he said he was in the mafia.

He couldn't get in touch with Ronaldo that night. Ronaldo's mom thought that call waiting was rude; Henry got a busy signal. That was fine. He didn't want to be told that he had made a mistake with Hines. He popped the bullets out of Hines's clip into the drawer in his armoire and threw the clip in after them.

He cleaned up his apartment instead of studying. In the bathroom he looked at the wall of the tub where the money was, and he felt like he was ruining the Hines family, though they had done nothing to him. Rather than dwell on it, he went to bed.

The coffin full of bricks–he pictured it being lowered down on ropes, though that wasn't done in this country anymore. Where did Mr. Bordelon go, while his funeral was going on? he wondered. If he could fake his own death and make off with a million in insurance money, Henry would go to the Caribbean, one of those little countries that don't care about passports, and for the first month he'd drink all day and exercise. He had read of such places. Or else he would go to Ann Arbor and live with Catherine, though she wanted nothing to do with him anymore. He would buy his own house and live there until she wanted him back.

Next he was half-dreaming, and it made no sense: the first thing Hines would do with a new life would be to rent a car and scour Northern California for his son. "This time we won't move, Paolo." This time you won't die.

9

Half of him wanted to concentrate on his career. He had to do well in school, and he had to do some research. Without research, all you would get would be snot specialties like pediatrics or family practice, and you would see colds your whole life. All the elite specialties started with "O." He should stop by otolaryngology, and orthopedics, and obstetrics, and ophthalmology to see if they'd take him on to a project. Residency was only three and a half years away.

He went by orthopedics. He would ask for fifteen minutes with the chairman.

"He's out of the country right now," said his secretary.

"How about next week?"

"Next week his surgeries are double booked because of his trip this week," she said, "And the following week he's in Miami."

He looked over the desk at the calendar she was reading. She wasn't lying. "Can I leave my name?"

She wrote it on message pad. "What year are you?"

"First."

She wrote that too.

"I have research experience."

"Good, good," she said, "Though I should say now that Doctor St. Germain usually says that first year students are best served by learning their basic sciences well."

* * *

The drudgery of class and lab was beginning to sap his enthusiasm, though. He found himself thinking of specialties so rarefied that the doctor would never be called, and a residency would be easy to get, because no one was practicing it. Trauma oncology: this is a specialty practiced by the trauma surgeon who only sees cancer patients, and then only if the tumor has been traumatized. "The bullet went through the patient's osteosarcoma and seeded metastases through the abdomen—page Dr. Marrier, the trauma oncologist." Every patient would merit a case report.

He looked and listened. First year students were welcome only in the lecture hall and in anatomy lab. But Hope Hospital for the poor was across the street, and word carried from there:

A young father without money or time for a car seat drove drunk with his baby daughter in his lap. He survived the accident, thanks to the baby. The ER docs call such a baby "an Arkansas air bag" to honor the hicks best known for the practice.

Or maybe they drown. St. Tammany Parish across the lake had the most drownings in America in the previous year.

Or lupus. The National Lupus Center was in Pennsylvania, but no one could explain why Louisiana had more lupus than anywhere else. *Lupus*—Latin for "wolf." You know how a trapped wolf will gnaw off its own foot? In Lupus your own immune system gnaws off your kidneys, or lungs, or brain, and you are freed from earth. Limp off into outer space. The only hope against lupus nephropathy was a renal transplant or daily hemodialysis—

Or so you hoped. Some Hope technician forgot to add osmolite to the dialysis solution. Distilled, clear water rushed into the vein, and billions of blood cells popped like the foam left by a wave. Three patients were found dead at the end of their dialysis sessions.

Or you could take a walk at night on the wrong street. Enter the morgue the next day as a "golf-course." That's what the ER docs called somebody with eighteen bullet holes in them.

Or just wait around for years. When he showered now, Henry noticed that left in the drain was a little hummingbird's nest of his own hair. He hadn't noticed himself losing hair before.

Or. Or. Or.... So many ways to die.

Fuck Hines. He wasn't giving it back. *I'm going to do something daring before I die.*

* * *

The one book he left in his bag before emptying it for the talk with Hines had been his dissector. It was now riding around with Ronaldo, so the next day he went to lab and couldn't read directions aloud. He could tell by Earnest's face that he took this as an affront, since he wanted to be read to while he dissected.

In med school slang, guys like Eric and Earnest were known as "gunners." Henry didn't see why guns should be so insulted.

They played surgeon. Henry played along, to get points for attendance. The cadaver still made him uneasy. Amanda got treated like the scrub nurse. Every day she came in, put gloves on, and stood at the head of the table, shifting from foot to foot, bored. The gunners asked her to hand them an instrument or to change a blade. She'd get glassy-eyed, pitying herself. Then she would go in the corner and study with her head in her hands. If you want to cut, say something, Henry thought.

Used to be that Eric and Earnest would place fat or skin on the table. Now they flung it, because that was what orthopedic surgeons did with pieces of bone. "Orthopods," as Eric called them. Lingo proves you're with it.

On Wednesday, Eric came to lab late. He and Earnest both wore scrubs now, like Henry. Eric had a length of clear plastic hose containing a straightened-out coat hanger. "If you guys want me to show you how to tube the cadaver, I can," he said, "I was a paramedic."

"When I worked in my dad's O.R. over the summer, I got to put the Foley's in," Amanda said. She was in a better mood because Eric hadn't been there; she was getting to dissect.

"I know this funeral home where they let EMT's practice on the corpses," Henry said. Ronaldo had said that renting out the bodies like that was easy money.

No response. From anybody.

Earnest braced one foot on the table and yanked on Mr. The Cadaver's wrist until his shoulder dislocated. "There," he said, "Now I can get at the plexus better."

Eric snapped his gloves on and walked toward the table with forceps—"pickups," he called them—in one hand, a scalpel in the other. "Move?" he said to Amanda.

She got out of the way of the scalpel and went to her place at the head of the table.

Now the race was on. Eric put his tube down on a stool. He and Earnest didn't know what specialty they wanted, but it had to have a really long residency. Pathology and radiology didn't count. Surgery was all that was left. To prove they deserved it, they came in every day and dug for the same structure on opposite sides. Whoever found it first won, and it was not a friendly contest. Keep the fingers away if they're using sharp instruments.

Earnest was sitting on a stool, with the cadaver's dislocated arm hanging off the table at a perfect angle. Eric would have dislocated his side, but that would be a point for Earnest. He had to angle his elbows in a weird way.

"Eric," Earnest said, "Do you have a dissector we can borrow? Henry forgot his."

Eric didn't want to leave the table for fear of losing his spot to Amanda. "I don't need it," he said.

The table was quiet. Amanda stared at the cadaver and sighed. Henry stared off into space and saw Hines. Hines and his SIG. Brazilian mafia or not, he didn't doubt Hines had more bullets and another magazine. What worried him more, though, was that Hines would call the cops. If he wasn't going to get his acid back anyway, why not just have Henry busted? He didn't like the thought of two NOPD officers in his apartment, which now contained guns and drugs. A Schedule I drug. Since LSD has no medicinal value, its possession and sale was prosecuted like heroin's. Nobody would understand. Maybe one of the cops would be Ronaldo's dad.

In the school library, he had found a legal pharmacology index. From what he could tell, he couldn't get in any really bad trouble, because the law didn't understand chemistry. To get prosecuted hard, he had to have a gram of acid. But acid's so powerful, it's dosed in micrograms. Even if the acid in his refrigerator were two hundred per tab, which was doubtful—that was hippie-era dosage—he didn't come close to a gram. This loophole must have been why it was possible in Berkeley to deal so easily. And why nobody was getting killed over it. The stakes weren't high enough.

He could just throw it away. Yeah—and then be as boring as Eric and Amanda and Earnest.

"Did you ever work in an O.R., Henry?" Earnest said.

"Nope."

"Me neither. I used to volunteer in the rehab unit."

Henry said, "I never did any volunteer work, actually."

Eric looked up. "None? What did you do, bribe the admissions committee?"

"I did a lot of lab work," he said, "Frog stuff."

Amanda said, "Do you want an MD/PhD?"

"Hell no," Henry said, and wondered if that was considered strong language, "No. I hate lab work. I think I want surgery."

"I thought you totally didn't like dissecting," she said. She smiled at him.

"I hate it," he said, "But I don't plan for my patients to be dead and brown and disgusting like this one."

She stifled a laugh and tried to catch Earnest's eye. Eric pretended not to hear. "Didn't you have to dissect the frogs?" Earnest said, without looking up.

"No. I sucked sperm out their cloacas," Henry said.

Eric muttered, "Thank you for sharing, Henry."

"I used a syringe," he said. "We dissected crawfish...." he was going to list all his dissections: a live worm and crawfish, a pithed frog, a cat, a pregnant shark, a squid. He had taken a pre-vet Bio class because they got to do surgeries in lab. He had taken out a live hamster's ovaries and sewn her back up, only to have her pant and roll over dead within minutes.

But he said nothing, because the next question would be, "Well then why does *this* bother you?" He was still breathing through his mouth. Some days his pulse would still go up when he saw the cadaver, if it's head was turned like it was sleeping. Flayed and sleeping.

"Did it hurt the frogs?" Amanda said.

Henry remembered grabbing the flippers and flipping a bullfrog's head against the lab bench to stun it. "I don't think they liked it," he said.

"I heard that next semester we have to operate on dogs in Physiology. I don't know if I can deal with that," she said, "I wouldn't mind if it were cats. I hate cats."

"Volunteer work is pretty pointless," Eric said, "All it helps with is the interview."

"The interview is pretty pointless," Earnest said, "'Why do you want to be a doctor?' They have to get the same answer all the time. No one is going to go in there and say, 'I want job security and a decent income.' What'd you say?"

"'I want to help people,'" Eager said.

"You stole my answer," Eric said.

"I thought everyone would say that, so I said, 'I don't like to see people suffer,'" Henry said, "Then my interviewer—she was some Hungarian lady in Pathology—said, 'Why not look the other way, then?' I didn't have an answer."

"So what did you say?" Eager asked.

"I said I didn't have an answer," Henry said, "She started giggling."

"Kind of the same thing happened to me," Earnest said. He didn't look up from his dissection and they had to lean to hear him. "I had Dr. Feldman, from Medicine. I said, 'I want to help people,' in so many words, and he goes, 'So why do this?'"

"What'd you do?" Henry said.

"I said, 'Well, I'm going into surgery because I like to work with my hands, so I guess I could become a carpenter. I'd still be helping people.'"

"Good answer," Henry said, "It must be true."

"No," Earnest said.

"I hate to tell you," Eric said, "But I got asked the same thing at Columbia, and I used the same thing, only I said I would be a barber."

"I would hate being a carpenter. I hate sweating. I think he believed me because I'm from Nebraska. If you're from the Midwest, you can get away with a lot," Earnest said.

"Did you know that most of the weed in the country comes out of Indiana now?" Henry said, "I read it in *The Atlantic*."

"I had heard that," Amanda said, "I don't get into drugs, but I had heard that."

Eric looked askance at the two of them and went back to work.

"That's why I want to go into surgery," Earnest piped in.

Amanda looked at him, confused. Henry said, "Because most of the weed in the country comes out of Indiana?"

"No," Earnest said impatiently, "Because I hate to sweat. I saw a parathyroidectomy at the hospital where I worked. The residents have to get in there early and get the patient prepped and opened up. Then the attending comes in an hour later and goes, 'What's the problem?' and gets the parathyroids out in fifteen minutes. Then he goes, 'Okay, close him up,' and goes back to the lounge to read the sports page and have coffee. And then they better not bug him unless the patient's crashing. It made the resident feel like complete you-know-what."

Henry had been wrong earlier: he had heard some students curse in the hall. His table-mates didn't. He wished one of them would.

"Dude, if you don't like to sweat I think you should pick another specialty," Amanda said, "My dad said it takes a totally long time before you're at that point. I never saw him when I was little."

Earnest shrugged. "What do you want, Amanda?"

"Derm or Optho. Something where I can watch my kids grow up," she said, "I'll get married too."

"I want to do surgery because my father had stomach cancer," Eric said, "Surgery saved his life. None of us doubt that."

Everyone cooed condolences. "How about you, Henry?" Amanda said.

"Well, it's nothing like Eric's reason. It's kind of weird," he said.

He should have shrugged and said he wanted to do surgery for the money. But of course, now they wouldn't let him rest.

"Okay, okay," he said, smiling. "I used to have really bad skin, and I would really enjoy picking at it. But I hated my dermatologist. So ever since I was fifteen I wanted to be a cancer surgeon because I thought it would be like popping giant zits out of people."

He thought it was funny. But they looked at him and waited for the real reason. But that was the real reason. Then they laughed–at him. Not at the idea. At him.

Henry said, "Y'all never had zit in your life? What's so fucking funny?"

* * *

He hadn't been joking. When he was thirteen, the zits started. You could have told him that acne was cancer of the face, and he would have nodded. He would sit on the edge of the bathtub and stare with sick fascination at the wheals and welts. His face was boiling over. Other kids at school had teased him, and the teachers asked if he had seen a doctor. He said that he had fallen off the steps and hit his head, and was knocked unconscious and foamed at the mouth; after that, the zits started. The zits were a form of seizure. After that story, the teasing stopped. He knew that he had done nothing to deserve his skin. Maybe he was being punished for something that his parents had done before he was born.

Two fantasies: he sold his soul to the devil, and all the zits he would ever get would gurgle to the surface and his face would slough off. The face that was left would be clean— handsome, even.

The other one involved a giant forehead abcess that his bastard dermatologist would have to lance, and he would get spritzed in the mouth. The guy was a bastard because he wouldn't prescribe retinoids. Retinoids would have cured him for life after one course of therapy. Even now, after his skin had cleared, and he understood that strong drugs had strong side effects, he promised himself that once he was a doctor, he would prescribe them to anyone who asked.

With skin like his, he had spent years trying to blend in with other kids. He had at first been too embarrassed to wear his motorcycle jacket, because it made him stand out. So now that he had been daring enough to stare down Hines, he decided to dare looking different.

"Give me a crew cut." He was in a hair salon on St. Phillip.

The hairdresser could have passed for a woman if his shirt hadn't been open. Lovely. Skinny. Rings in nipples and navel. He said not a word, even when he turned Henry to face the mirror.

It wasn't at all what he wanted. He looked like an astronaut.

The hairdresser took off more, until he was left with just an aura of fuzz. The haircut cost more than he had anticipated. At home, he checked out his head in the bathroom mirror. He looked dangerous, and he liked that. He toyed with the idea of growing a goatee and getting his ears pierced, but he remembered the rings on the hairdresser and thought, this is enough.

He checked from every angle: yes, his hair was going. The roots of his hair were black, too, like he had dumped ink over his head. That's because I'm rewriting myself, he thought.

* * *

How did he have time for this? After the first Embryology test—he Honored it, but so did a lot of people—he quit going to class.

The school library had stone busts of Hippocrates, and of Lord Lister, who first applied antisepsis and whose tribute is Listerine. If the med school knew anything about its students, there would be a monument for that unknown student who first thought of class note sets. An eternal flame would be appropriate.

Used to be that a first or second year medical student could go to class in his horned-rims and tie, and that would be enough. The doctors lecturing taught medical students with a blackboard and chalk. Compare a biochemistry text from 1966 with one only twenty years later—it's triple the weight. The only text that hadn't fattened was the one for Gross Anatomy, and Brewster students were still responsible for all of it. The reading for one subject alone was too much. One of Henry's Histology lecturers liked to run two slide projectors at once, and told them to follow along in the ten page, single-spaced handout on collagen types 1-23. A new collagen was discovered every year.

So years ago, some student somewhere had gotten this idea: why not have only one student tape record the lecture, take thorough notes on it, and distribute copies of the notes to the class via file drawers in the back of the lecture hall?

Class attendance dropped by half after students learned to trust the note sets. By second year, lectures would become seven-student seminars. Students would walk in during a lecture, pick up their note sets from their folders, and walk out. They only had to show up for exams. Professors' feelings got hurt. "You are not paying $28,000 a year to take correspondence courses," said the Embryology professor.

If I'm paying $28,000 a year, Henry thought, I can do whatever I want. Going to class was exhausting. That made him feel old, too. Just five years earlier, he had been seventeen, and went to school every day from eight until three with no problems. Now he got home and could barely keep his eyes open.

Then he quit going. He could wake up later, and had time to bike to a gym in a downtown hotel, where he started lifting weights again. On the way to the gym, he played a game: find the bullet holes. There was a stop sign that had been zinged through twice. Used to be that you had to go out to the country to see shot-up signs. There, that car that just went by: buckshot sprayed from a distance through the license plate. On Rampart one day, he found on the sidewalk an unfired 5.49 bullet, Chinese surplus.

The FBI investigated the police department. The police admitted that they only caught and convicted half the murderers—one in two. The FBI found the number to be one in four. At the bus stop Henry would see black kids of any age wearing plastic rosaries and death shirts: a photograph of the young dead man over dates. THERE'S A HEAVEN FOR A "G," the shirts read at the top.

On some days the stop sign would remind him of Hines and his gun. It was harder to be proud of what he had done when he didn't have Hines where he could see him.

Ronaldo called a few times and left messages, saying that he wanted to find out what Hines had said. Henry needed his bag back, but didn't return the calls. He still didn't want to discuss his meeting with Hines.

* * *

For the Anatomy practical examination, they would be allowed a total of ten minutes per lab room to identify three tagged structures per cadaver.

"I heard there was this guy last year who *slept* in the lab on the counter, he was studying so hard for the first lab practical. He knew the cadaver cold. He still failed," Eric said one day.

"I heard there was this girl who never went to lab, and just studied with one of those photo Atlases, and she Honored," Eric said another day.

"I heard this first practical was so hard two years ago that you might as well not study, and just start working on the next block," Eric said another day.

Eric also heard who was dating who. Eric heard that their lab instructor had failed Head and Neck when she was a student. Eric did not believe that he, or anyone else, should keep their mouths shut. Earnest and Amanda joined in on the gossip. Henry couldn't keep the names straight, or put faces to them.

He was smug after the first anatomy test, on Back and Upper Limb. He made sure Eric saw his exam paper—Honors for the written, and a High Pass on the practical. Eric hadn't heard this story, he witnessed it—there was this guy Henry who never went to class, and didn't touch the cadaver. He studied only from the Atlas, and when he took the practical, his brain threw color, labeled projections over all the brown muscles and nerves. There's a couple in every class—oddballs who can create a better dead body in their minds than the ones provided by the school.

"I think our table should be proud of Henry," Eric said, "What's important, though, is how much you *learn.*" Henry took that to mean that he had only Passed.

* * *

But then Head and Neck started. Do well on the first block, the lab instructor told them, because your grade needs the momentum for Head and Neck. Henry slept on the counter top in the corner. Half a paragraph of instructions from the dissector read aloud would take Eric and Earnest all lab to complete.

At the beginning of the year, all the students wanted to use the scalpel, because that's what they had heard the surgeons call for on TV. But in dissection and in real surgery, the blade is only good for getting in. After that you use fingers, or use the scissor-spreading technique like the instructors did: pop the tips between planes of tissue and pry them apart. Eric and Earnest both thought themselves good scissor-spreaders.

"Of course it looks good," Eric had said about his hand dissection last block, "I did it."

He was only half-joking.

But even the small scissors were too crude for Head and Neck; the tissue planes were too fine for their tips. They peeled off the face in strips, using the forceps. It took all three hours of lab for Eric to do one cheek; Earnest gave up. By the end of lab, he had only found the parotid duct, looping out of the fat of the right cheek.

Everybody was frustrated. They had all studied so much for the first block that they felt they deserved a week off; instead, they got this. Cadavers went un-wrapped and un-cologned, and they slammed the tanks shut in disgust at the end of lab.

On day two, Eric came in and said to Amanda, "Why don't you dissect? We've done it all semester."

Amanda brightened up. "M'kay," she said.

Jesus, Henry thought, give her the shit work, Eric. He settled on the counter with his hands crossed on his belly. He fell asleep. He dreamed that he bought a car with a coffee table in the back.

He was woken up by Amanda yelling, "All right, who the fuck took our fucking probe?!"

He must have slept long enough for her to get frustrated. He watched her huff around the lab: "Do *you* have our probe?"

That was the first time he thought she was cute.

10

Ronaldo left the message: he knew that Henry was too *good* to answer the phone, or even call him *back*, but if he wanted the money, he had another client's house for him to guard on Saturday. He would be there at 11 o'clock to pick him up.

He put his revolver in one pocket, and bullets in the other. His reflection didn't look suspicious. Better to have a gun and not need it than to need one and not have it, like the gun magazines said. It also sounded like something Hines would say. He put the thought away. Ronaldo showed up in the hearse at 11:20. Henry was sitting on a pile of books at the curb, reading an embryology note set. Ronaldo still had his bag. Before he had even gotten in the car, Ronaldo said from the window, "What happened with Hines. How come you don't call me back?"

Henry climbed in, sat down, and closed the door. His book bag was on the floor at his feet; he dumped his books into it. "You forgot that in here. I was trying to call and tell you," Ronaldo said. They pulled away. Ronaldo looked back and forth between the road and Henry's face. He was wearing a painted tie, with lines so fine that they must have been painted with a single boar whisker. "I like your hair, by the way," he said, "I cut my hair real short like that once, but my head was pointed."

"I tried calling you," Henry lied, "Your mom's always on the phone. Give me your cell phone number."

"I don't have that thing anymore," Ronaldo said, "It wasn't exactly mine."

"Your boss took it back?" Henry said, "I mean, our boss?"

"It wasn't exactly his, either."

"You stole it, then."

"You know what BellSouth makes on those accounts?" Ronaldo said, "Would you feel it if a little mosquito came up and took one hair off your arm? I don't call that stealing."

"You breaking into cars now?" Henry said, "Is that how you got it?"

Ronaldo made a swearing noise. "Give me some credit," he said, "Don't worry about where I got it. I don't have it now."

The curtain behind the seats was drawn. Henry pulled it aside with a finger, and saw a solid black casket, too dull to hold reflection. "Are we burying more bricks?"

"What bricks did we bury," Ronaldo said, "What's a brick?"

"Don't play dumb, Ronaldo," Henry said, annoyed, "Is there a person in there, or not?"

"Take a look," Ronaldo said.

"It's not locked?" Henry said.

Ronaldo laughed. "He's not going to escape," he said, "No, it's not locked. Take a look."

He twisted in the seat and lifted the lid. It was much lighter than it looked. The dead man inside had sideburns that ran to points at the corners of his mouth, a bald head, and a weak chin with a dimple. He looked like he'd sold tickets at a failing adult movie house. He looked so much like plastic that Henry thought he might find a seam running down his arms and over his head.

"He looks good, huh?" Ronaldo said, "I did his eyes."

False eye lashes peeled away from the eyelids at the corners. Henry closed the coffin and settled back into his seat. "Y'all ever cremate people?" he said.

"You can't cremate in New Orleans," Ronaldo said, "everybody's Catholic. Your body has to be intact."

"Why?"

"I think your body has to rise up and fight the antichrist."

"That's not why," Henry said, "It has to rise up and be judged."

"Why'd you ask if you knew?"

"I knew your answer would be better."

"They never taught us that. My dad said they used to teach him he was going to hell. All they did for us was tell us it's okay to have urges," Ronaldo said, "*Intact*, my ass. I don't think I want to be a mortician. I talked to these guys that work for Leinholder-Leggio—they're one of the funeral homes uptown—and these two guys are both licensed. They got a call from the police because these people over in the Marigny were complaining about the smell from next door. The police checked it out, and they wouldn't touch anything.

"So these guys are both licensed. They go to the house and they have on fucking air tanks they borrowed from the fire department, and white jumpsuits for contamination, and these gloves up to the shoulder they got from a slaughter house. This city is so pathetic they have to borrow. Most cities give the coroner's office the gear like that; not here. These two guys had to do this before. They got called because they have experience. They had to break in the front door with a crow bar. The cops and the neighbors all stood outside on the sidewalk and just watched.

"Inside, there was newspaper all over the floor—"

Ronaldo made a spreading motion of the dashboard.

"—like a bird cage. The smell was so bad that it was getting through their masks. Then in this giant bird cage they find this old fucking *man*, rotting into the paper on the living room floor."

As bad as Mr. The Cadaver smelled, Henry wondered what it would smell like uncut by formaldehyde and phenol, in an old man's dusty house, with the air conditioner broken. Flies and roaches. If their air tanks went out, those two morticians would have been like astronauts with their tethers cut.

"What was newspaper for?" Henry said.

"The old guy obviously lost his mind."

Ronaldo had not gotten on the interstate this time. They were heading uptown.

"That reminds me of something that happened to a classmate of mine," Henry said, "this girl who always wears tons of makeup. Amanda, my lab partner, says she dyes her hair. She was a tri-Delt at SMU. She won't talk to me. I got this story by spying.

"Just imagine this Southern Belle. She wants to go into emergency medicine because she wants to be able to schedule her own hours, so she can raise kids. And because of the TV show. She went on an ambulance ride, for experience. So she rode with one of the Hope crews one weekend, but nothing really happened all night. She was disappointed. But right as the shift was about to stop, they got a call about a car chase and a shoot-out with the cops, and a cop got hit."

"I remember that," Ronaldo said, "he almost died."

"So the ambulance turned around, and this girl was in the back. She said even the paramedics started to get worked up. They said they wanted to get the cop, because then they could get out of there.

"But another ambulance had gotten the cop first, so they had to get some of the civilians. She said that when the ambulance pulled up, she thought that someone was working on a car in their front yard and had removed the front end.

"Then she said they got out, and she saw that the car the cops were chasing had crashed all the way up to its windshield into the bottom of this house. There was another paramedic ripping the doors off the car with a giant can opener, and when they pulled the guy out his limbs were so all over the place that she couldn't even tell what was his back and what was his chest. There were cops everywhere, not doing anything, pacing around, crawling up the walls."

"They were scared," Ronaldo said.

"Her ambulance took one of the guys in the back seat. He had gotten shot, on top of having his legs broken in the wreck. Their guy had gotten shot in the both legs and stomach, somehow. I didn't think nine millimeters would go through a car like that. He was so messed up that they had this girl— this first-year med student— put on gloves and put pressure on his femoral artery.

"He was black and probably about 18—"

"Of course," Ronaldo said.

"He had shit his pants, or a bullet had ripped his bowel, because the ambulance started to smell. Then something happened, they hit a bump or something, and his artery just exploded. It sprayed out between her fingers and across her face."

"AIDS," Ronaldo said.

"No shit. Hep C. That's the end of the gross part of the story, but that's not the worst part. There's more. She said on the way to Hope, the driver turned up the radio up front for them to listen. They had on the police band, and the cops were saying, 'Somebody kill that nigger before he kills us all!'

"They got to the hospital, and they had to circle the neighborhood because they couldn't even get down the street to the ER because it was blocked with so many police cars. Just left running in the street. The cops were waiting to kill him. They didn't care who knew it. The ambulance crew was scared they would kill them, too. The girl in my class started to cry."

Ronaldo shook his head. "With the guy's blood still on her face," he said.

"No. She had wiped that off. By the time they got to the ER, the kid had died. And nobody was looking out for her. She ran in after the stretcher. It went to the morgue. Then another stretcher came in from the same scene. Two cops came in with this one. They weren't running. One of the cops kept saying, 'He died on the way over. He died on the way over.'

"You can't tell anybody this. I'm glad I spied and got it. She saw them take the guy off the stretcher, and she thought there was a dirty nickel in the middle of the mattress. But she looked closer....

"It was a bullet hole. She stepped closer, because she didn't believe it. When she looked up, one of the two cops was standing there with his hands on his belt, staring at her. She said he was black, too."

Ronaldo said, "What does that have to do with anything."

Henry said, "I guess you would expect that from some cracker Mississippi state trooper."

"So she's saying the policeman shot him. It doesn't matter if the officer's black or white, Henry," Ronaldo said, "They're all blue in uniform."

"That girl wants to be a dermatologist now," Henry said.

"Anyway," Ronaldo said, "what was I talking about?"

"The old man and the smell," Henry said.

"Oh yeah. They had to scrub him out of the carpet with a brush. His skin stayed there when they rolled him."

"So?" Henry said. Living gore seemed far worse. He was still thinking of the back of that ambulance.

"So I don't want to spend the money to get licensed just to shampoo some old fuck out a rug," Ronaldo said.

"Don't talk to me about debt," Henry said, "I'm borrowing a hundred sixty grand for the privilege of shoving my finger up people's butts."

"My story's worse than that," Ronaldo said.

"Did I tell you about the butt test? The school hires people to let us practice doing prostate exams on them. We pay the school tuition, so really I'm paying this guy to let me finger him," Henry said.

"What do those guys make?" Ronaldo said, "I think I'm going to be a police officer."

Not this again, Henry thought. "You don't want to be a cop, Ronaldo. You'd make a better living with a funeral home."

"I want to be a cop," Ronaldo said, not trying at all to sound sincere, "just like my dad."

Henry said, "Remember that time you and I were fucking with his stereo and he handcuffed us together?"

"He was always cuffing me," Ronaldo said, "He cuffed me to the lawnmower one time."

Traffic was slow on Magazine street. Ronaldo swore and turned up a side street. "So you never told me about your day with World's Greatest Dad. You should give Hines one of those shirts that says that. He really does a good job with his kids of his—whoops. I mean, 'kid.' He's got a daughter left."

Henry said, "He didn't really say anything."

"I find that hard to believe."

"He just kept saying I had taken something from him and wouldn't say what, and I said that I didn't know what he was talking about." If I say it, maybe I'll believe it, he thought. For the first time he wondered if Paolo had used Hines's SIG to kill himself. If that gun had killed somebody, he would have a harder time being cavalier. He had imagined until then the Paolo had shot himself some garbage .32 he had bought at school. At night now he sometimes thought of Hines's threats; and to stop thinking, he would think of Paolo's money inside the tub, and then he saw Paolo, animated from the photographs he'd seen. First in California, then in New Orleans. He rode the St. Charles streetcar, wearing his jeans and purple surfer shirts; he carried the garbage .32 in his back pocket with the hammer cocked, something Henry would never do. The streetcar had a lubricant on its axles that smelled like weed. The street lights came on before it was dark. Paolo did not know why he had bought the gun. He knew that at his age he deserved to be happier. But again and again he had been cheated.

He knew he would be better off not knowing, but he asked Ronaldo: "What did Paolo shoot himself with."

"What's a Paolo?" Ronaldo said.

"Shotgun? Pistol? Just tell me tell me if it was a little hole or a big one."

"I'm not a gun nut like you, Hank. I really don't know." Ronaldo said, "It was bigger than any hole I would want in my head."

"You have no idea what he shot himself with," Henry said, exasperated.

"I think it was a spear gun."

"Up yours, Ronaldo."

"And we buried him in flippers and a fucking snorkel."

They were weaving up and down old streets now. The houses were lilac or cream, with high porches behind short front patios behind black, cast iron fences. Cat's claw connected the fence of one house to the fences on either side.

"Are you lost," Henry said, "or is that something else you don't know."

"No, I'm definitely lost," Ronaldo said, "I always get lost up in here."

Some old white people on a porch watched the hearse pass. Then they pulled onto Napoleon Avenue, next to an apartment house from the days when they still looked like houses. The front yard was big enough to be a playground, and it was a playground. Swings with belt-seats hung straight as plumb bobs. The kids were in school. An old fountain with an iron boy on top had rusted dry.

"Finally," Ronaldo said, "Get out. This is the place—apartment G."

The house tapered up from the playground to the roof, until the top was a single room banded by windows. Henry hoped that would be apartment G; from up there, he could see everything. It probably wasn't apartment G.

"Who's letting me in?" he said.

Ronaldo jerked his head at the coffin as he dug in his shirt pocket. "That guy's son," he said. He produced a sheet of crumpled notebook paper. "What's this say? Mr. Landry's got the worst handwriting."

"Stumpey. Styoomp..." Henry read. He said, "How do I say it right? I don't want to offend him."

"Who gives a flying rat's ass," Ronaldo said, "This is another of one of Mr. Landry's charity cases. Asshole didn't have insurance and we're probably going to get stiffed. I'll be back in two hours. There's no wake."

Henry winced, because the man in the coffin could hear. But that didn't make any sense. He picked up his bag from the floor of the hearse. He put his hand on the edge of the door.

"Last chance," Ronaldo said, "what did Hines say to you. Tell me the truth."

Henry said, "You really want to know."

Ronaldo said, "How many times have I asked?"

"He said that he was in the Brazilian Mafia, and that if I didn't give him back the sheets, he was going to bury me alive in a coffin with someone else on top of me," Henry said.

Ronaldo went wide-eyed. "Like, doing it with you?" he said.

"No," Henry said, "the person on top would be dead."

Ronaldo was frozen in place, staring at him. When he got unstuck, he leaned back against the seat, shaking his head and shooing Henry away. "Apartment G," he said.

Henry was glad to see that this was no big deal. "You don't think that's anything to worry about," he said, to be sure.

"If he thinks he's Scarface for a couple sheets, then I was a goddamn one-man cartel. Apartment G," Ronaldo said. Henry shut the door.

But his walk must have looked worried, because before he pulled off, Ronaldo rolled down the passenger window and called out to him, "Don't worry about it. You work for Palace Springs."

II

The place had once been fancy. Wood columns stained almost black, rooted in carpet as faded green as an old pool table. The sun had bleached windows into the carpet. A receiving area larger than his bedroom sprawled to the right of the front door. It had once been a parlor; now there was no furniture, to discourage loitering. Built into the wall to the left of the door was one of those things— he didn't know what they were called. One of those things with a bench that opened, and at eye level, a long, narrow mirror, and above the mirror a row of coat hooks, from the days when men wore hats.

He looked down the hall. The downstairs apartments ran up to E. He went back to the foyer and took the stairs. If he walked in the middle and spread his arms, his fingertips would barely touch the bannister and the wall. It was creepy, like his apartment, but with sunlight.

The carpet on the second floor was red. Apartment G was at the end of the hall. He knocked. The door was thrown open by a black man, younger than Henry. He knew he had been back in New Orleans a while when he thought, this guy's robbing the place.

Henry held out his hand. "I work for Palace Springs Funeral Home," he said.

The guy absently shook his hand. "Can I see some sort of ID?" he asked. He didn't talk like he was black.

"I don't have anything from work," Henry said. He pulled out his wallet. Ordinarily, he carried it in the front to be safe from pickpockets, but the gun was in the front. "Here's my school ID." He offered the card, but the guy just looked at it.

"I'm Mr. Stumpe's son," the black guy said. He pronounced it "Stoomp-fa."

Henry said, "Oh." The man in the coffin had been white and ugly. Besides being black, this guy was handsome.

He didn't seem offended in the slightest by Henry's staring: "A later marriage. It's a long, awful story. They said you were a medical student. They said you were trustworthy. Is that Mr. Landry your father?"

"Well, some people feel a medical student's more responsible." Henry said.

"That's funny," the guy said, and he laughed as he spoke, not sounding at all funereal. That laugh belonged in a bar—no, a stage set of a bar. "Responsible for what? Golf?"

Old joke, Henry thought; safe joke; bad joke. "I'm into interpretive dance, myself."

"You can come in," the guy said, stepping back and opening the door. "Are you more trustworthy than the next guy because you're in medical school? Tell your boss that I would trust a singing mounty, or a Ghurka."

The apartment smelled like it was carpeted with lichen. A sofa faced an old television, with dials, not buttons. The sofa had been patched with silver tape; now the patches needed patching. The blinds were drawn and the lights off. Stacked four high against three walls were white cardboard boxes, about a yard long and a foot deep. Each had a lid. Each might hold two cinder blocks, snugly. Henry knew what they were: comic book boxes, for a collector. He had been a collector, when he was sixteen. He smiled a little.

"I'm sorry about asking for ID," the black guy said, "But your boss made it sound like we more or less could expect to get robbed. The television works, but it doesn't get sound."

The guy walked into another room—the bathroom, probably. Henry plopped his bag down on the sofa. His pants felt like they would fall down to his knees from the weight of the revolver. The guy came out of the bathroom slapping his neck and cheeks, wearing a black blazer over his black t-shirt, a blazer with no buttons and sleeves made to be rolled. He brushed past Henry. His aftershave in this apartment made him smell like a grandpa. In the kitchen he picked up the phone, held it to his ear with his shoulder, and started to dial a number from a business card. "Look in those boxes," he said to Henry.

Henry lifted the top off the nearest box. Just as he had expected: a column of comic books, each packed in a clear, plastic envelope on a white, acid free cardboard support. A hundred years would pass before the pages yellowed.

The son called out, "You know anything about comic books?"

"I used to collect," Henry said. But the guy was talking into the phone now, arranging a ride. He had sold his collection the Christmas of freshman year, and hadn't thought of comic books since.

The guy hung up. "You want to give me an appraisal while you're here?" he said, "He only had about ten thousand of them, including the ones in the bedroom."

"He's probably got a price guide somewhere around here," Henry said. He glanced around; dirt from the carpet burned his nose.

"So give me an appraisal," the guy said, "I have student loans."

"They're worthless," Henry said, "That's my appraisal."

The guy stopped in the kitchen door and stood there blinking.

"I'm just kidding," Henry said, "People don't get my sense of humor, sometimes."

The guy said, "I can see why. Get that fixed." He walked to the sofa and flopped down, "They're all he did. They have to be worth something."

Henry wanted to sit, but there was no place but the empty spot on the sofa, next to the son. He put his hands in his pockets, but his right wouldn't fit due to the gun. He put them on his back and pretended to stretch.

"Did you say you were in school?" he asked.

"I'm at Duke," the guy said, "I was pre-med freshman year, but then classes started."

It was an oft-repeated line, Henry could tell. He smiled. "Duke's got a good medical school," Henry said, "They rejected me."

"All of the medical students are unbearable," the guy sighed, "Every last one of them."

"So what's your major now?" Henry said.

"English," he said, "I'd like to be an essayist."

An arts major, Henry thought. An arts major who thinks that's important. "I didn't know anybody wrote essays anymore," Henry said.

"That depends on what you consider an essay," the guy said. He crossed his legs.

"I consider an essay those pages in *Newsweek* with the word 'Essay' at the top."

The guy raised an eyebrow and smiled. "Well, there you go. People writing essays," he said, "I think I'm going to wait for my ride out front." He stood up.

"Wait," Henry said, "Can I have a set of keys?" he remembered how he had watched the bolt close when the Hines family had left, and he didn't like it.

The guy hesitated. "There's only one set," he said. "My mother and I have to get back in here."

"Most clients leave their keys," Henry said, "I'm not going anywhere."

"Then why do you need the keys?" the guy said. He smiled. Here was a young man who didn't like to break rules.

"Put yourself in my position," Henry said, "Would you like to be locked into some stranger's apartment?"

After hesitating a moment, he reached into his pocket and threw Henry the keys. A rubber Batman with his fists on his hips had the key ring running through his head. "I'll see you in a couple of hours, then," the guy said. He walked out, still looking anxious.

"Have fun," Henry said, and shut the door.

* * *

The locked door was so heavy it was like part of the wall. He ran the shades up on both windows in the living room. The sun and the dust it showed made him sneeze. When he was a boy he thought that the dust motes seen in sunlight were the germs that gave people colds.

He looked through the kitchen door. The carpet ended and yellow linoleum started, the linoleum curled up and accumulating crud beneath. Two doors in the living room were closed; one the bathroom, one the bedroom where the man had no doubt died. That didn't scare him like Paolo's house had.

He decided to study at the kitchen table. It was the only table. The kitchen walls were yellow, but had once been white–seventy years of tenants had lit up in here. They leased by the year and by the year only. By the sink stood a wooden drying rack with a fork in it; the sink was full of dishes that smelled. On top of the refrigerator was a bird in a birdcage. It had started chirping when he had entered the kitchen.

He put his bag down on the table and stood on his toes to see the bird. It had an orange-combed yellow head and a gray body. With all the noise it was making, you would think it was frantic, but it squatted in one place and went on and on like an alarm clock.

"Shut up," Henry said.

The bird didn't notice.

The kitchen smelled like a cat. But there was no cat box or food bowl.

He looked into the sink. Mr. Stumpe had eaten off these plates and died. Drying spaghetti sauce ringed half a plate. The spaghetti was now in Mr. Stumpe's stomach. Soon the spaghetti would be buried. The remains of the last meal were floating here in sink water.

He turned on the water and jumped back. Judging from the plates in the sink, second-to-last through eighth-to-last meals were also represented. The stepson should have cleaned this up, he thought. But the stepson dared not sully his essayist hands. He looked for some dish detergent or bleach to squirt into the sink and mask the smell, but there wasn't any.

He moved his books and chair around to the side of the table facing the door, so he could see the whole apartment. He put the gun on the table. The bullets would roll off, so he left them in his pocket.

He took out his Histology notes. The Histology gut exam was next Monday, Halloween. There would be a slide practical: fifty slides would be passed out to the row of students sitting at microscopes. They had ninety seconds to identify the tissue, or whether the change in epithelium they saw represented the junction of the mouth and throat or the rectum and anus. If they were ever in any emergency room and couldn't tell one end of the patient from the other, they would be ready. Or there might be a tag on the slide that asked a question, like "What runs in the holes?" and they would write down the answer. When ninety seconds were up, each student was to pass the slide to the next student. If someone got so flustered that they dropped a slide and broke it, students were to sit in silence until the proctor replaced the slide. If someone got so flustered that he passed a slide before the buzzer, and the next student was so flustered that they took it, the slide flow would clot. Students were to sit in silence until the proctor straightened things out, and students would talk for the next three weeks about how much better they would have done if Grace hadn't screwed-up the exam.

Next, they would go downstairs to the auditorium, where tissue sections would be projected onto a twenty-foot screen. With a laser pointer, the proctor would circle a structure and ask, "What runs in these holes?" One minute per projection. Fifty projections. Students would vote whether or not to take a two-minute break after twenty five. The Histology department took the practical and its timing so seriously that you would think it involved a bomb.

After the practical, they got an hour for lunch. Then it was up to the lecture hall to take a three-hour written exam. At three o'clock next Monday afternoon it would all be over. Until Friday. That was the end of Head and Neck.

He opened his Histology binder at the page he had marked. It was like opening the phone book at "Miller."

He read and looked up. *The portal triad is made up of—*

"Chirp chirp," said the bird.

Portal triad—

"Chirp," said the bird.

Henry stood on the chair and pointed the revolver at it. "Shut up, I said."

It didn't. Henry rattled the cage and its wings went all over the place. Then he felt bad for scaring it. He could see square-ended feathers where its wings had been clipped.

Its food cup looked full, but maybe it was stale. He pulled the cup out of the side of the cage and looked for someplace to dump it, but didn't see a garbage can. There was a plastic garbage bag hanging next to an oven mitt over the stove, and through it he saw an empty tuna can. He picked the bag open with one finger and dumped the birdseed. At the bottom of the bag was the empty can and eggshells sprinkled with cigarette ashes. Stumpe had smoked in the kitchen to avoid damaging his comics.

He looked in the cabinets for birdseed. He found cat food in an open bag under the sink. Maybe the dead man had fed a stray, and that was why he had no litter box. He pictured a gray cat now eating on the floor of a three-girl apartment near Tulane. The man who had last fed this cat was dead. The college girls didn't know.

The bird had not stopped chirping. He held an asterisk of cat food through the bars. But the bird didn't want any of it. He dropped some pieces in its food cup. The bird stayed away.

He sat down with his notes in front of him and remembered how full the refrigerator had been at Hines's house. Now that he knew how wacko Hines was, he wondered where he had made enough friends to give him so much. Maybe his wife was more charming.

He wished that he hadn't seen Hines with his eyes red that day, begging him to stay and eat. He didn't want to feel sorry for him.

He checked to see that the revolver wasn't loaded. He always checked, even when he was sure. He imagined a TV show: *M.D., P.I.*

I really should get the bird something to eat, he thought. He stood up and pulled the keys out of his pocket by Batman's foot. He put the gun back in his bag.

At the door, he thought, I obviously don't really feel like studying.

* * *

There was a corner grocery one block up on Magazine Street. A movie was being shot on Magazine. That was why the traffic had been so slow getting here from downtown—all the cars had to take detours down side streets.

People in shorts and black t-shirts and tool belts. It was like watching a construction site. But then one walked by carrying an enormous horseshoe wreath, with a banner that said RIP. Then a female black-shirt hopped out of the back of a truck with a Colt .45, carrying it by the barrel, butt down. Bad idea with any gun, fake or not, Henry thought. A policeman leaned on his motorcycle in the shade, making sure no one from the real world broke into the movie. He looked bored.

The store owner was Vietnamese. He watched the movie from the corner with his hands in his armpits and followed Henry as he walked into the store. He bought soda crackers and two Diet Cokes, in order to wake up enough to get some work done.

The store owner said nothing. On his right forearm was a tattoo that looked like numbers and writing, so plain and even that the ink needles might have been fixed to typewriter keys. Henry couldn't tell what it said, because it had been ablated in the middle by a puffy scar. The scar might have come from a hot iron, pressed into his flesh with his other hand.

* * *

Back in apartment G, the bird hadn't shut up. The crackers did not make it quiet; he hadn't expected it to work, really. He put one Coke inside of the empty freezer with its empty ice cube trays.

He stared at his notes.

Maybe the black guy's mother had cleaned out the freezer and refrigerator. He imagined she was very dark, and short like her son. How had she ended up with Mr. Stumpe? The guy had said it was an awful story. Maybe she was a writer, too, and dug pathos. Better that than the thought of two losers settling for one another after failing all else. He pictured her in the corner, spinning a garbage bag and leaning away from it so it wouldn't ruin her widow's dress. It wasn't the first time she had cleaned up after him.

He looked into the living room at the bedroom door. Why not, he thought. After going through Hines's house, he felt almost obliged. There would be a dip in the old bed. No need for them to cut eye-holes: the ghost was *in* the sheets now, sure as Paolo's was in the bag of money at Henry's place.

He opened the bedroom door. The sheets were in a tangle, but the mattress was new, with no dip. Actually, the old man had probably died in the hospital, not in here. Otherwise, he would have rotted into a pile of comics before anyone smelled him enough to check. Everybody dies in the hospital now. But hospitals are never haunted. Sometimes he cut through the hospital on the way home, for the air-conditioning. It felt sterilized of ghosts, like a hospital should.

A broad, brown dresser topped with a square mirror faced the bed. On either side of the bed, piled up level with the bed, were two piles of comic books, as big as two people lying on top of one another. These comics weren't bagged; Stumpe had read these. The only room to walk was a corridor of carpet from the door to the far wall, where there was a beveled glass window that opened to an air shaft.

He opened the top dresser drawer. Inside were folded, half-cotton boxer shorts and undershirts. Either the writer-woman had come in here and folded them all like she used to, or as messy as Mr. Stumpe had been, he liked to keep his clothes neat.

The next drawer over was full of shoes. Stumpe couldn't keep them in the closet because there were comic books in the way. If he had kept his underwear neat, he didn't think footwear deserved it. Henry had to dig to match a pair of black deck shoes, made of plasticine leather. With his sideburns and these shoes, Mr. Stumpe had not been well-liked. And he tried to put those sideburns and these shoes with the widow he'd pictured in the kitchen. He couldn't do it.

Pressed against the inside of the drawer was an envelope. He wouldn't have seen it if he hadn't stirred up the shoes. Whatever was inside had to be bad or important.

He dumped the envelope out into his hand—pictures. He flipped through them, expecting to see a sad-eyed black woman holding the comic collector's neck fifteen years ago. Maybe one of the son when he was too little to understand that his new dad was white. But it was just thirty pictures of the collector with that stupid bird.

Here was Mr. Stumpe driving with the bird on his shoulder, the photo taken by someone in the passenger seat. He had an overbite which Henry hadn't seen in the coffin, or else Mr. Landry and Ronaldo had given him a stronger chin for his funeral. The car was just right for an older collector of comics: an American slab with brown plastic seats and no head-rests.

Another photo: Mr. Stumpe in a *Bill the Cat* t-shirt, sitting in a folding chair, behind a folding table covered with comic books in plastic. This was taken at a comic book convention. He was holding onto the edge of the table with his head thrown all the way back and his mouth open. The bird was standing on his chin, shoving its colored head deep down the collector's throat. He must have put food on the back of his tongue. Henry imagined that his eyes were closed. Though only the bird was naked, this picture seemed like it should have gotten Mr. Stumpe arrested. A boy wearing Spock ears in the background stared, unsmiling. He thought Mr. Stumpe was a child molester.

Mr. Stumpe had daydreamed about having his apartment open to boys. Only boys would coo over his collection and how it would never decay. He knew that they thought him a pervert, though. He got sexual with his bird because it showed the boys and everyone else that he didn't care, and that he was lonely. Without booze this apartment would be unbearable. Maybe the writer-woman had thrown out the bottles.

The bird was still calling in the kitchen to the man who had loved it so. There was a picture of him and the bird at McDonald's, with bird shit running down Mr. Stumpe's shoulder. He was smiling. There was a picture of the bird, Mr. Stumpe, and the Vietnamese store owner Henry had seen, taken in the store. Both of them were smiling. There was never any picture of whoever was behind the camera. Henry imagined it was strangers he had stopped.

There were eight pictures of the bird on the back of the chair in the kitchen, pictures that were attempts at portraits. All were blurry. He put the pictures back in the envelope, and the envelope back where it had been.

The phone rang in the living room. He didn't jump. On the third ring he picked up the phone. "Stumpe residence," he said. He expected the other end to hang up, and then the stringy looking white guy would show up, this time as an electrician with no tools. The thief's racket was probably to check the obituaries, just like Ronaldo had said.

He heard the other end exhale. "Don't leave that place," said a man's voice.

"I won't, sir," Henry said.

"You did," the man said.

He had been seen going to the store. By whom? This was a call from beyond the grave. Mr. Stumpe has called to make sure I keep his comics safe, he thought. He got goosebumps on one arm. "May I ask who's calling?" he said. "Is this Mr. Landry?"

The other end hung up.

He hung up and looked around the apartment. He felt someone watching now, through the sycamore tree outside the living room windows. Not likely, though; the leaves were too thick.

He didn't belong in the bedroom. That call was his punishment for being a snoop. He shut the bedroom door and went back to the kitchen to sit with his notes. If it had been Mr. Landry, he resented being checked on. He knew what his job was.

And just to prove that no one was going to tell him what to do, he was going back in the bedroom.

There wasn't much else there, besides the comic books. He pulled one from the pile to the left of the bed and started an avalanche. The voice on the phone had turned into a man, and he was in the other room now, waiting for him. He would have to wait, Henry thought.

He picked up the comic books. He had read some of them ten years earlier, and even then they had been old, used copies that were frustrating because other kids had cut out the ads to order pepper gum, years before. Here was the one that featured Thor talking to his father's left eyeball as it floated over the Well of Time. Henry remembered the story better than he could the anatomy he had studied yesterday. He couldn't accept the tail of meat that hung from the back of the eye. Now he knew that there was no muscle back there.

In an old *Legion of Super Heroes* he caught Lightning Lad, Ultra Boy, and Matter-Eater Lad reversing time. Overspecialized, Matter-Eater Lad was of little help.

Through the pile were covers reading, *Enter: The Puma!* and *Endgame!* But he knew from his days as a comic fan that the books were all enter and no end. Heroes only sort of died when sales were low. He could probably sift through this whole pile and find only one real death.

And he happened to find it.

He had picked up one of the four old Spider Man titles. To keep up with Spider Man took money. It was one of the reasons he quit collecting.

He hadn't seen this one. On the cover, a man in a purple ski mask and office work clothes pointed a double-barreled sawed-off not at Spider Man, but at the reader. Surrounding him were drawings of faces with a red X through each—dead people. These were just nameless victims to make a villain villainous; they weren't anything to worry about. Between the dead people were stark, orange question marks. The bottom of the cover read,

WHO IS THE SIN EATER?

The story inside was a meandering memoir by Detective Somebody. Henry couldn't remember her name. She had red hair and green eyes, and he remembered that in another issue she had been drawn wearing jeans entirely too tight for police work, and sort of arching her hips while dropping bullets into her service revolver. He could remember staring at that picture when he was fourteen and thinking with concern that he was getting too old for comic books.

He sat on the bed and read: she remembered growing up in a tough Irish neighborhood. She remembered playing stickball in pigtails. She had freckles. She remembered graduating from college in criminology, top of her class—drawing of her in cap and gown with chin held high. She remembered her first arrest, holding the crazed hatchet-man in the foreground at bay with an ill-rendered .357. The barrel was too long. She remembered being promoted to Homicide Division, the first woman in the history of the NYPD.

Henry turned the page. So how does all that, she mused, add up to this?

Here she was, sprawled backward over her desk in a dark office, with blood running from her nose and mouth onto the floor and her eyes rolled back in her head. Two policemen stood in the door behind flashlights. Except for his poor guns, the artist was good: the police silhouettes radiated alarm and fear.

Peter Parker—Spider Man in plain clothes—was on the killer's trail. This was a different sort of comic book. The people on New York streets looked less drawn than traced from photographs. Another homicide detective looked as ordinary as one might in real life, with a bulge around his middle.

The killer called himself the Sin Eater, the detective explained. At the scenes, he had left notes–notes and fruit. Peter and the detective faded away, but the detective's words continued in the upper left corner of the panel, like a movie voice-over:

Sin eater was a civic office in Appalachia. Every town had one. Here were some poor coal miners sitting in ill fitting, mail-order suits on hard pews. The women wore black veils. Even the veils didn't fit right. A candle sat at either end of the pine casket at the front of the dark church. In the casket lay a thin man in a string tie. Black lung got him. On his stomach sat a banana, an apple, and red grapes.

Up the aisle floated a chubby man in brown overalls, no undershirt, and a black, pointed hood like an executioner's. On TV, Henry had seen a mafia informer wear the same hood on the witness stand. The man wearing overalls and a hood in church had hair growing from his back and shoulders. He stood over the fruit in the casket. The red-sashed preacher turned away with sanctimonious resign. The people studied their hands in their laps. From beneath the hood came a horrible, fruity chomping.

The people believed that a man's sins jumped out of his body when they sensed that burial was coming. They would jump into the congregation. But the fruit fooled them, because they remembered being in the apple when Eve took a bite. And somebody in town got elected to be the sin eater and eat that fruit.

"And the town could go on," the detective explained, "because the sin eater saved them from the sins of the dead."

Henry wondered what happened to the banana peel. Impregnated with sin, it would constitute hazardous waste. Burn it. And why the pointy hood? You would know who the sin eater was in a little town when you saw who wasn't in church. He guessed that the hood was necessary because the sin eater had the dirt on everybody dead inside of him. The hood made things less awkward for the living. Everyone in town avoided the sin eater, who, to spite them, was a hairy boar. But who dared tell him to act otherwise? Who would take his place if he quit?

The phone rang again. Henry cursed and threw the comic book back on the pile. He let it ring twice more with his hand on the receiver. Then he lifted it and said, "Stumpe residence."

He heard his own voice say, "*I told you I would buy four boxes.*"

It was Hines, using the tape he had made when they had talked. If he wanted to intimidate, he shouldn't have used the recording; Henry hated the sound of his own recorded voice. It sounded high pitched. "Is that you?" he said, "Is that you, world's greatest dad?"

He heard a breath at the other end, and then silence. "Fucking loser," he muttered, hung up, and went back into the bedroom. He thought of the gun in Hines's glove compartment and drew a curtain across the image.

"Shitbag Hines," he said. He wasn't going to be intimidated by somebody who couldn't pass intro Chemistry. And to get back at Hines, he was going to look under the bed, like he had looked under Paolo's.

He had to lie on the edge of the bed and swipe the comic books away with his whole arm. They spilled in front of the door, and he didn't care. He stuck his head into the space he had made and took a look. The box spring wasn't slit open. What did he expect to find, anyway? Maybe a bottle the widow had missed. He stuck his head lower and looked under the bed.

Maybe not a bottle. He gave the dead man the benefit of the doubt and figured at first that the magazines stacked under the head of the bed were a secret cache of valuable *Conan*'s, but the magazines were too big. He knew from his boyhood that only porn got piled in the dark like this. It took two hands to pull the stack out, and some got left behind. *Juggs. D-cups. Stacked. Mature Nymphos. Barely Legal.*

He had some dirty magazines when he was growing up; he didn't know a boy who didn't. But he hadn't grown qualified to *review* porn until he was old enough to buy magazines at the newsstands. He had started with *Playboy*, but those girls were too much like a dream. Sleazier porn at first seemed better because the women looked real. No implants and no airbrushing. The women hadn't shaved their pubic hair. But in the end, sleazy porn—like he had here—reminded him how alone he was.

He shouldn't have looked under the bed. He wouldn't have wanted anybody digging under his bed in Berkeley. He had thrown out the magazines when Catherine began to sleep over, out of fear that she would dig around. Mr. Stumpe had lived alone, and still he was embarrassed enough to hide stroke mags under the bed.

He flipped through *Juggs*. The centerfold featured a pregnant Mexican woman with a tight perm and gold hoop earrings and crotch-less, red and black underwear. Pregnancy, or the need for money, or both seemed to have made her angry. She glared at him, with one hand on her belly like she was trying to pick up a basketball. Each areola had a halo of brown spots—prolactin working, he thought. Increased diameter of the areola enables the neonate to more easily find the nipple with its rudimentary sight. He had never seen a pregnant woman naked before. The next one would be his wife. Then he remembered that he was going to be a doctor; he would see lots of wives.

If this were his apartment, and he were dead, he wouldn't want his family to find these magazines. The widow would be forgiving. Her son wouldn't. He would write about it.

He took the magazines into the kitchen. He dumped them into his backpack.

Back in the bedroom, he re-heaped the comics he had knocked over. He took the chair from the kitchen and stood on it to pull the living room shades down.

* * *

The knock at the door didn't startle him. He called out, "Who is it?" instead of using the peephole, so if it was Hines he couldn't get shot in the eye. It's me, said the stepson through the door. Henry opened the door and gave back the keys.

The guy muttered, "Hey," sat down on the sofa, and pulled a corduroy pillow onto his lap.

I wonder what his name is—no, not really, Henry thought. "How was it?" he asked. He went to the kitchen to gather his books. Ronaldo would show up soon.

"It was very nice. Death...." Searching for a topic sentence, Henry thought. The stepson said, "You got my itemized appraisal?" and smiled slowly.

Henry chuckled.

The bird was still tweeting.

The stepson got up and ran straight at him, too fast for Henry to even think of pulling the .38. He backed against the wall.

The stepson ran past him, grabbed the bird cage by its handle, and carried it to the sink with the screaming bird hovering along inside. He threw open the kitchen window, opened the cage, and beat it against the casement until the bird fell out. Before either knew it, they were leaning over the sink and the window sill to see what would happen.

"The damn thing wouldn't shut up before, either!" the stepson said in his own defense.

The bird fell, sort of, and flew, sort of, into the sycamore tree. It watched them from a branch. It had never been in a tree in its life, but it rode the branch like a boat on swells.

"It can't fly!" the stepson said, "I thought it would fly off."

"His wings are clipped," Henry said, "They grow back. They either cut the muscle or cut the feathers. He just had the feathers cut."

The bird climbed into the leaves using its beak and claws. Not once did it splay its wings for balance.

The stepson was grinning. He couldn't stop. He couldn't believe what he had just dared to do. "My mom wanted to give it to me. She's going to wonder what happened to it."

Henry said, "Tell her I was playing with it and it got away."

The stepson composed himself to look sneering-smart again, like he had when Henry came in. He went back to the living room and sat down. Henry picked up his bag.

"Anybody ever told you that you look like a waiter in those clothes?" the stepson said. His arms were limp by his sides.

"I've never heard that one," Henry said. He moved to the door.

"As a doctor, can you tell I'm on Prozac?" the stepson said.

"I'm not a doctor," Henry said.

"Do you know how hard it is at my school to get a prescription? They want to *counsel* everybody. The only counselor I want is a lawyer."

Henry made a face like he understood, and it was so funny, and put his hand on the doorknob.

"This was on the door," the stepson said. He reached into his pocket and came out with a shrimp-colored piece of paper, folded in half.

Henry took it. Written on the flap was HENRY.

There was a drawing inside. It was a number two, surrounded by a one. In red ink, behind the numbers like a watermark, was a coffin.

Two-in-one. Hines must have gotten his wife to use her good pens for the message. He must have been calling from just outside the building, and put the drawing on the door after Henry had called him the world's greatest dad.

"Does that mean something?" the stepson said. He was leaning over the note.

He put the paper in his shirt pocket. He said something or other to the stepson and left. He stood outside apartment G and looked down the hall, and blew out his scared air. Then he breathed in some new.

It didn't work. Breathing through his mouth, queasy, he stood in the corner of the hallway and put his bag down, took out the .38, and loaded it. He retied his shoes in case he had to start running. How did this end up happening, he thought. He had six shots to Hines's sixteen. Even if Hines didn't do anything, the fear now was taking years off his life.

He wanted to keep the gun in his hand, but that would draw a lot of attention. He untucked his shirt tails and shoved the gun in his waistband. He opened the bottom button so that he wouldn't have to lift the shirt out of the way, and as he was cinching his belt around the gun he heard something behind him.

He looked over his shoulder. It had to look like he was taking a piss in the hall.

The stepson was standing there in the door. He said, "Are you taking a piss in the hall?"

"You fuck off," he snapped, "Go write a sonnet."

* * *

He watched for the hearse from the window seat in the foyer, with his back against the wall and his legs up. He could see all four lanes of Napoleon from here, but he didn't see the Hines frog-mobile.

This has gotten old, he thought. What if he had shot the stepson when he opened the door behind him? Forget med school. His life would be over. It seemed an affront to civilization that a man like Hines should own a gun. He had never thought guns should be outlawed until right now.

He tried to calm himself. The best he could come up with: Relax. He doesn't want to shoot you. He wants to bury you alive.

The Bronco hearse pulled up at the curb on Napoleon. He trotted across the park, worried that the gun was going to tumble down the leg of his pants.

Ronaldo leaned over and opened the door for him. "Nice shirt, slob," Ronaldo said, "You look like you just got laid."

Henry got in and slammed the door. "Go," he said.

Ronaldo pulled off. "What's up your ass?" he said.

Henry pulled out the note. "This," he said, putting it in Ronaldo's hand.

Ronaldo glanced back and forth between road and note. "One two," he said, "Twelve?"

"Two in one coffin," Henry said, "That was on the door."

"That's a coffin," Ronaldo said, still looking at it. "Did Hines leave this?"

"Unless you left it," Henry said, "If you did, it's not funny."

"I don't draw that good." Ronaldo handed back the note and set his jaw. "You see what happens when you don't listen to me?"

he said, "You see the trouble you're in? Being a doctor's not going to save your fucking ass now."

He thought Ronaldo was going to tell him not to worry about it, like before.

A few blocks later, Ronaldo said, more quietly, "I wouldn't worry about it. Like I said, we work for Mr. Landry."

* * *

He didn't feel the need to look after Stumpe's magazines like he did with Paolo's money. He took the magazines to the garbage can on the corner by his apartment, before he started to use them and made himself feel down.

12

The Histology exam went well. There would be a class Halloween party, but he didn't feel comfortable asking anyone for a ride, and the organizers were adamant about everyone showing up in costume. He didn't feel like getting a costume together. And since he had first stolen the sheets from Hines, this had been hanging over his head: *no more excuses*. If you want to be a drug dealer, you have to deal some drugs. There had been no more calls from Hines, and no more notes, so he believed Ronaldo: Hines was all talk.

He went home, took a shower, and took a nap. He dreamed he was back at Martyrs', because through an administrative oversight, his transcript had never been finalized, and Ian Hines was responsible in some unseen, dream way. The sun was going down when he woke up. At the Exxon on the other side of Rampart he bought beer and Doritos for dinner. Across Basin Street he saw St. Louis Cemetery Number One. A tourist had been killed there two weeks prior when she chased the man who snatched her camera.

He drank, did the dishes, listened to the news, and made his bed. Once it was as dark outside as it was going to get, he put on his dealer clothes: a shirt he had tie-dyed in an orientation activity at Berkeley, sweat pants he had cut off at the knees, and running shoes. You don't want to be wearing jeans and cowboy boots if you have to sprint from the cops.

He would need pockets. He put on his motorcycle jacket. About two years earlier to the day, Catherine had said she could stand it no longer: I hate that jacket, she had said, everybody in Berkeley has one. He hadn't worn it since, and hadn't missed it much, because with all the bikers and gutter punks up and down Telegraph Avenue, he hadn't felt that a Biology major had the right. He slipped it on and looked in the mirror.

With his new haircut, he had the right.

He didn't know how much acid to bring. If he did get caught, he didn't want get caught with much. He remembered hearing, or reading, that the maximum you could claim for personal consumption was ten tabs. With a sandwich bag over his fingers, he ripped off ten tabs from the corner of one sheet, then turned the bag inside out so that the tabs were caught inside.

He put the acid in the jacket's map pocket. Not once did he consider taking a gun. A gun and drugs would have made him too nervous to leave the house, no matter how much beer he got in him.

* * *

Bourbon Street was more alive than he had expected. He bought a beer from a window between two neon strip joints and leaned with one foot on the wall. Porcelain-brittle vampires wafted back and forth for the news cameras, hoping to be interviewed. He had seen at least two men in the Quarter who kept fangs glued in year-round. There were also the famous dead: several Kurt Cobain's with bullet holes in their heads; Jon Benet Ramsey licking a lollipop; a porn starlet Savannah with a bullet hole for a face.

And then there was the usual Bourbon Street crew of fraternity boys screaming at women on balconies to show their tits. They do the same at Christmas time. They do the same on Wednesday, if the crowd is big enough. The women sometimes obliged, and the boys would throw them Mardi Gras beads.

Okay, he thought. After I finish this beer, I'm going to ask someone if they want to buy acid.

But one beer didn't do it. Up the street he bought a Hand Grenade, which had a plastic hand grenade floating in it, and came with a flyer vouching that it was the most powerful drink in New Orleans. He noticed a steel drum band in the bar and watched them. He saw a good looking woman in a yellow tutu and tried to look at her without being seen. He finished two more beers.

Now he had so much booze in him that it could talk: *Sell.*

He took another sip. Just in front of him were three clean guys with ponytails; they might have been rock climbers. One of them was half turned his way.

"Dose," Henry muttered, and touched the tip of his tongue. That was Telegraph Avenue sign language for acid.

The guy ignored him. He was relieved–this was as bad as trying to meet women.

That didn't count, the booze said. He knew that. I'll ask three people, he thought. Then I get to go home.

Some high school boys with baseball caps pulled low over their eyes walked by. He wouldn't sell to minors. They were followed by two girls with dredlocks and what looked like staples in their faces.

"Doses," he said, and tapped the tip of his tongue twice. Then he looked around for police. Do it the other way around next time, he thought.

"Fuck you," one of the girls said. She thought he was offering oral.

I'll be home soon, he thought. It was getting late. The vampires had left in a huff over all the nudity and the people turning out in Mardi Gras costumes on Halloween.

He was ashamed of himself. He felt like the same nerd he had been in high school and college. All he was good for was reading books. He might as well just be a brain without a body, since he barely had guts enough to be alive.

"Doses," he yelled over the crowd, "Doses, goddamnit! Acid! 'Cid! Sandoz! Hoffman's bicycle!"

No one paid the slightest attention. There were tits to be seen instead. He turned to walk home.

He was touched on the arm by a frat boy in a COCKS baseball cap and a Grateful Dead skull on it, with a confederate flag where the brain should be. At the bottom it said, SOUTHERN BY THE GRACE OF GOD.

"Dude," he said, bright eyed. He touched the tip of his tongue. "Can you set us up?"

* * *

The frat boy had three friends. The one who had spoken to Henry was short, so he spent time in the weight room making his shoulders big. The other three had their backs to Henry, watching the balcony with the rest of the crowd. Two were lanky; both were wearing khaki shorts from J.Crew. The fourth was enormous. He might have had an extra brain in his back, like a brontosaur. They each held a twenty-ounce cup of beer, and each wore a dirty baseball cap with a frayed bill.

The little guy pulled one of the lankies down and shouted over the music into his ear. The lanky smiled and shouted into the big guy's ear and watched for a reaction. The big guy didn't turn. After a moment he began to chew his nails. Now all three of them were watching the big guy's face to see if he would eat acid for the first time.

Henry waited against a balcony's post across the street and hoped he didn't look suspicious. Even through the beer, this was making him nervous. He didn't feel good about selling to the big one. He was tall enough that Henry could watch his face over the crowd. He looked scared.

The short one and the other lanky walked over to Henry. "We're just waiting on them," shortie explained.

Henry could tell the lanky in the street was whining to the big guy, "C'mon, man. C'mon, dude...doo-ude—c'mon...." The big guy wouldn't look at him.

Exasperated, the short one said, "Wait here."

Henry and the lanky guy waited. The short guy went in the street, took the big one by the wrist, and led him over. The big guy's face was frozen. He needed to shave.

He didn't feel like selling to them anymore. But he had started this.

The big guy stood there and glowered at the asphalt. The little guy said to Henry, "You want to do this here, or...?"

"Let's go up by the cathedral," he muttered, and started walking.

"What?" the short one said.

"Follow me," Henry said.

They walked fast up Orleans Street. No one said anything. Behind him, Henry heard the big guy crush his cup and throw it into the street. He imagined him going out for freshman football and quitting after only making Junior Varsity. One of the lankies wore a t-shirt with fraternity letters on it, and beneath that TULANE SHROOM-FEST: *You weren't there, but I saw you anyway.*

"Y'all go to Tulane?" Henry asked.

The short guy was walking beside Henry. "Yeah," he said.

"I finished at Berkeley last year."

"Yeah?" the guy said. He didn't sound interested.

They turned into Pirates' Alley, to the side of St. Louis Cathedral. When dueling was outlawed, it was here that gentlemen would come to buy their weapons on the black market. When they went up the alley, some guy was pissing on the cathedral fence with a beer in the other hand. When he had finished, zipped up, and walked away, they moved closer to the wall of the cathedral.

The big one was chewing his nails again, looking over their heads for a way out. The two lankies seemed more excited than nervous. The short one had his wallet out.

You don't have to do this, Henry wanted to tell the big guy, I never have.

It's his decision, he reminded himself.

"How much?" The short one asked.

"Five apiece," Henry said. He reached into his jacket. Tomorrow the big guy would be worse off than Ronaldo had been that day at the stadium.

The short one handed over a ten.

They just wanted two. Maybe the big guy isn't tripping, he told himself. Maybe he was just scared to be around a drug deal. Henry used the bag like a glove again and tore two tabs off of the strip of ten.

While Henry's hand was still in the bag, the short guy handed him another five. "Five," he said.

Henry dropped three tabs into the short guy's hand. He stared at them, and turned them over with his other fingers. "Wait," he said, "What's this?"

"It's California Motorhead tabs," Henry said.

"I wanted five tabs," the guy said, as if Henry should have known, "Two for me and one for each of them."

A nervous smile crept over Henry's face. "Five will be twenty-five," he said. One of the lankies reached for his wallet. The short guy stopped him.

"I didn't hear you say five apiece," the short guy whined. The big one shifted on his feet.

"I told you," Henry said, "It's double dipped."

"I'm not some kid at the mall," the short guy said, "Come on. Five apiece? They're three back home, tops."

Henry put the bag back into his pocket. He swallowed and put his shoulders back. "I've been dealing here the last five years and it's been five each the whole time."

"Have a heart, man," the short one said, "Leave me some beer money. We're going to be out all night."

The lanky who had reached for his wallet opened his mouth to speak.

The other one nudged him.

"I'm sorry," Henry said. In memory, he would see that this was when he should have walked away. "Why doesn't each of you buy your own. Five bucks a piece is like, what, one beer each of you would have to pass up?"

"Two beers," one lanky said.

"I want this to be my treat," the short one said, "How about buy three, get two free." He nodded at the big guy, and said, "It's his first time."

The big guy snorted.

"The best I can do is three for ten," Henry said, "That comes out to $3.33 apiece. One beer."

"I can't get off on less than two," said the short one. He was getting louder. "Are you saying if we go over three, we have to pay two bucks more for each one?"

Why do I even care? Henry thought. But his mouth was already answering, "I can't sell more than three. I don't have more than three."

"Bullshit. I saw it there in your hand," the short one said. In high school, a short guy like this started a fight by slapping the other person with a straight arm, then staring up at them.

"I have other customers," Henry said, "Look, take those three you have there. Your friend here doesn't need his first time to be tonight."

The short guy threw up his hands. "I don't see what the problem is."

Then the big guy bassed down at him, "How about ten for three."

Henry had been right. The big guy didn't want to trip tonight. He said, "Okay, it's a deal." He reached into his pocket and gave back the extra five dollars.

The short guy took it and looked confused.

"No," the big guy said, "I mean three bucks for ten doses."

Everyone looked up at him. Then Henry looked at the four of them together.

"Where I'm from," the big guy said, "I know a guy who can get ten doses for a dollar." Being treated gingerly had embarrassed him. He took a step forward and his head blocked out the light from a gas lamp.

Henry took a step back. "So," he said, "Where are you from?"

The guy raised a hand. Henry flinched.

The lankies snickered.

"Give me *all* the fucking tabs," the big guy growled.

Henry reached into his jacket. The big guy jerked his hand away and reached in himself and pulled out the bag. "Sure," Henry said.

The short one said, "That's price gouging."

Henry couldn't see the big guy's face because the light was behind his head. But he could tell that he was staring down at him. After a moment, the big guy handed the bag back to him.

"What—?" the short one said.

"Now give them to me," the big guy said. He waited with his palm cupped.

Henry placed the bag there.

The big guy slapped his face with the other hand. Henry was spun around, into the short guy, who shoved him away and kicked his butt on the way down.

The Lankies stood back and said, "Holy shit. Holy *shit. Holy shit.*"

Henry was on his rear on the flagstones, his hand in a pool. Later, it would smell of urine.

"Thanks for your cooperation," the short guy said, "I'm in Econ and what you proposed was price gouging."

"Jesus," laughed one of the lankies, "Ethan, you want his wallet too?"

Henry pulled himself up and walked into Jackson Square. His face stung, but he wouldn't hold his hand over his cheek; that would thrill them even more. Just watching him walk away had the short one letting out a rebel yell.

He walked up Decatur Street and back down, and wiped his hand on posts and walls. Now that he was alone, he realized how drunk he was. Somewhere between Bourbon Street and the alley he had lost his Hand Grenade. He got a table at Cafe du Monde and ordered coffee and beignets. He was sure that the tourists behind him were talking in German about the American who had just gotten slapped beside the cathedral.

Well, he thought, I still earned ten bucks.

It didn't make him feel better. His cheek still stung. He could have just threatened me, he thought. He didn't have to hit me.

If I only had packed a gun...he pictured himself holding his Glock at the big guy's left eye. "Open your mouth," he would have said, and slid the barrel in—

He closed his eyes and held his head, with his clean hand. He had never thought before of doing that to anyone. He had never been hit before. He hoped the big guy flipped out and killed the short one, and then the two skinny ones got killed in a wreck on the way back Uptown.

He wanted to see them again, but didn't know what he would do. After finishing his coffee, he asked for a cup of water. They brought him a glass. He demanded a cup, and the waiter charged him a dollar. He poured the first cup over his hand and filled it again at a water fountain. He walked up Decatur Street and walked around Tower Records to sober up. Then he walked down Decatur in the other direction, all the way to Esplanade. He decided nothing, except that he wanted to see them when they were high, to punish himself for this whole stupid endeavor.

He walked back up Bourbon Street. The frat boys were back under the same balcony as before, and they had eaten their tabs. The short one stood in the street and showed his dick to the girls on the balcony, screaming until his face swelled. The lankies laughed until they sobbed, and moved in slow motion because of the drag they were getting from all the lights. And the big guy stared wide-eyed at the neon, with one hand dangling from his mouth by the fingers, like a baby.

Henry couldn't move behind them because the crowd was too thick. The short one was now playing charades with his genitals, yelling corrections at the crowd when they guessed wrong: "No! It's a pork chop!"

He saw Henry standing under the balcony. "Hey!" he screamed with his pants around his knees, "Thanks for your cooperation!"

The crowd didn't know what it was about, but raised a toast to Henry and his cooperation.

* * *

The worksheet: *Associations Re: REVENGE*

gun in mouth—his brain stopped the film before he pulled the trigger.

House on broadway—He remembered the house letters from their t-shirts. He knew exactly which one it was.

SHOOT HOUSE–He could use the AR-15. Flying glass. Screaming dates in formal wear hit the floor.

He didn't want to risk killing anyone.

The answer: *SHATTER BOMB*

Resolved: shatter bomb

13

When they were juniors in high school, Pierre had told Henry and Ronaldo that if you filled a plastic Coke bottle with dry ice, added a little water, and sealed the top, gas would build up inside and the bottle would explode with a crack so loud that it would shatter any windows nearby. On the way home from school, they stopped at a Korean grocery store and bought a brick of dry ice wrapped in brown paper and a two-liter bottle of Coke. They dumped it out in the parking lot. They would make the bomb in Ronaldo's mother's bathroom and see what happened when they put it in the abandoned car up the street. Ronaldo had already popped the lock with a coat hanger; he had taken a set of socket wrenches, and Henry had taken the bolo tie hanging from the rear-view mirror.

When Ronaldo opened the front door—the house was always dark, and it smelled bad—his mother called from the bedroom to see if it was him.

"It's me," Ronaldo called.

Henry had been so eager to make the bomb that he ripped open the paper and dumped the ice brick into the tub without making sure the tub was dry. It wasn't. The brick began to smoke. A lot.

"My Mom will fucking freak!" Ronaldo said, "Put a towel in front the door crack!"

Henry picked up a towel, then thought that a wet towel would make a better seal. In his panic, he ran the bathtub faucet, which of course made more smoke. "Dumbshit!" Ronaldo hissed, but they were both giggling.

Henry slapped the wet towel in front of the door. The smoke got to be just absurd. They were up to their elbows in it, using butterknives to hack up chunks of ice they couldn't even see. The ice squealed. The tub echoed. Ronaldo's mom would bust them for sure.

They were giggling like girls. "I think we're getting a buzz off this smoke," Ronaldo said, "Isn't this what comes out cars?"

"That's carbon monoxide. This is dioxide," Henry said, "This will just smother us." That made them laugh even more.

The ice ripped at their fingertips like it didn't want to go into the bottle.When it was three-quarters full of chips, Ronaldo took it over to the sink. Henry held the bottle cap at the ready. He didn't look at his face in the mirror. He didn't want to see the zits and shine.

Ronaldo turned on the water. "Ready?" he said.

Ronaldo held the bottle under the faucet for four seconds. Henry rammed down the cap and twisted it until it wouldn't move, then twisted it even more. The seal had to be absolute.

When she heard the front door open, Ronaldo's mom called out, When will you be back.

"Right back," Ronaldo said.

They hurried up the street. The bottle was already opaque with white smoke. Henry carried it, and Ronaldo walked as shy of him as he could without seeming scared. Henry placed the bottle in the driver's seat of the abandoned car and shut the door.

They crossed the street and watched. The more Henry thought of the noise that it would make, the more he wanted to hold his hands over his ears.

They watched. They waited.

After a few minutes, Ronaldo said he wasn't going to wait out here in the sun. Henry said Pierre was a moron. They walked back to the house.

Ronaldo had his own air-conditioner. They stood in front of it and waited for their sweat to dry. From outside, they heard what might have been a tree snapping. They went outside to check. Ronaldo's mom called after them again.

Pierre knew something after all: the passenger's window was in bits; the driver's side was gone, too. Fresh glass looked like the heads of engagement rings.

Ronaldo's mother didn't catch them, but she didn't need to. She saw the broken glass and grounded him. Who else would have done that to the old car and made such a mess?

* * *

He thought of other ways to get revenge. But nothing would embarrass and shock them like a shatter bomb. A shatter bomb would be most like a slap.

There were several problems. He had to plant the bomb under the frat house Uptown, and he didn't have a car. He didn't know where to buy dry ice Uptown; and even if he did, he didn't know where he could build the bomb without attracting attention.

And after a few trials, he and Ronaldo had never figured out how to time the things. They fiddled with proportions of ice and water and cap-tightness. A few never went off at all. A few went off so soon and so loudly that they decided to forget about shatter bombs. He had no doubt that a shatter bomb in closed quarters would leave a man bleeding from both ears.

Then he found out that the shrimp shop on Iberville sold dry ice. His plan was to fill three two-liter bottles with chips at home, and leave them capped loosely. In a separate bottle, he would carry the water. All of it would fit in a duffle bag. He would get a cab Uptown, assemble the bombs there, and roll them under the house. He would study somewhere close by, maybe in an empty class room, and watch the brothers get the hell scared out of them. In the open space under the house it wouldn't break anything or hurt anybody.

He figured that they would be most vulnerable while sleeping off Friday night. On Saturday morning he bought the ice, and wearing gloves he had taken from lab, he broke it up in the sink with an ice pick. He had dried the sink with his shirt, and threw the shirt on the table. The ice flecks burned his abdomen before melting to gas.

The doorbell rang. "Fuck." It was probably Ronaldo, or, less likely, the landlord. He didn't want either of them to see what he was doing.

The bell rang again. He ripped off his gloves, put the shirt back on, and ran to the bathroom for a towel. He threw the towel over the ice and ran down the stairs.

He opened the door. His breath left him.

It was a policeman. He looked familiar.

"Are you Henry Marrier?" the cop asked, not unpleasantly.

Of course the cop looked familiar—this was the bust he had pictured, he had dreamed about, ever since he had sent the first sheets to Ronaldo, years ago.

14

His guts shifted and set themselves. He must have answered, because the cop spoke again: "Are your parents Henry and Blythe Marrier?"

"Yes," Henry said.

The cop then offered his parents' address in Tampa, and asked if they lived there. He did not consult a piece of paper for the address.

"Yes," Henry said, "That's where they live."

"May I come in?" The policeman said.

"Sure," Henry said. *The acid*, his brain whispered. But he stepped aside to let him in. What happened to mom and dad, he thought. He also thought, I hope this is about them and not me. Thinking so made him feel like trash. The policeman walked up the stairs behind him. There was no kitchen door, and when he saw the kitchen table and its two chairs, the cop said, "Mind if I sit?"

The dry ice was in the sink under the towel, an arm's length away from the table. The two-liter bottle was standing empty on the counter, with the others full beside it. Without thinking, Henry had just tossed the gloves down next to it. The policeman took it all in with his thumbs hooked in his belt. He said nothing and sat down. Like the rest of the NOPD, he carried a Smith and Wesson automatic with a chipped, black finish, like a cap gun. He was a leftie; the gun was on his left hip. From the cop's other hip hung his PR-24 baton, the kind with a handle at a right angle to the shaft. They became common in the U.S. after an American cop on vacation watched a Taiwanese policeman use two to hold a small mob at bay.

Henry felt like he should offer him something to drink. He had nothing to offer from the refrigerator, and he didn't want to run water anywhere near the sink. "Do you need to use the bathroom-?" he offered instead.

"That's all right," the policeman said. He was probably in his early thirties. Beneath his hat he had ashy-blond hair that looked like wet feathers. This wasn't deja-vu, or a dream-cop—Henry was certain he had seen the man before; maybe he patrolled downtown, near school.

"So," Henry said, "What can I help you with?"

"We've got an investigation," the cop drawled, "That's all I can tell you. Other than that, I just want to ask you questions, like on TV."

Henry sat down opposite him. His hands didn't know what to do, so he laced his fingers together on the table.

"Wow," the policeman said, "These're some high ceilings." He contemplated the ceiling like he would enjoy a ceiling museum. His hat didn't budge. Henry thought manners dictated that he take it off.

He looked up too. "They built them high in the old days so the hot air would rise," he said, "You know what, why don't we go in the other room. I have an air conditioner." He wanted to get away from the sink. And away from the freezer, with its acid.

The cop stood up; his uniform pants made him look bow-legged. Henry picked up the kitchen chairs so they would have someplace to sit. The cop followed the sound of the air conditioner to the bedroom, and then tossed his baton onto the bed and sat on the bed's corner. He had seen Henry carrying the chairs. Henry put down the chairs and positioned one so that his side was to the cop. That made him feel less exposed. He wished there were still a table between them.

"So you're Henry Marrier?" said the cop.

"Yes," said Henry.

"And your parents are Henry and Blythe Marrier of Tampa." Then he gave their address again.

"Yes," Henry said.

The cop looked as if he were about to laugh.

Something's wrong, Henry thought. He read the cop's badge: brass crescent around a brass star and FRANK 665. The badge looked real to him.

"Your father's a CPA," said the cop, "You got no brothers or sisters."

The cop had lied: this wasn't like television. "That's right," Henry said. He added, "Did something happen to my parents?"

The cop leaned forward and retrieved a notepad from his back pocket. At last. This was what Henry expected.

He was about to flip open the pad. Then, absentminded, without looking up from the pad, he took his gun from the holster and stuck it under his left thigh, with the butt sticking out.

And that was not what Henry expected.

The cop flipped open the pad. "You own any weapons?" he asked.

Henry thought about how he should answer. "I own a couple guns," he said.

The cop read from the pad. "A Glock 17, a .38 revolver, a 12-gauge pump, and a Colt assault rifle."

"It's a rifle," Henry said. He felt himself sitting absolutely straight and still. That looked guilty, he thought, so he slouched with his arms crossed.

The cop looked around the room. "They in there?" he said, nodding at the steamer trunk.

This was a violation of his second amendment rights. Henry told himself that, and he hoped it would make his voice icy: "They're all registered. The handguns were purchased by my father, and he sold them to me when I turned twenty-one. I have a copy of the bill of sale. You can call him with any questions," he said, "I keep all my guns locked up at all times."

The cop looked up from the note pad. "I know they're registered. How do you think I got this?" He hit the notepad with his finger. "You think I'm stupid?" He stared with blue eyes.

When the cop didn't look away, Henry realized that he was expected to answer. He said, "No, I don't think you're stupid."

The cop flipped his notepad shut without taking his eyes from Henry's face.

"Henry?" the cop said, "You want to suck my dick?"

"Excuse me?"

"You heard me."

Henry squirmed in his seat. He put up a hand to scratch the side of his head, so that he could look away and decide what was happening. This guy wasn't a policeman. This was some sort of extortion con-job. He would have thought it was just a come-on if the guy hadn't talked about his parents and his guns.

"Put your hand down," the cop said, "Sit on your hands."

Henry saw the baton on the bed, and, real cop or not, that was a real gun. He sat on his hands.

The cop stood up. Slowly, he began to work at his belt buckle, unfastening.

A lazy thought went across Henry's mind, like reading a billboard from a backseat: go for the gun on the bed....

Then Officer Frank's hands slowed, slowed until they froze with his belt half unbuckled. "Henry," the cop said, "It's okay to say no."

"No," Henry said.

The cop re-buckled his belt in a hurry. "That's a relief," the cop said with a smile, "I didn't really want you to either." He sat down—back on the gun—took off his hat, and wiped his forehead with the back of his wrist. "I thought you were going to call my bluff. There's only so much I'm willing to do for this job."

Once he took off his hat, and smiled, Henry recognized him. It was the stringy pizza delivery man from Hines's house, this time done up as a cop. He was so relieved that he laughed. He put his hands back in his lap, and the man didn't stop him.

The man—whoever he was—laughed too.

"So," Henry asked, "How's the pizza business?"

"Are you gay?" The pizza-delivery cop asked, with another blue stare.

Henry figured that this guy still wanted to get into Hines's house. The rest—as he had himself said—was a bluff. Was there something in the house that Henry had missed? He didn't care. Hines obviously attracted crazy people as only a crazy person can, and now Henry had Hines's smell on himself. After he got rid of this "cop", he would take an eraser to Hines: flush the rest of the acid down the toilet, and let the dry ice smoke away, and spend Paolo's money. If Hines continued to bug him, he would call the real police.

"Look," Henry said, "I'm just assuming here. But I assume that this has something to do with whatever it was you wanted that day they were at the funeral. I really can't help you. I just work for the funeral home."

"It's a simple question. Three words," the delivery-cop said. He was getting loud. Henry wondered about diet pills. "You live down here in the Quarter, and you got butch hair, and you hang around that fruity pretty boy...."

"Ronaldo?" Henry asked.

"Is that your boyfriend's little namey-wamey?" said the delivery-cop.

Henry tried unsuccessfully to imagine kissing Ronaldo. He said, "I suppose stranger things have happened, but I'm pretty sure Ronaldo and I are not gay."

He guessed that he wasn't expected to be so calm. The delivery-cop looked confused, digging for something to say. He held his hat by the brim and scratched his forehead with the fingers of the same hand, then put his hat back on. He crossed his legs so that Henry could see his patrolman's boot. He said, "Henry, give me the acid."

The hat, the boot, the baton—he was drawing attention to his costume. Nothing else had worked. But that wasn't a costume gun.

Thirty-three percent of cops killed in the line of duty are snuffed by their own weapons. He had read that someplace. If that happened to real cops, then he could get the gun away from this guy. He had gotten the magazine from Hines. Now the cop was sitting with both hands on one knee, hoping Henry would look at his badge.

"Calling me queer. That's old," Henry said, "That's like accusing me of being a communist. I don't know what you're talking about. If you think I've got drugs, and you're a policeman, why not just arrest me?"

The cop got the baton in his hand, fast. He stood up and said, "You want me to arrest you, you little prick?"

Standing there, and with that voice, he seemed very real.

Henry said nothing.

"You sold it?" the cop said.

"Yes," Henry said.

"You sold two hundred doses of acid."

Henry swallowed. "Yeah," he said.

The policeman stared. Henry mustered up the guts not to look away, and hoped he looked honest.

The cop took a deep breath. "One more try," he said on the exhale, "Listen to me first. The D.A. likes to make an example of the white boys whenever he gets a chance. You hang around with that Ronaldo Pitero, who would be in jail if it weren't for his old man. That's common knowledge. That's old hat. And you got a trunk full of weapons in there. You know what a jury thinks when they see an assault rifle?

"You just confessed to slinging that shit. If I report this, Narcotics is going to come up in here and find those guns. I got friends in Narcotics. So they might find some other stuff you wouldn't even dream of. If you know what I mean. If you see what I'm talking about. I'm erasing your old answer from my brain. Give me a better one."

Henry sat very still. The room felt as though it were filling rapidly with water.

"Give me the acid, asshole," the cop hissed.

Without a word, Henry went to the kitchen and took the foil packet out of the freezer. The cop followed, sliding the baton back into the ring at his waist as he went. He stood next to the sink. Henry watched him regard the empty bottle on the counter, then throw back the towel covering the dry ice.

"You are one stupid asshole, you know that?" he laughed, "You're just begging for it. Who's the crackbomb for?"

Henry held out the acid to him. "It's not for anybody. I changed my mind."

The cop had the icepick in his hand. He took the packet from Henry and put it into his shirt pocket, then with the icepick went at the ice like he hated it. Henry thought he would punch holes in the sink. When he was done, he looked up with a face-splitting smile. "Let's put the son of a bitch together!" he said.

The cop shoveled in the chips with a spoon and his bare fingers, enjoying himself. Henry watched. He just wanted the man out of his house so he could be a student again; he never should have strayed.

The cop ran some water into the bottle and twisted down the cap one, two, three times. The last time he held it between his knees and twisted from the shoulders. He stood up and shook the feeling back into his hand.

He threw the bomb into the air and caught it with a slap, like it was a football.

Henry stepped backwards through the kitchen door.

"We used to use these to keep our math teacher in line. They work better with soda water," the cop said wistfully, "Where'd you go to school?"

In New Orleans, that question asks for high school. "Martyrs'," Henry said.

"I was at Aloysius," the cop said. He tucked the bomb under his arm. "I think you better come with me."

Henry didn't know what shaking up the bomb would do, and nobody was going to keep him around when that thing went off. "Fuck," he said, "that."

He had forgotten himself. But the cop just laughed, and spiraled the bomb six feet into the air. He didn't flinch at all on catching it. Henry did.

"I caught these two kids with one of these once. I made them play hot potato with it till it went off. Fucked up the eyes of one them," the cop said, "Follow me out to the car."

Henry didn't move.

The cop said, "Do you know how much trouble you're in? I got you now with intent to distribute." He tapped his shirt pocket. "This is enough for six-to-ten."

"You need a minimum of a gram for intent," Henry said. He felt weak. "There can't be more than a thousandth of a gram on that."

"They include the weight of the paper, Henry."

Henry felt the blood leave his face. "I don't believe you. That doesn't make any sense."

"It's the law," the cop said, "I'm going out now. If I get out that door and you're not behind me, I turn around and the bust begins. You got a choice: either become a convict, or become a doctor."

He went down the stairs. The bomb hung by the neck from between his two fingers.

Henry followed. Outside, the sky was the color of watered down, skim milk: clouds smeared from end to end. They still had to squint. The cop didn't have sunglasses, though he seemed like the type.

Parked across the street was a white van with a busted tail light. Henry saw Hines behind the wheel, wearing sunglasses. The cop walked ahead, and Hines rolled down the window and stuck his head out with a querying look.

"All through," said the cop. He handed Hines the foil packet from his pocket.

Hines put the packet in his breast pocket, and looked at the bomb. "What's the bottle for?"

"This is called 'the big surprise,'" the cop said.

Hines looked at him for an explanation, but the cop kept walking, to the back of the van. Henry followed because he had not been told otherwise. The cop pushed the button on the door handle, but the lock was being contrary. He cursed and yanked the door open with a sound like he had sheared the lock.

Inside was a refrigerator box, turned on its side. A hand cart was on its side next to it, to the right. And sitting on the wheel well to the left was Ronaldo, looking ashamed of himself. That's how Henry knew he was there of his own will. "Hello, Hank," he said.

15

The cop turned to Henry, who was still staring at Ronaldo, who stared at the bomb in the cop's hand. He knew what it was. Ronaldo had probably shown fear with his own dad's gun in his face, but that was how much it took for him to look scared.

Ronaldo looked scared when he looked at the cop. He watched the man's face when the cop wasn't looking, and looked away when he was.

"By the way," said the cop to Henry, "My name's Larry Frank. Say the whole thing." They shook hands.

"Get in. We're going for a ride."

* * *

Larry Frank closed the doors on them. There were no windows in the doors, or in the sides of the van; Henry couldn't see where they were going. He sat on the other wheel well, opposite Ronaldo, with the refrigerator box between them. He looked over the top at Ronaldo, but he wouldn't look back. The box of fire extinguishers that had been under the table at Hines's house rode on the floor between the front seats. Larry Frank wedged the bomb between two extinguishers and rode with his hat on his knee. The bomb had built up so much gas that the bottle was opaque; it could pass for solid ice.

Hines drove. Maybe he had just stepped in from a Saint Croix hammock, with that white linen suit. With that gray face and sunglasses, maybe he had just left a Saint Croix funeral.

He couldn't see Ronaldo now; he had ducked down. "Where are we going, Ronaldo," Henry whispered around the bottom of the refrigerator box.

Ronaldo didn't answer.

"Ronaldo," he said, louder, "Where are we going."

Still no answer.

Henry checked that Larry Frank wasn't looking, then stood and peeked over the side of the box. Ronaldo sat in a ball, with his eyes shut and hands pressed knuckle-white over his ears. Good idea— Henry did the same, to protect his brain from the shatter bomb. Larry Frank sat there with his legs crossed. Larry Frank grinned at the bomb now and again like he was a little kid spitting off a balcony.

Through his hands, Henry thought he heard his name being called. Then he was grabbed by the wrist and shaken for attention. Larry Frank had gotten up, and had one of the fire extinguishers in his hand.

I can tell you never been in the service because you love guns so much, Larry Frank's muffled voice said, What's this in my hand?

He didn't take his hands off of his ears. Fire extinguisher, he heard himself say from far away.

Larry Frank drew his beaten-up pistol with some difficulty and held it up. This is a people extinguisher, he said.

He turned back around and sat in his seat. He and Hines talked about something. Larry Frank threw back his head and laughed. Hey Ronnie! he yelled, Ian hasn't done one, either! *Two* cherries!

Henry let up on his ears in case the two in front revealed more. He heard Hines say, "Why are they sitting like that?"

He felt the van roll onto an uneven surface. They stopped. He had no idea where they were. Hines opened the back doors, with Larry Frank standing beside him. Even Hines's lips were gray. They had parked in a crushed-shell parking lot, by an abandoned okra cannery. Henry knew where it was: at the foot of Bayou St. John, on the seam between two neighborhoods. The Bayou here was only about one hundred feet wide, with concrete banks.

"So the young guys have the backs for this, right?" Hines said. The sort of safe joke you hear at a wake.

Ronaldo jumped out of the van. He said, "Hank, it's time you worked for a living."

Henry stared at him. Ronaldo was a traitor.

When he didn't jump out, Ronaldo turned and smiled at him. It wasn't his usual, spiky smile. It was an apology. "Pass out that hand cart," he said.

Henry wasn't going to let him off that easy, but he lifted the hand cart onto the top of the box and Ronaldo pulled it out. Larry Frank was looking at him, so he got out.

He and Ronaldo slid the box out. The top edge got stuck against the top of the door, and Ronaldo yanked hard on the corner until it popped free. When the box plopped to the ground, Henry guessed what wobbled inside. It was a dead body.

Ronaldo wriggled the foot of the hand truck under the edge of the box. "Get that strap, Henry," he said. Henry handed Ronaldo the yellow strap.

Bayou St. John was more of a canal. It had been carved to float barges of cane and cotton between the lake and river, right through the city. The end had been pinched off here, long ago. Mud turtles hung onto a swamped shopping cart. The okra cannery took up a block, on a lot the size of three. Mercy+Baptist Hospital peeped over the left corner. The cannery was made of pitted, red bricks and broken windows. Larry Frank waited for them to strap down the box, holding the bomb on his hip like a baby. How much longer did they have?

Ronaldo was thinking the same thing. They moved so that the box stood between them and Larry Frank and his bomb. Hines, the fool, stood right next to him, because he knew no better.

Larry Frank turned and walked toward the cannery. Without a word, Hines followed. Then Ronaldo gave the axle a shove with his foot and rolled after them with the box; the box rocked on the shells like a stagecoach. Henry had thought that Larry Frank worked for Hines, but now he thought it might be the other way around.

Look at his suit, Henry thought. His family—what was left of it—lived in a house with no books or much furniture, and Hines went around dressed like that.

No one in the passing cars looked at them with much interest. Larry Frank took them around to a back loading dock that looked as if it had last seen commerce when the bayou had. The rubber blocks for the trucks to bump were in shreds. Hines waved the box toward a loading ramp, which Larry Frank had already climbed. He waited at the top with the bomb, near a steel garage door. Oil had soaked a foot down into the concrete of the ramp. For some reason, Henry imagined broken bones; a workplace accident that left the bone sticking out. Ronaldo got a running start and got the box up the ramp.

Larry Frank produced a key from his pocket, placed the bomb on the concrete. The bomb wobbled and he jumped back. He was grinning with the tip of his tongue between his teeth; then that went away and he opened a heavy door with a cracked pane of square glass. He went inside and let the door slam behind himself. Then the garage door shrieked open and rolled up, driven by a black metal chain. Larry Frank stood inside with his hand on the switch. Henry wondered why the power was on. He looked at the bomb and thought that if they had to be around it, he would prefer they be outside.

"Come on, come on. Y'all're taking all day," Larry Frank said, picking up the bomb, "Henry and Ronnie know we ain't got all day, huh?" He winked.

"What?" Hines said.

Ronaldo went faster up the ramp.

Larry Frank closed the electric door. The inside of the cannery was a cavern; any machinery had been taken away long ago. Pigeon shit dotted the floor, and the girders above bubbled with the birds. A rectangular shack made of two-by-fours and siding stood to the left of the door—the manager's office. Henry imagined the green jumpsuit with the poking bone had been carried here and placed screaming on the desk.

Thieves had hacked the air-conditioner out of the side of the shack with an axe. Larry Frank reached around through the hole and unlocked the door. The door opened outwards, which looked wrong. Ronaldo tried to roll in the box, but it wouldn't fit.

Henry was right behind him. With one foot on the axle, Ronaldo let the box fall flat and said, "Get out the way," and pushed past Henry. He unlocked the holding straps with one hand, and with the other pulled a utility knife from his pocket. He belly-flopped across the box and cut around the bottom on three sides, then stabbed the side and sliced a line from bottom to top. Milky smoke wisped from the lines he had cut.

He didn't cut around the top; he just started ripping, and nodded at Henry to help. The cardboard was thicker than it looked. It did his nerves good to rip something. Then Hines joined in. The box made barking sounds as it came apart.

"Settle down. Christ," Larry Frank said. He had placed the bomb by the door of the shack.

Dry ice in chunks the size of feet fell out of the box; they produced the smoke. Beneath the ice was a six-foot mummy of newspaper and masking tape. Ronaldo pulled up on the paper and slashed the cocoon open from end to end, then split the paper wide with his fingers. Beneath the paper: black, cafeteria-sized garbage bags. Hines stepped away. He and Henry knew how it worked: one bag went over the dead man's head, the other over his feet, overlapping at the waist like the halves of a spy's cyanide capsule.

Ronaldo pulled off a bag. Henry braced himself for a bloated cadaver's face. He saw a pair of walking shoes and gray cotton pants instead. Ronaldo pulled off the other bag, the one over the head. The dead man was face down. He had a bald spot and gray hair. Henry found him small and surprisingly easy to look at.

"Shit for brains," Larry Frank laughed, "You opened him upside down."

"What's he going to do, get motion sick?" Ronaldo said with a weak smile. Sweat ran down into his eye, and he wiped it away. They were all sweating, Larry Frank the least. Henry felt sick to his stomach, and jittery, like he had had too much coffee after no sleep. He hadn't; that bomb was going to go off. He looked at it by the shack's door. He could almost hear it groan with the pressure. Even Larry Frank had gotten away from it now. He stood behind Henry, who stood behind Ronaldo, who was kneeling at the shoulder of the face-down dead man. On the other side of the dead man, closest to the bomb, stood stupid Hines.

"Get the gun, Ronnie, you worthless shitbird," Larry Frank said. He dropped his thumbs from his belt and put them right back. "If you unpacked him right, it would have come out on top."

The dead man lay on a bed of paper and dry ice. Ronaldo reached underneath and pulled out a Marlin .30 bolt-action, single-shot rifle. The stock was blue polymer, and taped to it were four cartridges in a sandwich bag. Ronaldo offered it to Larry

Frank with the barrel pointed at the ceiling. Larry Frank didn't take it. He nodded at Hines.

Hines took the gun. He looked like he had been sketched, he was so white, especially with those sunglasses. He took off his jacket, folded it, and laid it through the hole in the wall where the air-conditioner had been. He was harnessed to the SIG-Sauer. He carried it under his left arm in a pale, cowhide holster—a concealed combat holster that held the barrel parallel to the floor. No awkward dip into the armpit required. It pleased him that Henry stared at it. It pleased Henry that there was an empty slot in the holster where another magazine should go. With smoke from an ice chunk curling up his trouser leg, Hines pulled back the bolt and loaded the rifle.

Ronaldo had rolled the dead man over.

Henry remembered what his lab instructor had said the first day: "Cadavers don't look like people." Corpses were a different story. Before them was a corpse. Not an it, but a he. He wore a maroon golf shirt and gray slacks with a tab-fastened waist. What little hair he had died with had been messed up in the box. Henry looked at his jowly face and searched for what he should feel. All he got was a thought, a senseless one—this man once drove a car. Not anymore.

Ronaldo ran his arms under the dead armpits and gripped the corpse's opposite wrists. "Get his feet, Hank," he said.

Henry grabbed the ankles. They were cold from the dry ice, and he was heavy, and not stiff at all. A stiff body would have been easier to move; this was like dragging a garbage bag full of soup. Ronaldo walked the head into the manager's shack.

Larry Frank picked up one of the garbage bags and traded it with Hines for the rifle. "Ian, can you pick up the box pieces? And the paper?" The dry ice would turn to gas and disappear.

Inside the dark office, Henry made out two desks against opposite walls. No calendars hung from the nails above them. The office chairs had been stolen.

"Put him down," Ronaldo said, when they had walked him into the center of the room.

Henry placed the corpse's feet together on the floor. The body didn't revolt him like a cadaver would. He felt duty-bound to see that the man slept well.

As intent as Larry Frank was to play chicken with the bomb, even he was now moving fast. He stepped inside and pushed the rifle at Ronaldo. Outside, Hines watched with a fistful of newspaper and a garbage bag, sunglasses and a hung-open mouth.

"I got to?" Ronaldo said.

"You got to learn," Larry Frank said.

"What's there to learn?"

"You have to learn your lesson."

Ronaldo took the rifle. He didn't care much for guns, Henry knew, and he held the gun like it was a shovel full of dirt. "Henry's going to hold?" Ronaldo said.

Larry Frank nodded. Behind him, Hines walked out of sight.

"Hank," Ronaldo said, "Henry, you got to hold him up in a sitting position."

Henry looked at him, waiting for him to say something else; he looked at Larry Frank, who said, "Get down there and prop him up."

Henry waited, looking at him.

Larry Frank drew his pistol and pointed it at Henry's chest.

Henry felt his stomach bounce.

Henry slowly got down on one knee and pulled up the corpse by the shoulders. Because I got a gun on me; because I need to get away from the bomb; because Larry Frank will frame me; because

I'm a coward; not because I want to hurt you—he thought to the dead man.

He put his shoulder to the dead man's middle back and put his head down. He felt Ronaldo messing with the head, and heard his disgusted gasp when he stuck a thumb into the corpse's mouth to pull the jaw down. He did not slide the barrel to the soft palate, but pointed it up, just behind the teeth, where a straw would sit.

Henry made himself into a smaller ball and closed his eyes. I'm sorry, he thought to the corpse.

Ronaldo put the rifle butt to the floor and pulled the trigger. There was a sound of somebody clapping, once. Only the head moved, a little. It made no sense, but Henry wondered if the shot would have been louder had the body been alive. The pigeons made more noise than the gun as they rustled from beam to beam overhead.

Henry wiped the back of his neck; he thought he had felt some dead blood spritz across it. He gingerly put his hands on the shoulders and moved his own body to the side. He didn't want the mess above the jaw to wipe against him as he lay the torso down.

He looked; if he was going to be part of this, then he would have the guts to look it in the face.

What face? Where he had once worn the top of his head, his calvaria, he now wore a corona of nothing. The corona had slipped over his left eye: his left eye was gone. So was most of his nose. The brainpan must have collapsed, because the skull was flat as a paper bag. Henry knew that he was going to pay in a high, high court for this—too high for this world. He looked up, and Ronaldo was giving him a pleading look.

Officer Larry stepped forward and dumped the three remaining cartridges from the plastic bag onto the dead chest. Henry walked away and held himself up by the doorframe. He saw the bomb on the floor and turned back around. Ronaldo was lifting the dead man's shirt, and taped to the pale belly was a pint bottle of whiskey. He ripped it off. Hair came with it; he ripped off the cap, dumped half the bottle over the body, and threw the bottle away. It broke in the dark.

Henry turned around, to the door again; Hines was standing there, but didn't see him. He was looking at the body with his arms by his sides, his gun looking too big for him. He was thinking of Paolo. Henry looked down at the bomb by his left foot. He didn't feel like he was walking, but falling; he fell away from the bomb toward the door to the loading ramp.

It had locked behind them. He turned to see what was taking them so long with his hand on the door knob. Hines was reaching at arm's length for his jacket, trying to yank it from the hole in the wall without getting too close to the shack. He dropped the jacket, picked it up, and put it on. He looked like he might throw up. The two garbage bags full of cardboard and paper were on the floor behind him.

"Ian, what are you doing?" Larry Frank asked, "Get that stuff out of sight. Back there somewhere."

Hines dragged the two bags into the dark behind the manager's shack. Larry Frank kicked away chunks of dry ice, making a game of hitting the far wall. The pistol was still in his hand.

Ronaldo came out of the shack without the rifle. He joined Henry by the door and said nothing. They both wanted to get away from the bomb.

Hines drifted back out of the dark. "What about prints?" he said.

Larry Frank said, "What about them."

"Ronnie's prints are all over the gun. They're going to find they don't match when they do the autopsy."

Larry Frank let out a hacking laugh. "There's not going to be any fucking autopsy," he said. He looked at the bomb. He walked toward it.

Don't pick it up again, Henry thought.

Larry Frank picked it up. He brought it close enough that they all could look at it. Henry tried not to; it might pop his eyeballs. The sides bowed out, and the cap had rounded. "This should have gone off by now," Larry Frank said. He looked at Henry, "You make one shitty crackbomb."

Hines said, "That's a bomb?"

Larry Frank threw Ronaldo a key on a rubberband. "Ronnie, open that door and don't move," he said.

Ronaldo opened the door. They could feel warm, open air on the backs of their necks and arms; they wanted to run, but Larry Frank had told them not to move. He had holstered his gun.

With a quivering smile, Larry Frank grabbed the bomb like a football, dropped back three steps like a quarterback, and threw it. They ran through the door, and Larry Frank slammed it shut behind them. They waited with their shoulders hunched for the bang. Henry and Ronaldo had their ears covered. Hines looked at them and did the same. Larry Frank grinned at the door.

Nothing happened.

"Shit, Henry—" Larry Frank said.

Then it banged like a truck wreck. Pigeons blew out of the broken windows, dragging a shadow like a cloud's. Four crows on the roof maintained composure enough to scream at the noise.

Henry was the first to giggle, and Larry Frank looked at him and laughed. Then Ronaldo and even Hines caught it. When he laughed, Henry felt like he had done nothing wrong. When he stopped, he knew he had done something awful.

They walked back across the shell parking lot toward the van. "Give me the key," Larry Frank said to Ronaldo.

Ronaldo froze. "It's back there," he said, "In the door. On the inside." The door had locked behind them; there was no way they could get the key.

Larry Frank looked him in the eye. Hines and Henry stopped, and stopped breathing. Larry Frank looked back at the loading dock. "Oh well," he said, "The guy had to let himself in with something, right?" He kept walking.

A nine-year old black boy with a sinus infection, riding an adult's bike with a broken pedal, had stopped by the van. He watched them approach, looking ready to cry. "I heard a explosion," he said with concern.

"That's right. Why don't you go up in that building and see what it was?" Larry Frank said, "No, don't go up in there. If you go in there, I'll arrest you. They're going to lock you up in Angola. Where your daddy's already at. You're going to have to make your own clothes."

"That's fucked up, Larry," Ronaldo said.

"Larry Frank," Larry Frank said.

The boy's eyes welled up, and he tried to hop up on his bike and get away. Larry Frank smacked him on the back of the head.

Hines put his hand on the bike's seat. He bent down to the kid's eye level. "It's all right," he said.

That made the kid start crying. Hines pulled out a white handkerchief—just like Hines to carry one. He wiped the kid's eyes and held it over his nose. "Blow," he said. Larry Frank rolled his eyes.

The kid took "blow" to mean "exhale." His face would be a gooey mess under the handkerchief. Hines smiled. "Blow again?" Hines said. He wiped off the kid's face, folded the handkerchief, and put it in his pocket.

Surgeons don't mind blood or liquified fat, but they can't stand snot. "Gross!" Henry muttered, and looked away with his eyes shut. Larry Frank had walked around the van and was waiting with his hand on the door's handle for Hines to let him in. Ronaldo walked around to the back. Hines shook the kid's hand

and put a hand on his head, like he was wiping away Larry Frank's smack. But the boy still looked scared, and pedaled away.

* * *

Henry sat on the wheel well, holding his knees. He thought of the body they had left behind. If someone is dying, it's only human to help them; fail, and it's only human to bury them, not to leave them on a floor with half a head. One day I'll make a mistake and a patient will die, and I'll feel like I do right now, he thought. But this hadn't been a mistake....

"Do they really make their own clothes in Angola?" Ronaldo said. He sat opposite Henry, with his legs straight and his ankles crossed. He hadn't looked at Henry since they had gotten into the van.

"They grow their own food, too," Larry Frank said, "Cows and shit."

"I'd save a lot of money if I made my own clothes," Ronaldo said.

They drove. Without the box in the back, Henry could see that they were going up Orleans Street, taking him home. Without the box, it was harder for Ronaldo not to meet his eyes, but Ronaldo managed.

Hines turned on the radio, loud.

Larry Frank turned in his seat, drawing his pistol again. Ronaldo put up his hands and turned his face away. But it wasn't for Ronaldo; the gun swung past, at Henry.

"I'm sorry," Larry Frank said. He pulled the trigger.

Click.

Larry Frank smiled and put the gun to his own left temple. *Click, click, click.* "No hard feelings, huh?" he said.

Hines turned down the radio and the two of them laughed. Now Hines had gotten him back for taking his magazine.

Henry had convinced himself that Larry Frank was not a policeman. No real policeman would do this stuff in uniform. He could still go to the police if Larry Frank or Hines ever showed up near him again. What he would tell them, he didn't know, but he could still go to the police.

That idea changed when they dropped Larry Frank off: he climbed into a real squad car, parked in a loading zone because cop cars won't get towed.

16

Every day in high school he had thought it: if only his parents hadn't named him "Henry." It had a hunched, sebaceous sound. No wonder he had zits.

The strange names clumped together. At lunch the Matt's, Paul's, and Mark's held court in the cafeteria, or threw footballs in the parking lot. On the chapel bench sat Henry, Ronaldo, Dwayne and Pierre, and the occasional fat kid or pot head. Iago was there from time to time, because of Dwayne, but Iago was trouble and they were cold to him. They made fun of each other's names. "I'm Italian but my fucking name is Spanish," Ronaldo would say in self-defense.

The whole school was talking about the student who had hanged himself. Henry had known what he looked like: olive skinned, skinny. He looked quiet, and he was quiet. The priests had called a special assembly and told them that it was fine to feel confused, and maybe empty, after losing one of their own.

"I heard he was doing that thing where you choke yourself and beat off," Henry said to the guys at lunch. They pretended not to hear. Even Demon Dwayne wouldn't tell the truth, just because the kid was dead. Everyone had heard the rumor, and the kid was strange enough for it to be true—he took his big sister to homecoming.

The priests said that they should not forget to pray. There would be a prayer box outside the chapel where they might drop their anonymous prayers; at assembly, they would be distributed in a packet.

Honors Chemistry had Henry sold on science, and science made prayer seem quaint; but he played along, if only to set his naive classmates straight. He scribbled a prayer on a sheet ripped off of his assignment pad and dropped it in the prayer box on his way to class. On Friday they received the two-page prayer handout, mimeographed in purple ink. Ronaldo made them guess which prayer was his. It rhymed. Then Ronaldo read this one:

Dear Lord,

Help us see
He was here
Now he's not.

Amen

"That's the most fucked up thing I ever read," Ronaldo said.

It was Henry's prayer. He hadn't said so.

Six years later, he would regain respect for the dead. Mr. The Cadaver's smell commanded respect. Now he had helped shoot a corpse. A neurosurgeon guest lecturer had told them that the living human brain and spinal cord weren't rubbery like the ones they had dug out in lab. That was a trick of the formalin. The central nervous system was like nothing else on earth–electric, solid enough to cut, fluid enough to pour out of a bullet hole. This wondrous stuff made up a person.

If there had been a light in the shack, they would have seen the man's brain splattered on ceiling and wall. He deserved to have blood on him, as well; but he would find none when he later looked. It was a heresy. He didn't worry about a ghost at all; the dead man had seemed too helpless.

* * *

Hines dropped off Ronaldo and Henry at Henry's apartment. Ronaldo said he wanted Taco Bell and invited Henry along. Ronaldo's car was parked at an expired meter. He had gotten a ticket. He threw it onto the dashboard with two others.

They went to the Taco Bell across from the Orleans Parish Prison and Courthouse–A GOVERNMENT OF LAWS NOT MEN carved in granite by command of Huey Long. Ronaldo got four burritos and a drink. Henry had some ice with orange soda over it and moved it around in his mouth. Ronaldo said, "Eat," and threw a burrito in front of him.

They were not sitting across from one another, but at adjacent tables. Some deputies on break were standing at the counter. Henry said, in a low voice, "Do you plan on telling me what I've gotten myself into?"

Ronaldo took a big bite, wiped his mouth, and looked through the window at Broad Street.

"Hines said something about a 'money drop' that day he and I talked," Henry said, "I take that to mean that you and him were testing me in that house. Testing me to see if I would take the sheets and money. Why?"

Ronaldo mumbled. "That's what he says. That's him just rationalizing how he was suckered. You weren't supposed to take anything. You were just supposed to guard the house."

Henry waited. Hopefully, Ronaldo still had a big mouth, and would only need a little silence to get going.

"It's funny how you call him 'Hines,'" Ronaldo said, "That's like me. Everybody else calls him Ian. Even when I first met him, I never thought of calling him Mister Hines. I just thought of him as Hines. It fits him better because it sounds like 'heiny.'"

Henry said, "Everybody who?"

Ronaldo said, "Everybody nobody," and shut up again.

Henry waited, looking at him.

Ronaldo put down his burrito. "Henry, I wish you would just play along here. Don't worry about it," he said, "You're not in class. Don't ask so many questions."

"How come you get to know everything, then?" Henry said.

Ronaldo went back to eating. A burrito later, he said, "Just try and understand." He looked over his shoulder, which Henry read as melodrama meant to shut him up. The deputies had gone and there was no one else in the place. "Understand this. What we did isn't legal."

"No shit."

"The guy we work for knows what he's doing."

"Mr. Landry," Henry said. He wasn't sure he believed it. Mr. Landry seemed a sad sack not competent enough to drive a car. He would be the old man who rear-ended you.

Ronaldo shushed him and rolled his eyes. "His motto is, 'Don't play dumb, *be* dumb.' I know you because we went to school together. Those other two guys who were in the van?" He shrugged, looked confused, "What's a van? I'm too dumb to know."

"Okay," Henry said, "So tell me why we just went with Hines and Larry Frank and shot a dead man in the head."

Ronaldo chewed on ice, exasperated. He looked over his shoulder again. "This is being dumb," he said, "We don't even know what's going to happen. This morning, I had no idea what was going on. So don't get all mad thinking I knew we were getting you. In the back of the van, I couldn't even tell where we were. And I didn't try to know, because that's *being dumb*."

Henry lowered his voice. If he played along, Ronaldo would give more up. "So we take a dead body from the funeral home, shoot it in the head and dump whiskey over the body. It looks like he got drunk and killed himself. Then you provide a coffin full of bricks for the dead body's family to bury? It doesn't make sense."

"Because you're wrong," Ronaldo said, "That guy from today is really getting buried. The bricks were totally different."

"Why does this involve me?" Henry said.

"This wouldn't have involved you if you had just listened to me," Ronaldo said, "I told you to give Hines his acid back."

"So Larry Frank got it back. Why'd I have to come along and help out?"

"First off, you didn't really help out. You don't need more than two guys," Ronaldo said, "It could have been just me and Larry. It would be fine with me if you and Hines stayed home."

"So why didn't we?"

Ronaldo looked uncomfortable. "Because that guy you mentioned earlier," he said, "He didn't want it that way."

"Mr. Landry?" Henry said.

"Quiet," Ronaldo said.

"There's nobody here, Ronaldo."

"He's not as dumb as he seems," Ronaldo said. He went back to eating. Then he said, "Here's what happened. And you can't tell anyone.

"It was bad enough to take his drugs, Henry, but then you took his bullets. Hines is a drama queen. No wonder his son shot himself. My perfect example is a bachelor party we were guarding. There were more strippers than guys there. Hines is strutting around like a chicken. The girls were taller than him and naked. Russian girls. They want *money*. He's dressed like he's got some, like a director. He didn't give them dollar one, dude. Then at the end, he says, 'I'm fascinated by the stripper subculture.' That's what he got out a bachelor party for a guy one step shy of a pimp. I got drunk, high, and laid, and he got subculture."

"That doesn't sound so strange," Henry said, "He's married."

"When I say 'like a director,'" Ronaldo said, "I mean it. He was wearing boots and those pants that puff out. He didn't have the horse whip, but you just imagined it there. And you know he's got that gun on him the whole time."

Ronaldo was no longer talking under his breath. The story had picked him up and was carrying him.

"After you took his shit, Hines started being a complete baby. Our boss needed him working the phone, and he wouldn't even get out of bed. I went over to his house with Mr. Landry and Mike. It was nine in the morning and his wife is drinking wine out of a glass and making art, listening to space music. Hines had the covers pulled up to his chin and said he was too sick. To throw him in the ground with his son. Mr. Landry told him to get up. He didn't get up. It got to where Mike pulled on him, and he let himself fall out of bed. Then Mike dragged him over to the closet and tried to put a shirt on him, but he could only use one hand because he had to hold up Hines with the other one. Hines was moaning like he had a stroke."

"Mike got so frustrated that he just let him flop on the floor, and when we left the room, Hines's wife was waiting outside the door for us with three more glasses in her fingers, and her own glass and the bottle in the other hand. I felt sorry for their little girl."

Henry said, "What did Mr. Landry need him for so bad?"

Ronaldo looked impatient at the interruption. "To speak Portugese," he said.

"Oh," Henry said.

"So Mr. Landry wanted us all to do it today to straighten everybody out. I don't like doing today's kind of work either. It's disgusting. We could get caught. But he's been aggravated at me ever since that day when you and me went to the stadium. He looked in the coffin, and he wasn't happy about the mud. To tell the truth, he gave me money to buy bricks but I pocketed it. So I deserved what I got today. And Hines had to grow up."

Henry said, "Why did I deserve it?"

Ronaldo shifted in his seat. He thought for a while before he spoke. "Well, you shouldn't have stolen from Hines. It made it so he couldn't work."

Henry ran a hand over his head. Since cutting his hair off, he had developed the habit when feeling overwhelmed. "Ronaldo, I think that maybe it's best if I quit working for Palace Springs," he said, "I don't want to work for somebody who feels the need to 'straighten me out,' especially not like today."

"Don't think that," Ronaldo hastily added, "That's just the way I see it. Mr. Landry thought it wouldn't upset you, because you see bodies at school. He really likes you."

"He doesn't know anything about me."

"He knows you're going to be a doctor. That's enough. I don't know if he's worried about his health, but he wants a doctor around," Ronaldo said, "That's more than I can say about me. Nobody wants me around like that."

Despite himself, he felt flattered: if Ronaldo was telling the truth, Mr. Landry had the power to order around a crazy man like Larry Frank, and Mr. Landry found *him* valuable. Still, he must have looked anxious, because Ronaldo said, "Henry, he knows what he's doing. He's like you: he's from here, but he went off to California. That's where he got the name Palace Springs. I didn't feel safe with those guys at the vending machine company. I left when they tried to get me to start signing these blank invoices. I didn't know what they were going to fill in. But I feel safe with Mr. Landry."

"Paolo," Henry said, "Did he really kill himself, or was that fake?"

"Hines's son? He really killed himself. I told you before."

He didn't know why he had asked, because the answer made him feel no more at ease. "You said you didn't like doing stuff like today," he said, "So why do it?"

Ronaldo laughed. "Because today I made eight hundred bucks for twenty minutes work," he said.

"You don't feel like it's wrong?" Henry said.

"It's hard to feel like you're breaking the law when a cop is there in uniform."

"You know what I mean," Henry said, "*Wrong*."

Ronaldo shrugged. "Do you feel like what you do in Anatomy class is wrong?" he asked.

He did, but didn't know how to explain how he felt, and that embarrassed him. "That's different," he said, "That's education. That's not for money."

Ronaldo said, "You going to work for free? What's the highest paid doctor make?"

"It depends."

"How much."

"Ortho and derm can start at six figures."

Ronaldo looked at him flatly. "How's a guy like me supposed to make that kind of money?" he said, "At least I admit I'm doing it for money."

"Hey, " Henry said, "I'm going to *owe* six figures. Most of my class will."

"They wouldn't even let people like me borrow that," Ronaldo said.

"I never said I wasn't in it for the money," Henry said, hoping to make a joke of it, "Where's my eight hundred for today?"

Ronaldo gave him a slick smile. "Today was a training session. Seriously, though, Henry: I'm glad you're in on this. Nobody else is my age. Today's thing—that's really rare. Mostly, it's just odd jobs."

"I haven't agreed to be in on anything," Henry said.

"Come on, Henry," Ronaldo said, "What else you got going on?"

Henry tossed the burrito back onto Ronaldo's tray. "You eat that."

17

What else? Nothing else. Notes and lab. He decided not to get revenge on the fraternity. He would be nothing but a student again.

Head and Neck ended. The head and the neck were bad enough, but then they threw in the heart and lungs on the same practical. Henry again hadn't studied the cadavers, and again it didn't matter. Everyone else was just as confused. Henry's own lab instructor, whom he had previously considered a nice lady, tagged two cranial nerves as they entered the brainpan, but she left the dura over them. Only Gray's Atlas had a picture of the unpeeled brainpan, and nobody used Gray's anymore. They were allowed ten minutes per lab room, and before the buzzer went off, everyone was at the head of the table, stooped over and staring at the two little threads of nerve like they were lining up a putt. Some looked ready to cry.

One woman did cry, in the hall. "She failed first block," Eric told Henry, unasked, "And somebody on her table who will remain nameless told me that she's going to fail this one too." Even if she honored Abdomen and Lower Limb, she wouldn't pass. The summer between first and second years of medical school is the last summer any doctor ever has, and she would be taking Gross Anatomy over again. They had been warned: the previous summer the air conditioner had died. In order to see what they were dissecting, the summer students had to shoo away the flies.

After big exams like this, they repaired to the windowless bar across the street from the emergency room to get drunk. Once he could feel the beer, Henry thought of Palace Springs. He hadn't allowed himself to since the day they had shot the corpse. That was easy, with the worry over Head and Neck. The next day he had read the Times-Picayune obituaries:

Restauranteur Christopher Leggio, 55, was found dead in the abandoned Louisiana Okra Cannery building on Thursday, of what police say was a self-inflicted gunshot wound. Mr. Leggio was part owner of Leggio's Midcity Steaks and several other local eateries. He is survived by....

There was a picture of Christopher Leggio from that year. Larry Frank was right: there had been no autopsy. The coroner would have noticed that the "Christopher Leggio" found in the cannery didn't have thick, curly, black hair. Even with half a head he would have noticed.

He had saved the paper; remembering it now made his collar feel too tight, and he had the feeling that something awful was going to happen.

That went away after more beer. He ended up talking very loudly with five other students about what it would be like to win $125 million on Powerball. "To get the money, you have to let them publish your name and where you live," he explained, "If everyone in the city knew? You wouldn't be able to leave your house. You couldn't stay here."

A disgusted New Yorker said, "Why would you want to?"

Henry said that he would want to finish medical school. All present agreed that even if they won the lottery, they would still finish medical school.

A classmate was having a party. As the sun was going down, he stood on the sidewalk outside of the bar; across the street, a patient who looked healthy and bored was wheeled into the emergency room. He listened to the New Yorker offer him a ride from the passenger window of a car. More people sat in the back seat. Come with us, Henry; you'll have to sit on somebody's lap, but come with us.

He felt exposed out there on the sidewalk. "I have to go home first," he said, "I'll meet y'all there."

They gave him a ride home. Once inside, he thought that he should have gone along with them. It would have saved him cab fare. He finished half a bag of Doritos on the balcony with another beer. He didn't know why he had come home.

* * *

Ronaldo didn't call. It was like he wanted Henry to see how little went on in his life. The Head and Neck party hadn't been much. You could sit in the living room and watch *Melrose Place*; you could stand in the kitchen and talk about the test; or you could stand on the porch and get even drunker than you already were. Henry stood on the porch and talked a good bit to Amanda. She was friendly, and attractive, but belonged in the living room.

Then came the Histology final, and because it was on a Friday instead of a Monday there was no class party, since a free weekend meant an opportunity to leave town to see girlfriends, boyfriends, and family left behind. A lot of single students drove to Florida.

Not Henry. His street crossed Bourbon at the dirty end, where there were no jazz clubs or bars without strippers. When the sun was setting, he bought a giant beer from a bar's window and drifted up the street. The weather had cooled, though you had to stop and take notice. He had the feeling that he should be doing something, though there was no school work for him to do. School had kept him frantic for so long that he had forgotten how to be bored.

The strip joints had pictures of their girls tacked up in neon-piped cases by the door; he decided to pick the best one while finishing his beer. She had dyed black hair, curly. He wondered what she would look like wearing a shirt. These strippers used to look old to him when he was in high school.

He bought a large daiquiri, and while the bartender was drawing it, used the urinal, then with his new drink wandered up Royal Street. Here there were galleries which could only be visited by appointment, and an antique weapons store with an unexploded Civil War cannonball in the window for $500. The Royal Street police station was ringed by cop cars parked on the sidewalk. Anybody else's car would be impounded. He thought of Larry Frank.

He had not had a date since breaking up with Catherine, and had not had many dates before he met her. I never should have quit going to class, he thought, I should have bought a car and lived Uptown like everybody else. Then he would know more people.

He walked home and had two beers with AM radio, and took his shotgun apart. He put it back together with his eyes closed and wondered why the military made such a big deal of that. He would get drunk with this World War II music.

He locked the gun away, and before he could stop himself, he was on the phone, with the class phone list in his other hand. As much as he wanted to go out tonight, he was relieved when he got her answering machine:

"Hi. You have reached the home of Amanda, Kimberly, and Jean. Leave a message and *we* will get back to *you* as *soon* as we can."

He didn't know she had roommates. "Hi, Amanda. It's Friday after the Histo final," he said. He worried he might be slurring, "I just got back from bar-hopping with some friends from town, and if you weren't busy, or had no plans, I was going to ask if you wanted to do something. So I'm asking. But I guess you went out of town, back to Connecticut. I can't remember if you mentioned that in lab. Anyway. I'll see you in lab on Monday, hopefully. We're done with Histo. All right."

I sounded really drunk, he thought as he hung up. All right.

* * *

Now Anatomy would meet every day, with lab starting at eight in the morning. He hadn't gotten up at eight in months. He woke up too late to shower, and realized once he was outside that he should have worn a sweatshirt. The weather reminded him of San Francisco. He thought, if I could go to college again, I would try to have more fun. He would start going to class again, he decided, to socialize.

More and more students skipped lab. The cadavers no longer got the attention and care of new toys. Come noon, the people that did come to lab dumped on cadaver cologne and dissection kits and slammed the doors. Time for lunch. Mr. The Cadaver had dried out so much that he didn't stink anymore. Since they had cut his heart and lungs out, and his head was split down the middle, and his neck down the side, they kept his head folded up in his chest. Now he wasn't too long for the table. And the other day the guy at the next table cut the heel off of his female and handed it to Henry, saying, "Don't be such a heel." Henry had smiled to be polite but didn't take it.

This morning it was only going to be Eric and Henry. Henry was thirty minutes late, and Eric gave him a disapproving look.

Why, Henry thought, I don't want to dissect and you don't want me to.

Then Eric started smirking. He smirked at the thigh as he sliced it.

"Well," Eric said, "You certainly look like you're in a good mood."

Henry was flipping through the dissector. He thought a minute. "No," Henry said, "I think it's you that's in the good mood. I'm in a crappy mood."

"Do I seem happy?" Eric said, "I guess it's because I got ortho research lined up."

Henry looked up. "Bullshit," he said, "How."

"I walked in and asked for it."

"I went to the chairman's office and his secretary said I had to finish anatomy first."

"Well, I guess I walked into another office, because I start this Wednesday," Eric said, "I'm feeding the dogs in the vivarium. Gotta start at the bottom."

"That's great, Eric," Henry said. Asshole, he thought. "Good for you."

"Those other two aren't going to show up—gee, I wonder why," Eric said, "What a coincidence."

"I think Amanda went home for the weekend," Henry said.

Eric stopped flaying the leg and laughed. "I don't think so. Unless they both live in a bedroom in that condo in Florida everyone ran off to."

"Those two are doing it?" Henry said. He felt like he was watching a door slowly close.

Eric put up his hands. "I didn't say anything," he said. He turned back to the thigh.

Henry watched him dissect. "How do you hear all this stuff, Eric," he said, "You're like me. You never do anything. But you hear everything. I don't hear any of this stuff."

After saying it, Henry worried that he had hurt his feelings. But Eric grinned, then went back to work. Henry imagined him at home, reaching for the refrigerator door and naming the muscles that moved in his arm.

"Actually, I did something this weekend," Henry said, "I went out with some friends from town."

"What did you do," Eric said, "Go out drinking?"

"Yes," Henry said.

"I don't drink," Eric said, "I could use some help. Why don't you grab some gear and get to work on his foot?" He stared at Henry, steely. Henry had hurt his feelings after all. Eric might not drink, or do anything but study, but he could cut on this dead guy, and now Henry wouldn't have the stomach to do the same—or so Eric thought.

Without the smell, he could do it. "Sure," Henry said. He snapped on some gloves from the box on the counter.

"Are you sure it won't bother you?" Eric said, "I don't want you to be uncomfortable."

Henry picked up a pair of pointed scissors from the tank. All the instruments had rusted since he had last picked them up. He picked up a z-shaped leg-bar from the floor and slipped it into the slot at the foot of the tank, then plopped the ankle into the stirrup.

"Wait," Eric said. Early on, the next table over had thrown a bed sheet over their cadaver to keep it moist. "May I borrow this?" Eric said, picking up the sheet. He spread it over all of Mr. The Cadaver except the leg.

"That should make it easier for you," Eric said to Henry. "Just begin by skinning it." He handed him the scalpel handle first. He had put the sheet there so that squeamish Henry wouldn't get scared.

Sorry, he thought to the cadaver, and dragged the scalpel's blade down the sole of the foot. It rasped gritty across crystallized tendons. He peeled away the skin, and wasn't disgusted. He felt nothing at all.

He looked down at Eric, doing the same work the thigh. He had covered the body to make it seem less human, but now it looked ready for burial. That made him leery of cutting. And if I keep cutting, Henry thought, I'll be just like Eric, but with no research; just like Earnest and Amanda, but with no love life. Just a medical student.

He put down the scissors and forceps and snapped off his gloves. Eric looked up, pleased.

I'll give you some gossip, you dog-feeding bastard, he thought. "I have to go," Henry said, "There's something on my mind that I don't want to talk about."

"What," Eric said.

Henry sighed. "Well, it's my girlfriend," he said, "They want to kick her out of Covenant House."

"I thought that was where teenage runaways went," Eric said.

"It is," Henry said, impatiently, "But they want to kick her out because she won't get pre-natal care."

Eric's eyes gleamed, "You got your girlfriend pregnant?" he whispered, "How old is she?"

"Sixteen," Henry said, picking up his bag, "And I'm trying to get her in rehab so she doesn't have the baby on heroin."

He picked up his bag, walked home, took a shower, and went back to bed. This was the way to do medical school after all, he decided.

Then Ronaldo called, late at night. He was out of breath. "What are you doing the weekend before Thanksgiving?" he said.

"I'm going to Tampa," Henry said, "Where have you been?"

"You ever hear of Mac Donald?" Ronaldo asked.

"Old Mac Donald," Henry said. He had been asleep.

"No. The porno star," Ronaldo said, "He's getting married. He needs protection at his bachelor party and you and me are hired thugs."

18

Mac Donald was not only a porn star, but a Miami porn producer, his videos known by their Tartan plaid box; his latest was entitled *Penistroika: The Girls of Eastern Europe*; he was marrying a woman from New Orleans, in New Orleans, and Ronaldo was to be the bachelor party's master of ceremonies. Ronaldo wouldn't say how he knew Mac. He was so excited that you would think the party was for him, and he was doing his best to make it so: "Mac says that I can invite as many guys as I want!"

The party was the Saturday before Thanksgiving. Ronaldo needed some prostitutes with an act. The Banana Boat Twins canceled. So he got the Salad Sisters.

He and Ronaldo were eating at Popeye's Famous Fried Chicken on Canal and Carollton. "What happened to the Banana Boat People?" Henry asked.

"Fuck, Hank," Ronaldo said, "Boat people are from Haiti. The Salad Sisters are just as good. Better."

"What do they do with salad?" Henry asked.

Ronaldo smiled. "Bring zucchini. Or yucca root."

* * *

Their last experience with a prostitute had also been in November, when they were seventeen. They had gotten tired of ice bombs. They were both virgins, and there was no sense in saying otherwise, because they were around each other too much to pull off the lie. Henry knew he would never have a girlfriend as long as he had his bad skin; he didn't know what Ronaldo's problem was. Even with drugs, Ronaldo couldn't get anybody.

All night long they had tooled long, bored loops up and down Veterans Boulevard in Henry's van; and Ronaldo said, "I know where there's whores."

Neither of them had spoken in forty minutes. "Bullshit you know where there's whores," Henry said.

His dad had busted some prostitutes a few nights before, Ronaldo said, out on Chef Menteur Highway. He had told Ronaldo because Ronaldo was never, ever to go out there. Henry didn't say that he didn't know where that was, but he did say that he was not going to drive all the way out to fucking Chef. If he was going to drive all the way out there then Ronaldo could pay for the fucking gas.

Ronaldo handed Henry a five. He carried his money in a lizard skin wallet, the only one at Martyr's, like something an adult would carry. He had bought it with money made from dealing weed. His dad thought that he had made it cutting grass, not selling it.

Henry could just hear himself calling his parents, saying that he had been arrested with a hooker by Ronaldo's dad...but he took the five and put it in the breast pocket of his motorcycle jacket. He was too skinny for it then.

They took I-10 East towards the lake. The Chef Menteur exit was far away, past a chemical plant with flames on the smoke stacks, and over a canal stacked with barges full of gravel. Chef Menteur Highway was lined with bars, and hotels with ELECTRIC HEAT and hourly rates on their signs.

Ronaldo had eighty dollars in hand. "How much you got," he said.

"Six."

"Six bucks?" Ronaldo said, "Six dollars?"

"That's including what you just gave me for gas," Henry said. It was a lie. He had twenty, but he wanted to lose his virginity in a bed, with a girlfriend. Tonight they were stuck with the back of the van.

"I'm going to lay my pipe," Ronaldo said, hitting the money with his fingers, "She's just going to look at yours."

"I don't care."

"Cause you're gay."

"Like you."

"Whore!"

"Like you!" Henry said.

"No," Ronaldo said, "Pull over. There's a whore on the side of the road!"

Henry saw a black woman with gold braids walking away from them on the shoulder, wearing a black and gold jacket with tiger stripes. He slowed the van, and when she turned to face them, he knew Ronaldo had to be joking.

He wasn't. "Say, red–you for real?" he said, slurring to sound streetwise, "How much."

She studied them, and decided not to satisfy them by getting mad. Or even by talking. She stood there, with her arms up so that they could see all of her: *figure it out, idiot.*

Henry pulled away, shaking his head; Ronaldo called her a bitch.

"She was wearing a McDonald's uniform," Henry said, "She was getting off work and you tried to buy her ass."

"So?" Ronaldo whined, "You couldn't tell with that jacket on. And McDonald's doesn't pay that good."

"You're stupid," Henry said.

He drove. Neither of them spoke. They spent so much time together that sometimes Henry would punch Ronaldo in the side of the head. This felt like one of those times. But it also felt like it could turn into a real fight, because Ronaldo was fed up, too.

He turned around before Chef lifted from the ground and became a long, slow bridge over the canal. We could have stayed in Metairie if we were just going to drive around, he thought. But he was also relieved to still be a virgin.

They stopped at a light. A white woman sat in the glass shelter at the bus stop on the next corner. "There's one that looks like your mom, Hank," Ronaldo said.

"It probably is," Henry said.

As they drove up, Ronaldo leaned out of the window and said, "Hey baby, I want to lick—"

She put one leg in the air and grabbed her crotch. She was stick-skinny and wearing black jeans so tight that she must have been stitched into them. And her legs were stuck in soft, red boots bunched down around the ankles.

"Stop," Ronaldo said to Henry, staring at her. Henry already had. The light was green. The only other car on the road pulled around them. He thought of pulling away, but then thought that they couldn't be arrested for watching someone knead herself.

Her fur coat was fake, and by the way she glared at them, she didn't care that they knew it. Now she had her hands up under it, running them over her chest, with her face still flat with hatred for them both.

"There's something wrong with her, Ronaldo," Henry said. She had curly black hair that looked like it had been combed through with grape jelly. She stood and walked away from them, into the empty parking lot of a Korean-run convenience store. CHINESE PO BOY painted on the side.

"Follow her, Henry," Ronaldo said.

The light had turned red, so he couldn't drive off. Still, he hesitated.

"What's the matter with you?" Ronaldo said, "Are you scared?"

It was the concern in Ronaldo's voice that made him follow. That's what did it. If he had just been making fun, Henry wouldn't have turned the van after her.

She was standing between the store and the garbage. Ronaldo opened his door. It sagged on the hinges like the gate to a yard. A year later, Ronaldo would open that door and it would fall off the hinges, and they would both fall on their butts laughing.

She ran toward the open door like they were her getaway ride. She jumped for Ronaldo's lap headfirst. "Go!" she said, with one leg not yet in the van, "What are you waiting for?"

"Go, Hank!" Ronaldo said. For some reason, he turned up the radio. Henry stepped on the gas and Ronaldo slammed the door.

Aah! he heard her say under the radio, Aah! From the corner of his eye, he saw her twisting on Ronaldo's lap. He was pulling at her arms and shoulders.

Oh yeah, baby, Ronaldo said, Yeah.

You fucking prick, she said, opening the door with her other hand, you slammed my finger in the door!

Henry looked over. The door must have been loose-fitting enough that Ronaldo had closed it without feeling her finger in the way. She had now closed the door again and was shaking the pain out of her right hand. She held it against her stomach and doubled over on Ronaldo's lap. Ronaldo looked with worry at her fake fur back.

She snapped off the radio and hunched back over. She was a tiny woman. "Put on the light!" she said. She had a cigarette voice, from up north. Ronaldo turned on the overhead light. "Are you hurt?" he said, "I'm sorry."

Henry pulled down a side street and stopped by a dumpster.

They could hear her breathing through her mouth, watched her turn her finger in the light. Bright blood ran from the nailbed. Her nails were not painted; she chewed them, you could tell. She said something they couldn't make out.

She sat up and said, "I said who sent you?"

She sat up and looked at Ronaldo's face; she stared at Henry. He was certain that she would remark on his bad skin.

"How old are you?" she said.

Before either of them answered, she reached into her right boot and pulled out a gun. Henry collected gun magazines then and knew that it was a .380. She held the barrel against Ronaldo's throat.

She said, "Both of you: anything of value is mine." She was wide-eyed, and looked scared; but the gun didn't move.

Ronaldo had rolled his eyes up toward the van's roof and heaven, but they kept dropping back to the gun. He snaked a hand into his jacket. She didn't think that he was reaching for anything but his wallet. He put it into her hand.

Henry looked at the gun and thought, is that real? Is it?

She said, "I'm going to kill your friend. I'm going to shoot him through the heart."

Henry reached into his jacket and gave her the six dollars. She traded hands on the gun, reached for the door handle without looking, and stepped out backwards. Her blood spotted Ronaldo's collar.

Ronaldo's revenge: by the time they were 22, he had slept with 24 women, four of them the eastern European prostitutes that filled the condos in the warehouse district the day after the casino bill passed. That was when he was selling X. And Henry now had his four guns, all of them real.

* * *

Their job was to guard the guests' cars, because the party would be held in an empty house in a bad neighborhood, right up the street from the St. Bernard projects.

It was cold. Ronaldo pulled up at seven; he was wearing a zipped up, red skiing jacket that made him look like he was in college. His car's heater was dead.

Ronaldo got out of the car, pulled a rod out of his pocket, and snapped his wrist. The thing turned into a yard-long, black steel baton. "Cool, huh?" he said, "I took it from my dad's car."

Henry took the baton and tried to push it closed like an antenna. Ronaldo snatched it back and stabbed the end into the ground. It collapsed and he hid it back inside his jacket. He was getting back into the car. With one foot inside he said, "You're not bringing a gun, right?"

"No," Henry said. He was wearing his motorcycle jacket, with the Glock in his left inside pocket; the magazine was zipped up on the opposite side. He hadn't shot a gun in a long time, and his .38 six shooter hadn't felt like enough when he had picked it up earlier.

"Better to be judged by twelve than carried by six." That's what the gun magazines said. Of course there was also what the news magazines said: you're most likely to be shot by someone you know, and he knew no one in the St. Bernard projects. When he studied now, these pictures fell between his eyes and brain, blocking out Netter Atlas watercolors of the intestines: Larry Frank with the bomb in his hand. The empty head on the cannery floor.

The Glock was a seventeen shooter. His dad had bought it for him on his twenty first birthday. He remembered how the plastic magazine had felt silly, like a toy candy bar. The gun was deceptive that way, and he had never much liked it. Of his guns, it seemed the one most likely to kill somebody.

"Is Larry Frank going to be here?" he asked as he got into the car.

"He shouldn't. He's not invited." They pulled away.

Henry said, "I forgot to buy salad ingredients. I had some Doritos I could have brought."

"Taco salad doesn't count," Ronaldo said, "And anyway, the Salad Sisters can't make it. They had a scheduling conflict. But I got replacements."

"What's their name?"

"They don't have a name," Ronaldo said, "Are you scared of Larry Frank?" Ronaldo said.

Henry looked away. "I don't see why you're not," he said to the window.

Ronaldo drove without saying anything for a while. "I'd like to say that his bark is worse than his bite," he said.

"I know what you mean," Henry mumbled, "I thought that same thing."

Ronaldo drove along the bayou, away from the cannery, toward the lake. They crossed the bayou on a low, concrete bridge, and Ronaldo parked on just the other side, underneath a sycamore tree. It was dropping orange leaves big enough to write on, and stemmed seeds that looked like little bombs.

"That's the place," Ronaldo said, pointing across the street.

The house had been designed in the seventies by someone with a lot of bad ideas. A stupid little wall surrounded the yard. The roof looked like a witch's hat with the tip snipped off, and with only one window facing the street the house had just one eye. There didn't seem to be a door. To find it, they had to follow a line of concrete discs that snaked too much on their way across the lawn, like they were in line at the bank. The front door was on the back, opening onto another lawn which sloped right into the bayou.

Here the bayou was wide enough that you could just make out a person on the other side, with the lights from the City Park driving range just behind them. The house was in the corner formed by the water and the bridge. Henry remembered a story of a Lincoln Continental being dragged out of the bayou some years ago, but there was no one behind the wheel but crabs.

Ronaldo hit the door once with his fist and opened it. It seemed like the door should have opened onto a living room and stairs, but instead of stairs there was a yellow wall. The living room was empty except for metal folding chairs stacked against the wall and three guys in golf shirts sitting around a keg. They watched Henry and Ronaldo walk in.

Ronaldo said, "I forgot something in the car. Y'all meet each other."

All three of them sat with both feet on the floor and their arms folded. There was a chair in the middle of them with a deck of cards sitting on it. They didn't offer to move the cards.

Henry walked over and offered his hand. "I'm Henry."

"Eddie."

"Andrew."

"Charlie."

Eddie had been the wiry kid who started fights with anybody. He nodded at the cards. "Cut you for five," he said.

Henry didn't get it.

"Cut the cards," Eddie said, his arms still folded. "Then take a card."

Henry did. Then Eddie swiped one.

"Six," Eddie said.

Henry showed him his card. "Eight of diamonds."

Andrew slapped Eddie on the back, hard. "It's all over now!" He laughed, "Streak's over! Give it up!"

Eddie didn't smile. He reached into his back pocket, pulled out a wine-colored wallet, and gave Henry a five. Eddie wore a gold bracelet; Henry had never met anyone his age that did.

Henry said, "I don't want to take your money. It's all right." He tried to give it back, but that offended Eddie even more than losing.

Ronaldo came back, carrying a gym bag with a broken strap. He knew Eddie and Andrew, and gave them complicated, popping handshakes. Eddie picked up the cards, and Ronaldo put the bag down on the chair, then pulled out three gray cell phones. Eddie and Andrew sat and got back to brooding.

Charlie was the only one wearing shorts, and his hair was lighter than the others'. He stood up and shook hands with Ronaldo. "I'm Charlie," he said, "You're Ronnie."

"You from Florida?" Ronaldo asked.

Charlie nodded.

"Then I'm Ronnie," Ronaldo said, holding the phones with both hands. "Where's the bachelor?"

"Where's the Salad Sisters?" Charlie asked. He reached to the floor behind his chair and picked up a paper grocery bag. A dozen carrots rolled around loose in it.

"They'll be here," Ronaldo said, "Keep your pants on." He handed Charlie a phone, then gave one to Henry.

"Okay. I'm one. Charlie's two. Henry's three," Ronaldo said, "Go down to the word and we can call each other. Like this." He scrolled down and hit TALK. Seconds later—it seemed too long—Henry's phone rang. He answered it, looking at Ronaldo. "Why do we have the phones," he said into it.

Ronaldo hung up. "These phones are our communicators," he said smartly. "Come outside. I'll show what we're going to do."

"Wait," Charlie said, "Security is just us three?"

Ronaldo stopped with one side to the door, the other to Charlie. "Yeah," he said, "So?"

"Two of you and one of me?" Charlie said, sputtering out a laugh. He looked at Henry like he would agree that this was just absurd.

"We have these guys, too," Henry said, pointing at Eddie and Andrew, who were arguing about cards.

Charlie didn't look any more relaxed.

19

Here was Ronaldo's plan: Everybody got a beer. They would patrol the block every twenty minutes. One man would stay at the gate. A second would walk ahead to the corner, followed by the third man. Once the second and third met at the corner, one of them—they would take turns—would walk to the next corner, while the other watched his advance. In this way, they could be in sight of each other the whole time and signal each other.

"Ronaldo, you are really fucking scared of black people," Henry said.

"I want to be the man by the house," Charlie said.

"Why do we have the phones if we're going to signal each other?" Henry said.

"We have the phones in case we have to sneak up on somebody," Ronaldo said.

"I'm going to be the man by the house," Charlie said.

"What are we going to do when we sneak up on them?" Henry asked.

"Just use the damn phone, Hank," Ronaldo said, "Okay. I'll go first."

Charlie said, "I'm going to be—"

"Fine," said Henry and Ronaldo.

This side of the street was lined with magnolias, making the sidewalk into a dark tunnel. Ronaldo went first and was swallowed up.

Henry waited, and turned to Charlie. He felt bad for snapping at him. "What drama, huh?" he said.

Charlie smiled without showing teeth.

Ronaldo popped out of the shadows on the next corner and stood under the street light. Henry walked after him. In the magnolia tunnel he put the phone in his back pocket, switched his beer to his left hand, and when he was sure neither Charlie nor Ronaldo could see, reached in and put a hand around his gun, playing like he was going to quick draw on somebody. He had forgotten to eat dinner, and the beer was getting to him.

He pulled his hand out of his jacket before he reached the corner. He didn't see Ronaldo there anymore. He must have walked ahead to the next corner. His phone rang.

He answered. "Ronaldo?"

"Keep talking on the phone," Ronaldo said.

Henry turned to the voice.

"I'm right here over by the tree," said Ronaldo's voice over the phone.

"I know, Ronaldo. I'm looking at you."

"Is he watching you?" Ronaldo asked.

Henry looked back down the sidewalk. He could see Charlie's silhouette glance up and down the street, take a sip of beer, and then look at him through the magnolia-tunnel. Henry waved. Charlie waved back. "Yeah, he's watching," Henry said. He turned and looked down the block. Charlie would think Ronaldo was on the next corner.

"What a bunch of bullshit," Ronaldo said, "Look where we are. Look at this neighborhood."

Blue television light came around the curtains of a picture window.

"I'm hanging up, Ronaldo."

Ronaldo stepped away from the tree, but not close enough that Charlie could see him. "The project's like five miles up that way. Nothing's going to happen."

"So why are we out here? It's cold."

"Mac Donald's from Florida. All these Florida guys just got back from shooting porno in Bosnia, and they're afraid in New Orleans. We have to keep up the guard."

"How'd you come up with this phone thing?" Henry said, "No wonder Charlie's nervous."

"I had time restraints."

"Constraints."

"I didn't have much time," Ronaldo said, "My first house fell through, the Salad Sisters fell through. The phones were just a last minute opportunity." He flipped his open. "I'm going to call beach boy and tell him that we secured the perimeter."

"Who was that Beach Boy that died?" Henry said.

Ronaldo was already talking into the phone. "All clear," he said, "Okay. Bye."

"How did you get the house, Ronaldo," he said, "Or let me guess—I shouldn't worry about it."

"Right." Ronaldo walked back into the light on the corner. Charlie would see him now.

"If you can get a house on the bayou, maybe you can move out of your mom's," Henry said.

Charlie was waiting with his hands jammed into the pockets of his soccer shorts. He looked worried. That made Henry nervous. He was beginning not to like Charlie.

"If anybody's messing with the cars, we'll call back on the phone, get a bunch of guys together, and rush him," Ronaldo said, "They're going to be so worked up after the girls I got, the spade will be lucky he doesn't get raped."

"Do you guys have guns?" Charlie asked.

"Has anybody else shown up yet?" Henry said.

"A few people. I told them to go inside," Charlie said. "I don't know if you heard. Mac's not, you know, only worried about black people."

Ronaldo slapped him on the back. "Chill out, Chuck. Let's wait for these girls away from this cold—"

Charlie pushed Ronaldo's hand off of him. "Look. I work for Mac. I see naked girls all the time. I want to know about security. Like you promised."

Ronaldo was still smiling at him. He tapped his cell phone against his leg four times. Then he said, "Charlie, those guys you saw inside are good. Everybody coming here tonight from my end is good. That's your security. These girls are good. They're not just naked. They're the Salad Sisters."

"I'll wait out here," Charlie said, "Bring me a beer, though."

"Then don't let anybody park in front here. These spots are for the bachelor and the strippers."

Henry and Ronaldo started back to the house. "I thought you said that we didn't have the Salad Sisters," Henry said; Ronaldo pretended not to hear. Four weightlifters—not the short kind, the tall, fat kind—had joined Eddie and Andrew by the keg. They all had goatees and baseball hats, and they all knew Ronaldo. Henry offered his hand. One of the goats shook it without looking at him.

Eddie was still sitting next to his deck of cards. "Spent my money yet?" he said to Henry. He smiled unpleasantly.

Henry was filling up his own cup and Charlie's from the keg. "You want to try and win it back?"

He didn't mean it as a challenge, but Eddie took it that way. He bristled. "I'll get it back," he said, "Don't worry."

No one was talking to him, so Henry went back outside, using Charlie's beer as an excuse. Charlie was smoking and sitting on the wall by the sidewalk, his hands squeezed between his knees for warmth. He should have worn jeans.

Henry handed him the beer, sat down on the wall, and Charlie thanked him.

"You're from Florida," Henry said, "My parents moved there."

"Mmm," Charlie said, "You don't happen to have any sort of weed, do you?"

"No."

"That's too bad," Charlie said. He realized that Henry wasn't going to leave, so he might as well talk. "Do you work for the funeral home, too?" he said.

"I'm a medical student," Henry said.

Charlie raised his eyebrows and threw his cigarette into the street. He said, "I was going to be a doctor."

Henry wondered how old he was—late twenties, probably. "What about you?" he said.

"I'm a film editor," he said, "I'm a film editor for Mac Donald."

"They edit porno movies?" Henry said.

A Honda with five men inside holding bottles pulled up to the curb. "Is that Mac?" Henry asked.

Charlie was staring at the car and shook his head.

"You can't park there," Henry yelled, "That's the strippers' spot."

The driver waved, nodded, and backed up.

"Yes they edit 'porno movies'," Charlie said, "I went to film school."

"Where?" Henry said. He had never met anyone who had gone to film school.

"Well, I took classes," Charlie said, "Everybody always asks that—'do they edit.' And no, I don't get to make it with any of the girls."

Henry said, "I guess I won't ask then."

The five men had gotten out of the car and were retrieving grocery bags from the trunk. They walked toward the house and nodded at Henry and Charlie.

"You know them?" Charlie said.

"No."

"Then who are they?"

"I don't know. Ronaldo will know them. Relax."

They sat for some time without saying anything, watching more guests walk by. They were all white men who might work the doors at bars, or in contracting. Several carried bags of produce. Henry went back inside for more beer for the two of them.

The party sounded bigger than it was, because the room was bare. There was now a chair in the center of the room. On the floor in front of it were zucchini and bananas arranged in rows, and next to them, a short toilet plunger. That has nothing to do with salad, Henry thought.

Everyone still thought the salad sisters were coming. "They're not going to be disappointed in my girls, though," Ronaldo said. He had set up a card table and was pouring a bag of Zapp's Crawtators into a bowl. He checked the presentation once he was through.

"I didn't know you could cook, Ronaldo."

Ronaldo looked around for a garbage can. When he didn't see one, he threw the bag on the floor. The house either didn't have a heater, or Ronaldo hadn't turned it on; almost everyone still had on his jacket. That was fine with Henry. He didn't want to feel obliged to take his off, because that would mean shoving the gun into his waistband. He had tried that at home. It was uncomfortable.

"The girls I got aren't just strippers, they're prostitutes," Ronaldo said, "They're some of those Russians from the Warehouse District. They got bad teeth."

Someone had brought a funnel, and the weight lifters were funneling beer into each other. Someone else had a balloon full of nitrous. It reminded Henry of a fraternity at Berkeley he used to hate. "I'm going back outside."

Charlie was smoking again. He drank about half the beer. It seemed to be calming him down. "I was watching the History Channel the other night," he said, "There was this show on about the St. Valentine's Day Massacre. One of the people killed there was a doctor."

"Yeah," Henry said, "Doctor Schwimmer."

"Did you see it?"

"I just know about that kind of stuff."

"You probably know this already then, but the guys who did it were dressed up as cops."

Henry wished he hadn't reminded him; he pictured Larry Frank.

"The other thing I thought was interesting is that not that many people were killed. It was only like eight, or eleven. I thought to be called a 'massacre' that it had to be like ninety people."

"That's like the Boston Massacre. That was only eight people," Henry said.

A new, dark Land Rover came slowly up the street.

"That's Mac!" Charlie said, standing up.

The Land Rover was allowed to park right up front. The driver got out first. If this was Mac, his movies must have been big among sadists. He was enormous, alabaster white, and his head was shaved bald. In the locker room, he bought pirate growth hormone squeezed from the pituitaries of dead men.

Charlie went around and slapped hands with the man, whose scowl didn't change. The four guys who climbed out of the back were softer, and bland. All of them were drunk. Then the passenger got out, slowly. He was older than the rest, and cartoon-handsome.

Charlie was smiling for the first time. He grabbed the passenger by the shoulder and introduced him to Henry. "Henry, meet the bachelor," he said, "Mac Donald."

Mac smiled and shook Henry's hand. Mac had a split lip and blue eyes. Henry stared at the lip.

"I slid right into someone's foot playing softball," he said.

One of the drunks said, "He was trying to let the camera in and her foot slipped and kicked him."

Mac play-acted innocence. "Me? I'm getting married in two days! How dare you!" he said. He turned to Charlie: "We have the Salad Sisters?"

"They backed out," Henry said.

Charlie looked panicked. "What?"

Henry thought he shouldn't have said anything. "No. We have, uh...the Turkey Twins."

Mac said, "The Turkey Twins. I guess that's because of Thanksgiving."

"Yes," Henry said, "I hope y'all brought your frozen turkeys."

Mac Donald laughed. "That's good. You want to be in a movie?"

Henry felt his face go red.

They all laughed at that. Charlie said, "Don't get your hopes up. I've been getting the same offer for two years."

Mac was walking away with his people behind him. He said, "Maybe the 'Turkey Twins' want to be famous."

* * *

Charlie had gone inside with them. Ronaldo called Henry on the cellular and asked him to stay outside until the prostitutes showed up. "Don't call them the Salad Sisters," Ronaldo said, "They might get offended."

Not long afterward, a white 1975 Stingray with salt rot pulled up to the spot just in front of the land Rover. Salt rot—that was strange for this far south. The windows were tinted. One of them hummed down. Henry felt like he should duck.

An insincere looking man with his flat top gelled into needles looked back at him. "Is this the bachelor party?" He sounded like he was from Long Island.

"Yes."

"The bachelor party for Mac Donald?"

"Yes." Henry tried to look into the car. He couldn't see the driver.

The car's headlights went out, and the engine stopped. The driver got out. He was a heavy black man, bulkier than Mac's driver, wearing a blue sweatshirt with the sleeves ripped off and wristbands.

The passenger got out. He was dressed like Ronaldo, but the ski jacket was purple. He let the two hookers out of the back seat. They were pale and looked like they understood not a word of English. The driver went around to the trunk, pulled out a portable stereo and a duffle bag big enough to smuggle a kid.

The strippers were wearing short t-shirts and didn't have jackets. They shivered at the curb, holding their elbows. Henry imagined them being mugged.

"Where's the way in?" the passenger said, looking at the house.

"Follow," Henry said.

He opened the door and let them in. The room smelled like weed. The black guy went in first, then the white guy. When the girls came in, everybody smiled, or whistled, and a few barked.

In the light, Henry could see that they were pretty, with delicate folds at the ends of their eyes. The blonde one—dyed blonde—looked at the floor. Flat top pulled her along by the arm.

"Where's the bathroom," he said.

Ronaldo showed up, red-eyed. "Bathroom!" he said, "This way!" He pushed his way through.

"Hi. Hi," the brunette stripper said, smiling at the room. Her teeth were in stacks.

All four of them went down a hallway and into the bathroom together. Ronaldo turned to Henry and said, "They always do this. They have a white guy for a handler, and some big nigger to keep the girls from getting raped. He works the radio."

"How many of these have you done?"

Ronaldo walked over to the keg. "I talked to Hines the other day," he said in a low voice, over his shoulder, "He said that you sold some of his shit."

"Why doesn't he think I ate it?"

"Henry," Ronaldo said, "You don't really seem like the type. Don't take that the wrong way."

Henry recalled getting smacked in Pirate's Alley. Talking about it would make it less shameful. "I got ripped off, actually."

"The dudes that ripped you off," Henry said, "Was that shatter bomb for them?"

Henry was amazed. And suspicious. "How did you know that?"

Ronaldo was eating potato chips by the fistful. "This Deadhead ripped me off once. I traded him a sheet for half a pillowcase of mushrooms he said he dug out the cow shit in Slidell," Ronaldo said, "They were just grocery store mushrooms, dried up. I got the idea to shatterbomb his car, like we did that time? But when I finally saw his car, it was in the Quarter, and I was drunk, stoned, and tripping and there was no place to buy the ice. So I went to the Farmer's Market. They were delivering the fruit for the next day. I bought some bananas. Then I went back to his car and ducked behind it, and slid eight or ten bananas up the tailpipe. Then I very carefully mashed up the rest into a fucking paste and smeared it all around to make a fucking seal, and waited in the bar across the street. He had some girl with him. He started the car and it had banana diarrhea out the back and jerked up the street. I could see them inside screaming in terror."

Henry said, "That's brilliant."

"Drugs expand the mind," Ronaldo said.

The crowd stayed away from the chair in the middle of the room. With the fruit and vegetables there, it looked like a voodoo altar, calling a spirit to sit in the empty chair. It had gotten louder since the girls had arrived. Mac Donald sucked on a joint, chased it with nitrous, and puffed a cigar. Henry had another beer; he would need the bathroom and need it steady after this one. Somebody asked him if he was someone else. After a while, the flat-topped handler came out. He found Ronaldo and whispered something in his ear.

Ronaldo unzipped his jacket and threw it across a chair. It was now warm, but Ronaldo had left his on, like Henry. Henry had done it to hide the gun. Ronaldo had done it so that he could unveil the shirt at just this time. Henry and Catherine had driven to Cambria one weekend; Catherine had not been spinning a tall tale: bits of jade really did wash up out of the sea. Ronaldo's shirt could have washed up in Cambria.

The handler said, "I like that shirt, man."

Ronaldo pretended not to hear. He stood on the chair in the middle of the room. He said:

"HEY! Everybody shut the fuck up if they want a show!" The room got quiet after two more tries.

"This is Scottie. He manages the girls."

Ronaldo stepped down. Scottie didn't take his place. He spoke from the floor. Henry noticed one loop from a set of handcuffs peeking out from beneath his shirt tail.

"I want to congratulate Mac. I want everyone to enjoy themselves. But we have rules:

"Keep your thumbs out of their buttholes and pussies."

Henry saw Mac roll his eyes. "Everything but thumbs is okay?"

"They'll let you know what's okay," Scottie said, "And no whipped cream in their hair. It's hard to wash out." He put a hand up. Those were the rules.

Scottie smiled for the first time that night. "Sit down, Mac," he said. He stood behind the chair in the center of the room.

A snicker seethed through the crowd. Mac walked out with a huge grin and sat down. Scottie pulled the handcuffs from his belt, took Mac's wrists, and pulled them back. They heard the locks click.

It seems like the girls should be doing this, Henry thought. But then Scottie pulled a black blindfold out of his back pocket and put it over Mac's eyes. "You can't see the bride," Scottie said, "That's bad luck."

Scottie walked back down the hall; the crowd parted for him. Henry looked down the hall after him: he hit the bathroom door with two fists. From behind the door came the muffled sound of an organ playing, "Here Comes the Bride." The door opened and the black guy came out, unsmiling, holding the boom box out in front of him. Once in the room he stepped against the wall. Everyone watched the hall to see what would come out.

Out came the blonde girl, wearing a white veil and a short white cheerleader's uniform with the insignia torn off, and white vinyl boots with needle heels. She carried a plastic bouquet over her belly.

Behind her, carrying the veil, was the brunette, done up in a black vinyl nun's habit and holding a riding crop in the other hand. She used the crop on the bride. They marched around Mac one time. They did that shuffle step they use down the aisle.

Blindfolded Mac heard the crowd cheering and beamed.

They marched around again. And again. They kept marching. The crowd stopped cheering.

"This isn't the Salad Sisters!"

"I didn't come to see art! Take it the fuck off!"

"What," Mac said.

As the music ended, the vinyl nun whipped the bride so she was facing Mac. She threw her bouquet backwards. It let off big, white splinters as it flew. The black guy started some metallic thump music.

One splinter hit Henry in the head. He caught it as it bounced off. A joint. She had thrown fat joints at them. He wondered if Ronaldo had paid for this.

Charlie plucked the joint from his hand. He pulled out a lighter, turned to Ronaldo, and mouthed the words, *Thank you* under the music.

They got lit up and passed around the room. The black guy handed each girl a spray can and a rag. The bride borrowed a joint, sucked on it, then sprayed the tip. Flame shot in a plume. People jumped back.

While she was up to that, the vinyl nun had taken a drag off another, and had straddled Mac to blow the smoke into his mouth. Mac held it in and began to redden in the face. The vinyl nun sprayed her rag and waited with it draped over her hand. The bride waited behind her.

When Mac exhaled, the vinyl nun clamped the rag over his nose and mouth. Mac cried out, but had to breathe through the rag if he wanted to breath at all. The nun got off his lap. The sprayed rag made Mac sway in the chair. The nun and the bride each took an end of the blindfold and pulled it off.

The spray made Mac look like he had just been told terrible news. He said, "Oh."

The girls didn't even have their clothes off yet. Two guys got Ronaldo by the arm and said they wanted him to do their bachelor parties, too.

* * *

They took off their clothes, with no ceremony to it. They left the boots on. The black guy snatched the nun's habit away from some jerk in the crowd and stuffed both costumes into the duffle bag.

The blonde tied Mac's ankles to the chair with her veil. The brunette had the sort of body that porno magazines achieved with an airbrush; Mac was allowed to lick parts.

The spray cans and rags went around the room. Henry took the can just to read it: *ROYAL FLUSH* (a picture of four cards) *This product is not to be used for other than its stated purpose. This product has been shown to cause CANCER in the state of California.*

But the can stated no purpose. The albaster bald man, Mac's driver, was standing to Henry's left. He asked, "Are you through?" and took the can from him. He sprayed it onto the rag and smothered himself with it. His head was still wobbling when he passed the can. His white head shined.

Every so often some idiot would mimic the strippers and blast a fireball from the tip of a joint or cigarette. No one was burned, but Henry had the feeling that it was only a matter of time.

20

Time jumped. He was very drunk. He looked at his watch. Only an hour had passed since the Turkey Twins had arrived. It seemed much longer; maybe he was getting high off the smoke and can fumes. The floor listed to the left beneath him, and he thought he should have eaten before he came. He wouldn't be as drunk now if he had. He pushed his way to the table where the chips had been. All the chips were gone. The table was gone, too—in two pieces on the floor. Someone had tried to stand on it.

The girls were taking turns going around the room with cans of whipped cream. A dollar paid to Scottie gave you rights to squirt cream anywhere on the woman then lick it off. Below the waist was two dollars. The other stripper would stay with Mac and rub against him. Tied down, all he could do was smile, though he tried more with his tongue. This is what it's going to be like being married, he joked again and again.

Henry had to piss. The bathroom was on other side of the room. He opened the window by the broken table and pissed through it onto the lawn.

Still zipping his pants, he turned around. Everyone was looking at him, waiting.

"What?" he said.

They laughed. Someone had taken the roll of toilet paper from the bathroom, and threw it at him. It hit him in the chest and he caught it and threw it to his right.

Then he understood: the brunette was standing to his left and behind him, offering the whipped cream. The blonde was blowing more smoke into Mac's mouth. Henry was expected to use the brunette and pass her on.

He looked at her; she couldn't have been more than twenty, and maybe it was because this was his first bachelor party, but he felt much older. The room was now webbed with toilet paper. He saw Ronaldo slap Scottie on the back and give him a ten dollar bill. He pointed to Henry and said, "Give the jerk off all he wants."

She sprayed cream in a circle over one nipple and pointed it at Henry. She smiled, showing her bad teeth. One of them had a gray pinhole. She needed braces. He could see her in braces.

He bent down and licked it off. She sprayed the other side; he did the same. Then she turned, spritzed on a bunny tail, and bent over. He slurped off the tail.

He stood up and the guy next to him clapped him on the back. They laughed together. He had that feeling again, but hazy, through the beer: something bad was going to happen.

She hadn't made it three feet before Eddie with the gold bracelet made a grab for her. Her ankle folded. She yelped and fell on her side. He had never seen anybody take a spill like that naked. Everything about her shook when it hit the floor.

Scottie hauled her up by the arm pits. He wasn't concerned with Eddie. The big black guy was already there, plowing him into the wall with a forearm as big around as Eddie's neck.

Everyone in the room was too high and drunk to do anything but watch.

Scottie pulled the black guy's shoulder, and said, "Don't worry about it. It's time, that's all."

The black guy stepped back. Eddie gasped for air with his hand on his throat. Scottie said something to the two girls. Henry didn't know the language, but he could tell that Scottie spoke it poorly, with a strong American accent. Scottie pushed his way toward the bathroom. The girls went after him, followed by the bouncer. They left the music playing.

Mac had heard them talk, too. He wasn't smiling anymore.

One of the weight lifters lit the toilet paper roll on fire and threw it across the room. It exploded against the far wall.

"Assholes!" Ronaldo screamed, "You're going to burn down the fucking house."

The burning core had been kicked to the floor behind Mac. Ronaldo unzipped his pants and pissed on it to put it out. As far as the pot-smokers were concerned, this was wit of the highest order. Many fell over with laughter. Charlie was reduced to an invalid.

Mac wasn't laughing. He saw that Henry wasn't either.

"Hey," he said, jerking with his head, "Come over here."

Henry walked over. "Congratulations," he said.

"Were those Ukraine girls?" Mac demanded.

"Something like that," Henry said.

"Look," Mac said. He looked at the hallway where the bathroom was, then back at Henry, craning up as much as he could. "You have to help me get out of here." He was trying to seem calm. But his chest was heaving.

Henry looked behind him. Mac's arms were locked through the back of the chair. His ankles were still tied with the veil. It was netting. It would have to be cut off.

"Why?" he asked.

Scottie was back, not smiling. Mac watched him. The girls were dressed in their jeans and t-shirts again. Henry figured they were leaving after getting grabbed.

"What kind of shit is this?!" Eddie screamed.

"Act Two!" yelled Scottie. He held up two fingers on each hand.

When they had come back out, Henry had moved away from Mac, to the wall opposite the window.

The black guy had the duffle bag over his shoulder. He picked up the radio and turned the volume up even louder. He walked in front of Henry to stand by the front door.

Across the room, people did stupid, stoned dances. Ronaldo stuck out his tongue and pumped his crotch at the girls. They were standing in front of Mac. Mac was pale, and held his mouth as tight as a pencil drawn line. He didn't want any more smoke or spray.

The girls touched tongues, then let their tongues pull their bodies together. Guys quit dancing to watch, with their mouths open.

The brunette broke the kiss, and snatched a zucchini from beneath Mac's chair. She whipped her hair and body like she had gotten high on something in the bathroom. She threw her head back and tongue-flicked the tip of the zucchini. The blonde had walked past Henry. The black guy put down the radio, and pulled from his back pocket a bread bag. The blonde pulled the bag over her hand.

She saw Henry looking and turned her back to him. The black guy stared at him in a way that made him look away.

The brunette was sucking the zucchini.

The blonde pulled the brunette away with her left hand. Her right arm was in the bread bag up to the elbow. In her right hand was a gun.

She shot Mac in the eye.

She stitched him twice in the chest.

That didn't happen, Henry thought.

Mac now had a black dot instead of a left eye.

The brunette was running for the door. Scottie was already there, and pulled her by the arm. She jerked her arm away but ran outside after him. The black guy was gone. The blonde was sidestepping after them, squeezing the trigger again and again. Not at Mac; at everyone.

Henry ducked into a ball and threw his arms over his head. I should have ducked long before this, he thought. But a bullet would go right through his arms into his skull and he knew it.

The music had stopped. The gun hadn't. POPPOPPOPPOP. POPPOP.

She's going to kill everyone. It came to him so clearly that he knew it had to be true.

He half-crawled, half-jumped across the floor, toward the window. Everyone was on the floor now, rolling on top of each other, screaming, trying to get anything between themselves and her. Even if it was someone else, that was all right.

He had to pass right in front of her to get away. Something hot hit the back of his neck, like a burning cigarette. He clapped his hand over the spot. A bullet doesn't slam you, like in the movies; it burns. He had read that in a gun magazine.

Now a line burned down his back—blood?

He was at the window. The alabaster baldie threw himself in front of him, to hide from the gun. His eyes were very bloodshot against his white skin. Henry grabbed him by the collar and yanked him out of the way.

With one hand he threw open the window and fell out. His foot got caught on the sill and he jerked it free. He was face down in the grass and he smelled his own urine, from earlier.

The shooting had stopped.

A chain link fence woven with wooden slats separated this yard from the next. The fence ran right to the edge of the water. He ran to the end of the fence and tried to swing around it and hide. He was too drunk for it, and dunked his foot in the process.

He squatted there and heard himself breathe. He hadn't moved his hand from the back of his neck. He prepared himself to see his hand come away bright, wet red.

There was no blood. The gun was part of the act, he told himself. I'm not shot and neither is Mac.

He stood up. Something moved in the back of his shirt. He shook it out. A 9 mm casing, still warm. It must have hit him on the back of the neck and rolled down his collar.

He threw it into the water and pressed his hands into his eyes. The world listed to the left, and he fell onto his butt. His ears were ringing, from the music and the beer and the gun shots. What am I supposed to do, he thought.

Check to see if they're all right.

He pulled out the Glock and loaded it. It felt impossibly light. He crept up the lawn with the gun pointed at the ground. He had done it in the mirror and had seen it in the movies.

The white Stingray rumbled across the bridge, not speeding. Why it had taken them so long to leave he didn't know. He didn't care. He aimed and let five go. The flashes looked big as pie plates.

For a second he thought the car was going to go into reverse and come back for him, like when he and Ronaldo used to throw eggs. It didn't even slow. But shooting had made him feel better. He moved toward the window again.

A square carpet of light was thrown onto the lawn by the window. Someone fell through the window and landed in the light on all fours. He was wearing a gold bracelet.

Henry reached out to him. "Eddie!"

Eddie's head turned. He saw the gun and ran. His feet made no sound on the grass.

In the light, he saw smoke curling from the barrel. You shouldn't have shot the gun, he thought. You shouldn't have it at all.

To stop thinking, he looked inside. He saw Mac sitting with his head to one side. Someone was screaming for help. Someone else, just screaming. He saw some feet as they ran out of the front door.

He ran to the other end of the yard, with the gun just hanging from his hand. This edge of the yard was made by the bridge. There was another fence here. He pulled himself around it and hid under the bridge. A steep, dirty concrete slope ran down into the bayou. His feet slid on the dirt; he had to shuffle backwards to stay out of the water.

Why am I hiding? he thought. The answer: because he didn't want to see any more of what was in the house. She emptied that gun.

And because he had just fired one.

He unloaded the Glock and shoved into his pocket. He remembered the cellular phone, punched up Ronaldo's number.

It rang twice. Then, "*The cellular subscriber you have called has left the vehicle—*"

He flipped it shut. He didn't trust the phone now. Anybody could be listening. Ronaldo had probably turned his off for the same reason–he hoped.

He called Charlie. He would use the code names Ronaldo had given them. It seemed long ago and moving farther and farther away.

"Hello?" Charlie answered.

"Two," Henry said, "This is Three."

"Henry!"

Henry closed his eyes and took a breath. "Charlie, what's happening?"

"It's bad in here," Charlie sobbed, "Mac's dead. There's blood on the wall. I've never seen so much blood."

"Where's Ronaldo?"

"I don't know," Charlie whined, "I'm in the shower. I don't know." There was a catch in his voice; he had been crying.

"Charlie," Henry said, "Listen to me. I need you to go back in there and tell me if Ronaldo's hurt." He swallowed. "Dead."

Charlie whimpered. But Henry heard the shower door slide open, and movement down the hall. He heard cars moving at high speed over the bridge above him. Guests who hadn't been hurt getting out of there.

Charlie breathing. Charlie sobbing. That man screaming. Someone screaming at Charlie to call 911.

"Charlie, is he there?"

"No!" Charlie said, "I don't know where he is."

Henry pulled the phone from his ear to listen. Sirens.

"Charlie, get rid of the phone," he said, and hung up. That stoned moron is going to say he talked to me, he thought, and he was disgusted with Charlie, and himself, and the phone, and he threw it into the bayou. He pulled out the gun and broke it down by feel and threw the parts in, farther away. Seven hundred dollars worth of gun, gone like that. His dad had given it to him. He imagined the parts darting away like fish.

He closed his eyes to think. The dark spun clockwise.

He gagged himself to get some of the beer up and clear his head. It worked, but only a little.

Red and blue light dragged back and forth over the open water to his right. A yellow spot light cut over the lawn. The cops had turned off the sirens for the final approach. He heard shouting between officers.

He slid further into the dark. I didn't do anything, he thought. Before long they would be down here with their flashlights. Then there would be the other light, the blue light he had seen on a cop show: it lit up the flesh of the hand that had recently fired a gun.

He squatted and slid both hands under the water and rubbed them on the concrete.

He imagined the cop with the flashlight. The cop was Larry Frank.

"Why were you hiding?"

"I was scared."

"Those other guys inside were scared. They ain't out here with you."

"I was more scared than they were."

"Why should you be more scared than them?"

"I was scared for my life. There's nothing wrong with that."

"If you didn't do anything wrong, Henry, then why am I talking to you right now, you cocksucker?"

And then to the patrol car in cuffs. Despite the scrubbing, the blue light would make both of his hands glow.

He had crept through the dark under the bridge, and then came out on the other side. He was now on the opposite side of the street, in the backyard of a bigger house. A line of cypress trees marched down into the water.

He snuck up along the trees, and looked across the street. There were three cop cars pulled up onto the sidewalk, with all their lights scraping every tree, house, and sidewalk for him. The neighbors on that side of the street were already out, watching from down the sidewalk. The neighbors on this side would be out soon. They would see him.

An ambulance was coming up the street. The victims would be taken to the Hope ER. His lecture hall was across the street and seven floors up. He never thought he would wish to be there like he did right now.

Maybe Charlie had called 911. The cops would find the phone.

"Charlie here is too high to lie and he says that you called him on this phone. Where is your phone? You threw it into the water because you were scared. Whose house is this? Where's Ronaldo? What else did you throw in the water 'because you were scared?'"

Let me get away. I'll serve mankind. I'll go into pediatrics. Just let me get away.

He exhaled and stepped out onto the sidewalk. He made himself walk. There was no reason anyone should be walking around a quiet neighborhood like this, day or night. Not if he didn't live there.

The leg of his pants was caked with mud and bayou-slime. He could feel how pale he must look. A car passed, and he felt the lights follow him like the eyes in a painting.

He made it across the bridge. He had to cross to the other bank. Plenty of teenagers parked in cars. Their eyes would already be pealed for the cops, especially with all the commotion across the bridge; and who was this guy in the leather jacket with the muddy leg?

But he made it past the bank. Across four well-lit lanes was the City Park golf course. He would be safe once he reached the golf course. He would be able to see the park police headlights long before they saw him. And once he was far enough away, he would say he had gotten in a fight with his girlfriend because he was so drunk, and she had dumped him in the park. And he had stepped in a puddle when he got out of the car.

But once in the park, there were the trees. The Spanish moss on some of them hung all the way to the ground. His first thought was that the trees were trolling for him.

He walked across the golf course with his hands in his pockets, to look rejected and just-dumped. And because he was resigned to it: he wasn't going to feel safe anytime soon.

21

He woke up holding the pillow over his face to keep out the light. When I move this pillow, he thought, last night will not have happened.

It didn't work. He squinted against the sun. Mac was still dead and who knew how many more.

After crossing the park, he had washed his leg with the water hose at a gas station. It had seemed impossible, but it wasn't even ten o'clock. He had caught the bus downtown, then walked the long way home, up Bourbon Street, so that he wouldn't be alone. At home he had showered and fallen into bed. He remembered the empty space above the bed and how it had once felt haunted.

But he couldn't think so softly anymore. All he got now were pictures. There's Mac with the black dot in his face. He was in the shower and saw Mac's albino driver cowering in front of him, right before he had jumped out of the window. Mac had brought the driver along as a bodyguard. He was sure of it.

The sky was so clear that he could smell the blue. He stood on the balcony and looked up and down the street, hard. Then he crossed Rampart to the Exxon for a newspaper. He stood in the window so that he could watch the street and snapped the paper open to the front page:

BAYOU BLOWOUT!

This year's Grambling-Southern game promises to be one of the biggest.

He turned to the bottom of the page: *CORONER SAYS N.O. EAST BONES HUMAN.*

Since his return to New Orleans, the Times-Picayune had begun treating shootings like old news. At the top of the Metro section:

RUSSIAN STRIPPER TURNS PARTY DEADLY

Three slayings at a Mirabeau Ave bachelor party marked a bloody Saturday for the city, police say, and a Russian strip dancer performing at the party is believed responsible.

"For no reason, she started shooting," said Charles Sullivan, a tearful party guest. Sullivan is currently in custody for possession of several marijuana cigarettes, hidden in his underwear.

The celebration was being held for Peter "Mac Donald" McDonald, 34, who was to be married to a local woman today. The woman has refused comment and has asked not to be identified. McDonald was an independent film producer from Sarasota, Fla.

A nine-millimeter pistol was recovered from the scene.

Also killed were Andre Dilaberto, 24, and Thomas Nicholls, 27, both of New Orleans. Several other guests were wounded and treated at Hope hospital. One remains in serious condition. Police have no motive for the slaying, and the alleged killer is described by Sullivan as "Ukrainian, blonde hair, and big t__s." Police say there is no evidence of connection to Russian organized crime.

In two unrelated killings, Reginald Antoine, 18, was found early Sunday morning dead of a gunshot wound to the face, lying beside his burning car on First Street Uptown. And an unidentified man in his early twenties was found shot dead and stripped in the courtyard of the Florida housing project at about the same time. Police have no motives and no suspects in either slaying

If you have information about the above crimes, call Crimestoppers at 882-2000. You may be eligible for a $1000 reward.

He folded the paper in half, dropped it into the garbage, and walked out.

Mac shot dirty movies in Russia; Russians shot Mac. And Andre. And Thomas. He remembered meeting Andre, over the cards. Andre Dilaberto could be alive right now, thinking, I met that guy Henry Marrier, over the cards. Henry wondered: would anyone reading the paper think they were white?

I'll get up to date with note sets today, he thought, Lower Limb is easy.

Eight dollars bought him a meat omelet at a Greek restaurant on Dauphine. The heavy, woman cook slit the chorizzo and red, serous fluid ran from the wound. He watched from behind a glass shield and thought, I deserve an expensive breakfast.

The Salad Sisters canceled at the last minute. At the last minute, the Turkey Twins. The bread bag prevented prints on the gun.

He ate and told himself that he was not watching the street with one eye. I am not watching the street with one eye. Watch the sky: plane load of bad teeth and pistols, coming over on fake visas.

I'm almost through with my first semester of medical school, he thought as he walked home. I'm going to high pass everything, without mangling Mr. The Cadaver. Today I'll get through all the note sets.

The phone rang soon after he got home. He didn't feel like talking, and whoever it was didn't leave a message. He made some tea and turned on the radio. He turned up the radio. One word of a commercial and he changed the station. He found himself scouring the sink. The phone rang four times, but he didn't answer it.

Ronaldo was the one who got the Turkey Twins. Ronaldo was in charge of security at the party. Ronaldo had disappeared.

Ronaldo had known what they were going to do.

He went to lie down, and held a pillow over his stomach. That made it no easier to breathe. If I don't trust the police, I can call the FBI, he thought.

The phone rang. He still didn't feel like talking, and let the answering machine get it.

"Hey. Henry. Where you at," the mouth speaking sounded far from the receiver. Now it closed in: "I know where you're at. You at home, hearing this. You just got back from the Exxon. Then you got some breakfast. You might be thinking of calling the police.

"This is Larry Frank. This is the police calling you. Mr. Landry thinks we all need to meet and have a long, sit-down talk. If you hear from Ronnie, you call Palace Springs. It's real important that we get this straightened out so we can enjoy the holidays."

Larry Frank hung up.

Henry moved the pillow over his face.

* * *

She was walking them through ligaments of the gut. Henry sat on the counter and chewed the skin around his nail.

"Take your right hand like this," hollered the lab instructor. She held up her hand with the palm toward them, "And slide it down along the right side of the abdominal wall just below the spleen. Do this now."

Eric, Amanda and Earnest stood around the cadaver with gloves and gowns on. Amanda kept pinching Earnest's glove and letting it snap him; he would play at being stung. Eric was pouting because today he wouldn't be allowed to cut anything.

The liver was too high, too big—a gray pillow under the ribs. The stomach was too small. The small intestine was just right. Henry looked at his own belly and imagined the same gray-pink rope. Amanda was petite, but even she could snap it with her hands.

"The layer you feel between your fingers, running perpendicular to the floor, runs between the bottom of the spleen and the top of the colon. It is therefore the spleno-colic ligament."

Earnest removed his hand, and Amanda took a feel. Eric gnawed at the leg with hemostats.

"Next, take your right hand—"

Heads turned to see what had stopped her. Henry stood on a stool so he could better see.

Ronaldo was standing in the doorway in his jade shirt and his hair bleached to snot-color. Even at his most depressed, a punk skater like dead Paolo wouldn't suffer hair so ugly.

This is the end, Henry thought.

* * *

They stood outside the lab, by the case containing the hydrocephalic's skull. "What'd you do to your hair," Henry said.

"Bleach and peroxide." There was a warble to Ronaldo's voice that had not been there before.

"Why didn't you just dye it blonde?"

"I don't know how dye works. I think you need a shower to use dye." Ronaldo touched him on the arm, then pulled his hand away when he saw the wary look on Henry's face. "I haven't been home. I need you to help me."

Henry could remember trusting him. "Help you what," he asked.

"I'm hungry."

He expects me to pay for it, Henry thought. "All right," he said, "We can go to the hospital cafeteria. They have Taco Bell now."

Ronaldo bought the Manager's Thanksgiving Special instead, and paid for it himself. He refused to sit by the window, and insisted on a corner where he could see the room. Henry ate his burrito without saying anything.

"So," Ronaldo warbled, "You're being quiet."

Henry wiped his mouth. "Why the hair," he said.

Ronaldo's eyes shot left, and then back. "It's a disguise."

"It's not a very good one," Henry said. Ronaldo was scared, and that made him feel good. "Why do you need a disguise?"

Ronaldo's eyes slipped again, and began to well up. "I am in big, big trouble, Hank." He turned his face to his plate and tore at the turkey leg.

Henry watched him. He handed him a napkin and looked around; two surgery interns at another table looked away. "Don't cry, Ronaldo. Wipe your eyes."

Ronaldo ground the paper into his eyes. Henry considered what to say. It occurred to him that he was now taller than Ronaldo; and the tears and silly hair made Ronaldo smaller still. He could say whatever he liked. "So how much did you get for it?" he said.

The skin around Ronaldo's eyes had reddened into a cartoon-robber's mask. He didn't look up from his plate.

I hope I'm wrong, Henry thought, I hope this makes him start laughing it's so absurd. He lowered his voice so the interns wouldn't hear. "Here's what I think. I think the Salad Sisters were available. But then these Ukrainian people approached you. I know you. You wouldn't take them just because they were cheaper. They offered you money."

Ronaldo didn't laugh. "I wanted a new car," he said.

Henry went numb over the nape of the neck. "You knew what they were going to do," he said, "and now you expect me to help you."

"You've known me ten years," Ronaldo said, "You know me better than anybody. You know that I have never done anything to hurt anybody. Maybe their property, but not them."

"Remember that time you sprayed catnip with roach spray and sold it to those kids who wanted weed?"

"I don't remember that," Ronaldo said, "I didn't know they were going to do that at the party. They told me they were going to do...something else."

"What?" Henry said.

Ronaldo sighed. "They told me they were going to get Mac fucking one of the girls on video and blackmail him with it."

Henry slouched back in his chair. "Fucking him on video."

"That's what they said." Ronaldo looked dismayed.

"Ronaldo." Henry leaned forward again. "Did it occur to you that this guy fucks people on video for a living? They could just rent a tape."

"Yeah," Ronaldo whined, "But he had told his wife—his girlfriend—that he had quit. She didn't even know that he had left the country."

"I don't want any part of this. As far as I'm concerned, you killed those people," He noticed that his voice was rising and he stopped. "Go to the police. I don't want any part of this," he said in a low voice.

"Did Larry Frank call you?" Ronaldo asked.

Henry did his best to make his face blank. "Why would Larry Frank call me?" he said.

"He wants to make sure I don't go to the police."

"He is the police," Henry said.

"He doesn't want me telling the police or anybody else," Ronaldo said, "We've done a lot of shit, him and me. He would get in more trouble than me if I said anything. I know he called you."

"Why don't you go to your dad?"

"Henry," Ronaldo looked around. The surgery interns had left when one of their pagers went off. "Remember that thing in the can company? Me and Larry had another one of those a while ago. I told him the scene looked wrong for suicide. He said, you want it to look wrong? And he took his pistol off his belt and shot the body seven times. The paper reported it as a suicide."

"What's that got to do with your dad?"

"My dad doesn't have connections like that, that's what it means," Ronaldo snapped, "And if he put a gun in my face when he caught me selling, how do you think he's going to handle this?"

Henry didn't believe all of this; he refused to. But he wouldn't let on that he didn't believe. "Larry Frank called me and said that Mr. Landry wanted to have a sit-down talk with all of us there."

Ronaldo said, "Larry Frank is going to kill me."

Henry looked at his face, and now it was his turn to look away. He wadded up his napkin and placed it in the right corner of his tray. "Why do you think that?" he said.

"I told you why. Mr. Landry wants to talk because I got dirt on him, too. But I know more about Larry. And Larry...you know how he is."

"So what do you want to do, Ronaldo?"

"I need to borrow some money to fly to California. Then I can call Mr. Landry for people out there I can stay with."

"Why don't you use the money the Russians gave you?"

"I never got it. Henry, I don't even have a bank account. It's taken this to wake me up and see what kind of a life I've been living. I have to get out of here."

Ronaldo seemed to have thought out all of his answers ahead of time; there were half-truths in there, somewhere. But Henry said, "All right."

* * *

Ronaldo wanted him to buy the plane ticket over the phone with a credit card, and then he would catch the airport shuttle from one of the hotels by the medical school. He insisted that he did not want to leave the building. He wouldn't even cross back from the hospital to the medical school on street level; he demanded that they take the bridge. The sky over the glass bridge looked like rain.

Back in Berkeley, street hustlers had a scam: I'm a college student whose backpack got stolen. Can you give me fifty dollars for a bus ticket back to Stanford? I'll mail you a check. No, we can't go to the bus station; give me the money right now.

Henry thought of this while he went back to lab for his backpack and jacket. Ronaldo was hiding behind a potted plant in the lobby.

"I have a better idea," Henry said, "Where's your car?"

Ronaldo looked wary. "I parked it at that tire-shop by your house. I went there looking for you this morning."

"Let's walk back to your car and take it to the airport."

"I want to take the shuttle from the hotel," Ronaldo said, "I told you."

"Thanksgiving is in two days. You might not get a ticket by phone. If we go to the counter, we might be able to get you a no-show. If I lend you my credit card, you can buy a connection to California from wherever you end up. The important thing is to get you out of town."

"It's going to rain. My car won't start if it's wet," Ronaldo said.

"That's why we need to hurry to my apartment and beat the rain. I've flown a lot more than you; trust me."

Ronaldo was still apprehensive; in the last ten years, he had gotten better at secrets and lying, but Henry didn't doubt that his fear was real. So on Henry's suggestion, they improved his disguise: they traded shirts in the bathroom, and Henry gave him his leather jacket. It went well with his hair; he looked like he was in a band, not like Ronaldo at all. Ronaldo had left his ski jacket at the party when he ran from the gun; Henry shivered as they walked.

He didn't tell Ronaldo, but he kept a sharp eye for awhite van, and for cop cars. And for the Hines frog car. But he saw none.

He pulled the blanket off of his bed. He would not bring a gun; since the bachelor party, he had felt—irrationally, he knew—that if he left guns alone, they would leave him alone. He had a scheme, one he hadn't told Ronaldo. Ronaldo waited outside, ducked down by his car.

Henry traded him the blanket for the car keys. "Lie under this in the back seat," he explained. Ronaldo started the car, then slinked into the back seat, curled up in a ball, and pulled the blanket over himself.

Henry got behind the wheel and looked over the controls several times without touching anything.

Ronaldo peered at him with one eye from under the blanket. "When was the last time you drove a car?" he asked.

"About two years ago. At Christmas with my parents," he said. Catherine had done all the driving after that. He found reverse. "How hard can it be? You just keep the painted part up."

Ronaldo didn't laugh.

Henry pulled away. To get on I-10 West to the Airport, he had to go left on Claiborne. He stifled a giggle and went right—I-10 East. Ronaldo didn't see.

Maybe he noticed because they weren't slowed down by traffic. Ronaldo peeked out with one wide eye. Then he threw down the blanket and sat up. "You're not going to the airport!" he cried.

"That's right!" Henry laughed. "We're going to Florida! We're going to my parents' house!"

"My car can't make it to Florida!" Ronaldo said.

"You're going to have Thanksgiving dinner with my parents. My mom is going to ask you why you don't have a girlfriend. She gave up on me," Henry said. His trick had made him giddy. Larry Frank had threatened him and Ronaldo tried to fool him, but here was, fooling them all. A raindrop hit the windshield with a crack, followed by more.

"You're driving into the rain," Ronaldo said. He continued to bicker with him. But Henry refused to turn around.

A white van was behind them, in the same lane, coming faster than it should. Henry stopped laughing.

The van, close enough to see inside now: Hines at the wheel, Larry Frank in the passenger seat, out of uniform. The rain on the roof was so loud that Ronaldo had to shout over it and the motor. Henry didn't understand what he had said, because Ronaldo was twisted around and watching the van approach through the back window. With the blanket wrapped around his middle, he looked like a little boy.

The car began to drift to the left. Henry straightened it and slowed down.

"I told you that my car wouldn't work in the rain," Ronaldo said, "I told you!"

"I thought you just said it wouldn't start when it was wet."

"It won't start when it's wet," Ronaldo said, "and it doesn't work in the rain! Not in rain like this!"

"At least the windshield wipers work," Henry said.

Henry headed toward the nearest exit, creeping along at twenty miles per hour down the ramp, with the van just behind them. It wasn't much of a car chase. He would go somewhere there were crowds. A line of cars flowed through an intersection and under the interstate, and he followed them. Ronaldo was cursing and pleading behind him.

They ended up in the parking lot of Sam's Wholesale Club. The lot was full; but in the corner, to the right of the entrance, there were four empty spots. The spots were there to save them; why else would they be empty?

He pulled into one and found out why: they were flooded. The car hit the pool of rainwater and the engine quit. Water lapped at the bottom of the door.

The van pulled in next to them, throwing waves at the car. Larry Frank already had his door open. Tied around his left wrist was a clear plastic garbage bag of yellow popcorn, the kind sold by the stale dozens to school fairs. He pointed the popcorn at them. "Out of the car, assholes," he growled, as only a city cop can.

He could have a small rifle in that bag, buried in the popcorn; a sawed-off shotgun, easily. Henry put his hands up. Ronaldo, who didn't know guns, put the passenger seat forward, opened the door, and ran. Henry heard his foot's *sploosh* in the water; when he looked, Ronaldo was running stooped over along the row of cars, back toward the interstate.

Larry Frank jumped out of the van and half-raised the popcorn bag, holding up the bottom with his other hand. The van jerked into reverse. Larry Frank cursed and hollered at Hines, "Wait for me! Damn it!" He watched Ronaldo run away, with his hand on the van's door and one foot in the puddle.

Ronaldo hopped into a drainage ditch. He didn't come up on the other side. Then they saw him pop up a hundred feet away, running into a wooded lot. If he had run into Sam's, Larry Frank would have pulled out his badge and arrested him; store security would have helped. If he had stayed on the road, they would have hunted him down.

Larry Frank was standing in water half way up his calves, hunching his shoulders against the rain and the cold. He blinked the beads of water off of his eyelashes and said to Henry, "You get out of the car, then." He bopped Henry in the nose with the popcorn.

Larry Frank reached in and took the car keys. Then he made Henry squat in the water and let the air out of the back tires. Bubbles drained up in clusters and then in singles and then nothing, like he was drowning a kitten or rat. He had to keep his head down to see through the water running down his face. Maybe someone will think we have car trouble and offer to help us out, Henry thought, and then I can get away.

Cars passed, and he had to stand so as not to get hit in the seat by the waves they made. No one offered help.

Larry Frank handed the keys to Henry. "Take the car key off the ring," he muttered. Muttering wasn't like him. Henry peeled off the key; the popcorn bag was pointed at his groin.

Unhurried, tired, Larry Frank opened the gas cap, let it fall into the puddle, and pushed the key into the gas tank. Then he nodded toward the van door. Hines had closed it.

Henry looked at Ronaldo's car, dragging its haunches in the puddle. Even if Ronaldo had a spare key hidden at his mother's, he wouldn't get anywhere in this car. He climbed into the back of the van and sat on the wheel well. Larry Frank flopped into the passenger seat. Henry covered his nose and sneezed.

Hines said, "To Palace Springs?" Since he was on a manhunt, today Hines was dressed as a Texas Ranger. He was wearing denim head-to-toe, and gray, ostrich-skin boots. And a cowboy hat. He was actually wearing a cowboy hat.

Larry Frank nodded. The van pulled away. He turned to Henry and ripped the bag from his wrist. Popcorn flew everywhere, and revealed Larry Frank's hand holding an arthritic shotgun, so old and sawed-off so short that it looked almost as dangerous to Larry Frank as to Henry.

"I'm not mad at you, Henry," he muttered, "But Henry, I hate cold water."

Hines snuck a glance at them, and didn't protest or slow down.

Larry Frank lifted the shotgun and held it in Henry's face. He had never seen a double-barreled before, and couldn't tell the gauge, but the barrels were big enough that popcorn had nestled inside. He could see it.

They rode that way long enough that Henry started to worry about hitting bumps, and the rickety gun going off. Larry Frank pulled it back, cracked the gun in the middle, and pulled out two shells.

Loaded, this time.

* * *

They parked under the carport at Palace Springs. Larry Frank went inside first, with the empty shotgun in his hand. He opened the door to the front office and said, "Ronnie ran off."

Mr. Landry was wearing a yellow shirt and red tie—odd for a mortician. He sat forward and spread his fingers wide on the desk. The desk was bare except for a water spray bottle, the kind used for delicate plants. "In this rain?"

"Henry here tried to help him. We fixed his car so it won't go nowhere."

Mr. Landry gave Henry a smile and wink, the way his dentist used to.

Mike, the one who looked like the high school football coach, was sitting in one of the two chairs in front of the desk. He stood up and looked at Mr. Landry. "What are we going to do?" he said.

Mr. Landry hid his mouth under his mustache and put his hands in the air. Then he looked at Henry and said, "Henry, do you know Mike?"

"We met," Henry said.

"Look at how wet y'all are," Mr. Landry said scoldingly, "You going to catch a pneumonia."

Larry Frank walked over to Mike and handed him the shotgun without looking at him, followed by the shells. "You have to make this one worth my while, Eddie," Larry Frank said to Mr. Landry. He wasn't muttering anymore, and Henry was relieved. "I got no more sick days. I get sick real easy, too."

As soon as Henry saw the gun out of Larry Frank's hand, he got mad. Hines was standing next to him, and he stepped away.

"We'll talk about it, Larry," said Mr. Landry. He got up and walked around the desk, for no other reason than to put a reassuring hand on Larry Frank's shoulder. It was almost noon, but Mr. Landry had just shaved. He had used bits of white toilet paper to stop the bleeding. The skin of his neck looked like he made it bleed every day.

"So what now, Eddie," Larry Frank said, "Don't just throw up your hands again."

Mr. Landry was about to, but stopped his hands halfway and put them in his back pockets. He thought that was funny. No one else laughed. "I think we should try again when Ronaldo shows up," he said, "He'll show up."

"He'll show," Hines said.

"Maybe he'll show up on a boat, Hines," Henry said, "Then you can wear your sailor suit."

All of them looked at Henry. Mike giggled behind his hand; Larry Frank looked Hines in the face and laughed. Hines gave Henry a look that said, please quit picking on me. And give me back my magazine.

Mr.Landry scowled behind his mustache; he didn't approve of the teasing. "Why don't we all just try again. I'll call everyone, just like this time."

Henry remembered the phones at the party. "Calling each other doesn't work," he muttered, rubbing his eyes.

"And Henry, if you have time, I'd like you to stay here with me and talk right now. I don't blame you for being sharp with us. I don't think that we been fair to you. We've kept you in the dark for too long."

"You want me to stay?" said Mike.

"No," Mr. Landry said. He gave Henry's arm a squeeze. "He doesn't have a gun. You don't have a gun on you, do you Henry?"

Henry said no, and thought, we're following orders from this old, touchy-feely idiot? He mangled himself shaving: red blood on white paper equals a target.

22

They were left alone. Henry sneezed.

Mr. Landry offered to turn on the heater; there was a window unit behind the desk. He fiddled with it, looking through the bottom of his glasses. "This is an air conditioner," he declared.

"I haven't been in this particular house through a winter yet. I don't even know how the heater works," he said. He laughed. Henry didn't. "So how about a dry shirt, Henry? I have one in the other room."

"I don't want some shirt you have lying around a funeral home," Henry said, "I don't want to think about where it came from. How about a towel?"

Mr. Landry hurried off. He had been wearing a suit the last time Henry saw him. Now he saw that Mr. Landry's body came to a point from wide hips. It did not make him more confident in him. He peeled off his soaked sweatshirt.

Mr. Landry handed him a hand towel, and told him he could just put the sweat shirt flat on the floor, to dry. The carpet would dry okay. Henry dried his head and pulled the towel around his shoulders. Mr. Landry wanted them to sit beside each other, in the two chairs facing his desk. "No more formality," he said. He put the spray bottle into a desk drawer and walked around.

These were the chairs Mr. Landry used for ripping off families. Henry sat down anyway.

"So you ready to fix my back?" Mr. Landry said, "This one doctor gave me some pain pills for it. They always ask me if I did something to hurt it, but I don't remember. I fell off a ladder in 1980. But I had the pain before that. I didn't want any pills, but this doctor said to me, did I want my life back or not? So I took the prescription. They were diamond-shaped pills. I had never seen a pill like that. I took them a couple days, and then I woke up at night and I saw all these Chinese people in my room, looking at me, sewing these veils on machines. I hollered for Mike. He put the pills down the sink."

"Mike lives with you?"

"What kind of doctor you want to be, Henry?"

"A trauma oncologist."

"That would be a hard specialty."

"A penis enlargologist."

"Don't be nasty."

"Mr. Landry, I'm a medical student. I've spent my whole life in school. I took a part time job with you in September. Since then, I've had my life threatened three times. It's only November."

"The end of November," Mr. Landry said.

"So excuse me if I have a smart mouth. I'm trying to pretend this is all a joke. Otherwise, I feel like I'm being punished for something I never did."

"Three times. Let's hear those times," Mr. Landry said.

Henry counted on his fingers. "With Hines, that day you made me go off with him. He threatened to blow up my head. That bachelor party. Just now in the van, Larry Frank put that shotgun in my face. Because he was cold."

Mr. Landry said, "I was thinking about Ian and Larry the other day. I was thinking that they're two sides of the same coin. Ian Hines thinks that he's in a movie. He's getting worse since his son died. But he can't back up what he says. So that one doesn't count.

"Larry Frank, on the other hand, on the other side of the coin, knows he's not in a movie, but he acts like he is. In other words, he doesn't care about his safety, or anybody else's. So I'll talk to him about what he said. But Henry, can you really blame him? He told me about the guns you have."

"It's not my fault it's raining and he got cold," Henry said, "I don't carry guns."

"I said I'll talk to him."

"I notice you left out the bachelor party. Rationalize three dead people."

Mr. Landry looked at the floor and cracked a testy smile. "Henry," he said, fidgeting, "do you think I'm some kind of big boss? Was I present at any of these situations? The bachelor party—I had no part in that. I put two people in touch over the phone. Ronaldo and some other guy. Don't blame me if your friend drags you into the shit with him.

"And my experience with those diamond pills taught me something, Henry: leave the drugs alone. Leave them to people like you and Ian, right? Like you and Ronaldo, right? Monthly packages from Berkeley, right? Maybe you're being punished, Henry, but don't sit there and tell me you never did nothing."

* * *

Ronaldo used to talk for hours about his drug dealing, if he didn't check himself. It was natural: he wanted appreciation for ingenuity and hard work, and work kept quiet wasn't appreciated. Henry hoped to get Mr. Landry to start talking. "I don't believe you're a mortician. I don't know what you are. But it's not that."

Mr. Landry laughed. "I got licenses for California, Utah, and Louisiana," he said, "You mean you don't like my shop. That's because the funerary business has been locked up by the old families.

It hasn't happened here yet, but it will. In California, all the little mom-and-pop funeral homes were bought up on the sly. Then the price of caskets and services creep up and up. If you want crime bosses, talk to the old families."

"Ronaldo showed me your book with the repeat photographs."

"I got to make a living. I know who I can touch. I use that book on the ungrateful kids. One thing I can't stand is these fucking kids who want to bury their parents in cardboard, practically. No offense, but I've seen more than one doctor like that. If they had any respect, a doctor wouldn't even come to a funeral home like this. I never use that book on the people who come here because they really need me. My families can't afford the big homes."

"What did you charge Hines for his son?"

Mr. Landry scowled. "That was free," he said, "Henry, sometimes your jokes aren't funny."

"What's your charge for burying bricks?" Henry said.

"Hmm," Mr. Landry said, "Did Ronaldo explain to you the Palace Springs policy of being dumb?"

"If Ronaldo wasn't so dumb," Henry said, "Those people might be alive right now."

"The bricks. What's there to say about the bricks," Mr. Landry muttered.

Henry waited.

"I like it when I put together a good service. Paolo's service, that was really fine. Ian is going through hard times now, but the service was fine," Mr. Landry said, "But what I really enjoy, Henry, is the bricks. I don't mean any disrespect, but a priest just promises heaven. I can get it for you now, financed by the insurance you've paid for years."

"I thought insurance didn't cover suicide," Henry said.

"I'm not talking about that. The man who killed himself, Chris Leggio—he had tax problems. Legal problems. That was a real tragedy," Mr. Landry said. He didn't do a good job sounding ignorant. "Insurance companies should cover suicide. Some do.

"Insurance, now there's a racket. You want to talk to crime bosses, talk to insurance. Look at the biggest building in any city. It's insurance. You lived in the Bay Area: look at the Transamerica building."

"I don't think Transamerica is the biggest in Frisco."

"It's the pointiest," Mr. Landry said, "It's the most distinct. You caught me: I never even been to San Francisco. That's the point, Henry. There are no more secrets between us. I'm a half-ass mortician who rips people off. You figured that out. I can't feel bad about the life insurance companies, either. If a mosquito flew up and took a single hair off your arm—"

"—'Would I feel it?' No," Henry said, "Ronaldo said that one time. That's strange behavior for a mosquito."

"So let's talk about Ronaldo," Mr. Landry said, "Let's talk about Ronnie. What's he said. Why did he run."

"Ronaldo ran," Henry said, "because he believes that Larry Frank is going to kill him."

Mr. Landry scoffed.

Henry continued, "He's going to kill him because Ronaldo knows too much about him," Henry said, "And I don't feel too safe around him either."

"Larry Frank will not kill anybody," Mr. Landry said, "He's crazy, but he listens to me. You saw that earlier. Ronnie's not in danger from him. Not from him."

I wish he could have lied and said it would all be fine, Henry thought. "Why?"

Mr. Landry sighed. "What Ronnie has done," he said, "is turn a muffaletta situation into a mafia situation."

"What's that supposed to mean?"

"A muffaletta is an Italian sandwich. It was invented by New Orleans Italians. It's made of olive salad, pastrami, Genoa cheese—"

"I know what a muffaletta is."

"—And the real mafia people call people like me muffalettas. It's like an insult. Like I'm small fry. I've had some big-fry friends. I'd rather be called a sandwich than dead or in jail.

"Some bachelor party you and Ronnie set up. Eight friends of the groom, the rest Ronnie's muffaletta friends. These are guys who work real jobs, then get a hard-on when they buy or sell something that fell off the truck. They read crime books and play with guns."

I'm a muffaletta, Henry thought.

Mr. Landry said, "So you and Ronnie see that real mafia people don't play with them."

Henry kept his voice steady. "So they wanted to kill Mac. They did it. Big deal. What's that got to do with Ronaldo."

"How's it affect Ronaldo?" Mr Landry said. He chuckled nervously. "I'm worried about how it affects me. You ought to worry about you. You saw how Mike was scared, too."

"I don't understand."

"Henry. American Mafia, even Italian Mafia, are all Catholic. These Russians are communist. Or used to be. They have no respect for human life. I'm not racist, but not even some project coon would shoot up a roomful of people to get one man. These Russians have a special, separate word for what they did. I can't pronounce it. It's not enough just to kill him, you make a party of it.

"Mac has to have Russian people too, or else he couldn't have worked over there. So I don't know if these were enemies of his people. What I know is this: the clock is ticking. By tomorrow, at the latest, Mac Donald's people are going to find out that Ronnie sold him out. That's who he should be scared of. Not of Larry

Frank. I'm scared of them because Ronnie works for me. I should have had my dog on a leash."

"The people who shot Mac," Henry said, "Maybe they were Mac's people from Russia. Then that's the end of it."

"That's even worse," Mr. Landry said, without any hesitation, "They know where I am. They actually talked to Ronnie. They got to know by now that even in New Orleans, you can't get away with one like this. I don't know if you've been following the news: the paper's picked up on the stripper-sex act part. It made national news. That means the police have to solve it. It's like when a tourist gets killed."

"So why me," Henry said. He had begun to breathe harder. "I was just in the room. Like another guest."

Mr. Landry shook his head. "Like you said, you been in school your whole life. They don't need to make sense. Everything is based on what they heard. You're his best friend. What if they hear that you were in on it?

"Our only chance is to meet as a group. We can circle the wagons. We'll order food. There's an Indian place up the street. We can plan, and get Ronaldo out of here. If we do it fast enough, then I can convince them I don't know where he is."

"What if that's not enough?"

Mr. Landry threw up his hands.

"You wanted me to work for you so bad," Henry said, "Since we're being honest, tell me why."

"I'm starting an eye bank," Mr. Landry said.

"I don't know anything about eyes."

"Yes, you do," Mr. Landry said, "Yes, you do, Dr. Marrier. You'll get used to how that sounds. Don't be so modest. I need someone with a science background to prepare the tissues."

Henry remembered eyeball day in lab: Eric freed it up with the scalpel. Then he made his fingers into a beak and plucked it out.

Amanda nicked the ball and the lens fell out. The dissector said, "carefully remove and appreciate the cornea." That meant cut off the front of the eyeball and look at it. "Mr. Landry, you don't need me for eyeballs. They're easy."

"I know that's not true," Mr. Landry said, "I have some doctors lined up, and they said, get people with some training. Doctors would be best. But I got a doctor to be." He squeezed Henry's arm.

"Who are these doctors?"

"They're in Brazil."

"And that's why you have Hines," Henry said, "He can speak Portugese."

Mr. Landry looked at him, guarded, but then his smile returned. "Right. Very good, Henry. Very smart. You're so smart I want you to work for me. You want the job?"

"Eyes are cheap in Brazil? Or are you providing eyes?"

"We'll talk about that later," Mr. Landry said, "Honestly."

"School keeps me busy," Henry said. He imagined a sign in a parking lot: PALACE SPRINGS EYE BANK. The image sickened him.

"I have antennas that sense money," Mr. Landry said, "My antennas are vibrating over this eye bank. I know how to make money and stay out of trouble, Henry. Including tax trouble. I have a television at home–you should see it. Football season, you can see the blood on the field. Larry Frank is in my pocket. Police don't come cheap."

Henry smiled and said, "I think you should find someone else."

"Listen to me," he said, "Talking to a doctor about making money. Think about the people you'll help, Henry. I'm going to give people the chance to see again. Lens transplant is the number one surgery in the country. Everyone is going to get cataracts if they live long enough. Look at my eye. You can see I'm getting one." He spread his lids and leaned forward.

Henry knew that now lenses were usually polymer prosthetics. Mr. Landry was taking the Brazilians, or they were taking him somehow. Let them have each other.

Mr. Landry was holding his right eye open, waiting. Henry looked and said, "I don't see anything."

* * *

The rain had stopped. Mr. Landry drove a clot-colored Lincoln. He drove Henry back downtown, and was still pitching the job. "These Brazilian doctors told me they can get this to count for research."

Henry wasn't interested. "It never bothers you, doing this?"

"I'm just making a buck, Henry."

"What you do to these bodies never bothers you."

Mr. Landry looked over at him. "I supplied cadavers to Brewster Medical School. I'm surprised what I do would bother you."

"I'm asking you," Henry said.

Mr. Landry stared at the road. "When I was a little younger than you, I got into some trouble. My father sent me away to California, to work at his friend's funeral home.

"We didn't do a lot of the actual burials. Our money came from the cremations. Out there, bake-and-shakes are big business. Nobody's Catholic. Everybody wants to be dumped in the ocean from a plane. We had the oven, and all the homes in the central coast contracted with us. My job was to put the remains in the oven.

"They would be delivered at nine and two. The homes around there, they used to pride themselves on their hearses. Every remains got its own hearse, I don't care how many trips it took. Nowadays, they use trucks.

"For a week I did them one by one, sifted them, put them in the urns they came with. I had never been around dead bodies before, but by the end of the week I was fine. Then my old man's friend came back there. I had one on the rack, ready to go. He was annoyed with me.

"He made me pile on two more. We pushed them in. Then he made me help him bend another one around the first three. He picked up this old lady by himself. She had one leg. He stuffed her in at the edges. There was a two by four lying around and he used that.

"He said it was illegal to mix remains, but he would go broke running a crematorium the way I had been doing it. We just sifted equal amounts into different urns. You want to know what bothers me? That bothered me. One of those urns was going to one of our families.

"Anyway, we gave them the urn, and they never found out. No family ever found out. My daddy's friend was very, very good with the families. I figured that if anyone could tell the difference, it would be the families. But...." He shrugged.

The radio was on AM, playing old, sugary jazz. Once Mr. Landry stopped talking, the smell of his aftershave grew stronger. The music, the smell—Henry thought of an old, stooped barber sweeping up hair. It was sad; he looked at Mr. Landry to see if that was where the sadness came from.

It was gone. "We also used to pry out the gold fillings. But that was real common at that time. Eyes are going to get the same way. That's why we need to get in on the ground floor." And he started pushing the job again.

They stopped in front of his building. Henry hadn't told him where it was. He thanked him for the ride.

"Henry," Mr. Landry said, "You didn't have a gun at that party, did you?"

Henry was out of the car, and stopped with the door half-closed. "No," he said.

"Because, Henry, I heard this rumor that you were seen running around behind the house with a gun in your hand. People might think that you did it. The police, and other people besides."

"Everyone there saw the girl."

"Well. They're drunk, and who knows what else. I wonder if that girl threw the gun in the bayou. That's the thing. People always think that under water's the best place to hide something. So many people think so that under water is about the worst place."

"They found the gun, Mr. Landry," Henry said, "I didn't have a gun there."

Mr. Landry's face was stony. "I believe you, Henry," he said, "But it's a rumor. When Ronnie calls, tell him it's time to circle the wagons."

Henry thanked him for the ride. He went inside without waiting for the car to pull away. Once inside he washed his hands without realizing it. Then he went to the armoire. There was a box of 9mm's inside. Seventeen were missing. They would find the gun in the bayou and fit the seventeen from it right into this box.

He would throw them out tomorrow, with other garbage. He pulled the Glock's registration, shredded it, and flushed the pieces.

23

He didn't go to lab the next day. After trying to study, he cleaned his bedroom again. He called Ronaldo's mother in late morning.

"Ma'am. This is Henry Marrier. From Martyrs'?"

"Henry!" she shrieked, pleasantly, "Ronaldo's not here. I don't know where he is, but he's not here."

Henry remembered that flirting worked. "Well, maybe I was calling to talk to you."

"Well," she said, "Maybe you were."

"And how have you been," Henry said, "Do you have a new, uh, 'friend' now?"

"What about you?" she asked, "You tell first."

"School keeps me busy, Ms. Pitero," Henry said.

"Nicole," she said.

"Nicole."

"Henry, if you were here I'd smack your behind. Make time for girls," she said.

So they knocked it back and forth more, real easy, like ping-pong, then Henry said, "Nicole, if he's there, he'll talk to me."

The other end of the line was silent. He heard a breath, then a pause, then Ronaldo's voice. His throat sounded tight. "I told her not to tell I was here."

"Ronaldo," Henry said, "I'm sorry I tried to drive to Florida. I thought it would work."

"It didn't. I'm still here," he said, "I can't quit smoking. I'm smoking my mom's cigarettes, I'm so scared to go out. They're like lollipop sticks."

Henry told him about his talk with Mr. Landry. He didn't tell him the rumor about himself and the gun. It took some convincing, but Ronaldo agreed to circle the wagons. He hung up with a finger, and without putting the receiver down, he called Palace Springs. Mike answered. Henry told him that if he were picked up at noon, he could take them to Ronaldo.

He shaved his left ankle up to mid-calf. With wound dressing tape he had stolen from the hospital, he taped the revolver to the inside of his leg. He experimented with taping until he could rip the gun off, easily and quickly. He didn't know what would happen with it after that.

* * *

They pulled up in the van early. Hines was behind the wheel. Henry had never known anyone who wore camel's hair, but he guessed that was what his coat was made of. The jacket had no lapels. Under it he wore a black turtleneck shirt. He had gotten his hair cut like Caesar, and wore a pair of wraparound, yellow sunglasses.

Larry Frank was sitting next to him, in uniform. A lawyer once said on TV, it's easier to convict a nun than a police officer in uniform.

Henry stood in front of the van, lifted his sweatshirt and shirt, and twirled for them on his toes, showing them his back and gut.

Larry Frank stuck his head out of the window. "Are you doing ballet?" he asked.

Henry walked toward the van. "I'm showing you I don't have anything," he said.

Larry Frank turned around in his seat and watched Henry climb into the back. He didn't look at Henry's leg or anywhere else he might have a gun. He looked at Henry's face.

Henry stared back.

Larry Frank turned away, bored. His baton was on the floor between the seats. Hines pulled off.

Henry said to Hines, "Are you, like, spy-a-go-go today?"

Hines said nothing.

"I have to go before the fucking ethics review board today," Larry Frank said.

"What for?" Henry asked. I hope they nail your ass for corpse mutilation, Henry thought.

"I called a meter maid a meter maid."

"What are you supposed to call them?" Henry asked.

Larry Frank shrugged. "They probably won't tell me, either. They don't care if anybody learns from their mistakes."

Henry said, "Speaking of mistakes, Mr. Hines, this is yours." He pulled Hines's magazine from his back pocket and handed it over. "We're all on the same team, right? The Palace Springs team."

Hines looked genuinely moved. He took it back. "Thank you," he said.

Larry Frank smiled, looking out the window so they couldn't see.

Hines didn't ask why there were no bullets in the magazine.

The only talking was Henry directing them to Ronaldo's mother's house. Hines said, "You've got to be kidding me. He's here?!"

Henry was opening the side door. "He lives here."

"I've been coming by here five, six times a day," Hines said, "I never saw him."

"Good work," Larry Frank said, "That really fucking inspires confidence, Ian."

Henry rang the bell. Ronaldo came to the door, blinking against the gray sunlight; under his arm, he had Henry's jacket. He handed it back, looking over Henry's shoulder at the van. Larry Frank gave him a lazy salute.

"He has a gun on him?" Ronaldo asked.

Henry slipped on his jacket. "Yes," he said, "I have something, too." From the van, it would look like just a conversation.

Ronaldo went pale.

"That's just insurance," Henry said, "It's going to be okay."

Ronaldo walked past him to the van.

* * *

The Bronco Hearse was parked in the alley, blocking any passage beyond the funeral home. Larry Frank told Hines to back in. Once it was under the carport, he came around the back of the van. Henry and Ronaldo watched the door open from the inside. Hines stood at one door, Larry Frank at the other.

"Well," Larry Frank said, "Here we are. Going to have a little talk."

Henry and Ronaldo both looked at him and didn't move. Something was wrong.

"Come on," Larry Frank chuckled. His left hand, his gun hand, was on the door. They could see the gun snapped in his holster.

Henry got out first. The leg of his jeans caught on the gun, but Hines and Larry Frank didn't notice. He shook his leg and there was no gun again.

Ronaldo stepped out.

When his foot hit the concrete, Larry Frank blasted him in the face with the pepper spray he had hidden behind the door. Hines looked as surprised as Henry felt. Ronaldo yelped and grabbed his face with both hands. He fell to the ground in a ball.

Henry turned to run down the alley, but that seemed a terrible mistake. There would be no witnesses in the alley, which Larry Frank would like when he shot him in the face, chest and gut; then he would call it suicide. Instead he ran right into the funeral home. If Mr. Landry wasn't in the office, he would run out of the front door.

Mr. Landry was sitting behind the desk, wearing that yellow shirt again, this time without a tie. On the desk was the white spray bottle again and a box of tissue. Mike stood up from one of the two rip-off chairs with the sawed-off in his thick hand.

"I thought we were going to talk!" Henry said.

"Yeah," Mr. Landry said, "What?"

"Larry Frank is a fucking crazy man, that's what!"

He didn't have time to explain. Hines came in the room first, watching behind him as Larry Frank herded along a hunched-over Ronaldo. Ronaldo was sucking air through clenched teeth and grunting. Clear syrup ran from his eyes, nose and mouth.

"Damn it, Larry!" Mr. Landry said, "What did you do?"

Larry Frank started laughing.

"This isn't funny, Larry. This is serious, serious business," yelled Mr. Landry, "That spray stuff and your gun—give them here. Give them to me."

Larry Frank's laughter sputtered away. "Fuck, Eddie, you told me to—!"

"I told you to bring him here so we could talk!" Mr. Landry said, "How can we talk if he can't breathe? Give them here. I'm serious."

Sulking, Larry Frank handed over the gun and spray. Mr. Landry held them in one hand. "All right. Ian," he said, "You too. Play time is over." He held out a hand in front of Hines.

Hines reached into his jacket and handed over the SIG. It seemed impossible that that tight jacket could have hidden it. Mr. Landry stuck that one in his pocket. It made his hips seem even wider.

He then held the hand palm-up in front of Henry and waited. "I don't have anything," Henry said.

"Are you sure, Henry?" he said. But he was looking at Larry Frank for the answer.

"He doesn't," Larry Frank said.

Mr. Landry placed the two guns and spray in a desk drawer. He made Mike put the shotgun on the desk and sit with his hands folded. Ronaldo sat opposite him in the other rip-off chair, rocking back and forth with his hands held just off of his face. He had discovered that rubbing made the burn worse.

Mr. Landry picked up the spray bottle and tissue paper. "Let me clean you up, Ronnie," he said, "I'm sorry about this. All of this."

Ronaldo's eyes had swollen shut. He let Mr. Landry squirt mist over his face. *Kiss kiss kiss* went the bottle with each pump.

"Everybody makes mistakes," said Mr. Landry, "Larry Frank has the ethics board again today." He let Ronaldo take the bottle, and wrapped his hand around the tissue paper box for him. Ronaldo wiped his chin, and went back to spraying himself. "You made one big fucking mistake, Ronnie."

Mr. Landry walked behind the desk and pulled out a wad of empty produce bags from a grocery store. *SCHWEGGMAN'S*, in green letters. He smoothed them on the desk.

"Henry," he said, not looking up from the bags, "do you know Mike?"

Kiss kiss kiss went the bottle.

Why was the spray bottle on the desk last time? Henry wondered. "Yeah, I met Mike a couple of times," he said.

"That's right," Mr. Landry said quietly. He looked up and nodded at Larry Frank.

Larry Frank asked, "What hand you write with, Henry?"

Henry held up his right without thinking. He was watching Mr. Landry.

Mr. Landry said, "Of course y'all know each other. I must be getting senile. Mike kills people."

Ronaldo stopped spraying.

"Excuse me?" Henry said.

Larry Frank speared him under the ribs with his baton, and Henry's legs crumpled under him. Larry Frank kicked him onto his chest and put one knee on his back. He grabbed Henry's right wrist; Henry felt the cuffs click around it. From the floor he could see Mike on his knees in front of Ronaldo, hugging his arms to the chair. A crescent of gut hung out beneath Mike's shirt.

The spray bottle was on the floor in front of his face. The bottle had been here last time because Mr. Landry had planned the pepper spray, this knee in his back, all of it.

Larry Frank cuffed his right wrist to his left ankle. He found the gun taped there and said, "Son of a bitch."

The bottom fell out of Henry's stomach. Ronaldo squirmed in the chair and screamed. Mike clapped a hand over his mouth. That big hand could cover Ronaldo's whole face. Larry Frank ripped the gun off of his leg, and then it felt like he was dropping quarters onto Henry's head. He opened his eyes and saw that they were the bullets from his own gun.

Mr. Landry stood behind Ronaldo and pulled the plastic bags over his face in a sheet.

"Wait, wait!" screamed Larry Frank. Henry saw Larry's fingers pick up bullets from the floor.

This whole time, Hines had pressed himself against the wall, a fist up by his mouth and his head turned like he might get splattered.

Mike drove a shoulder against Ronaldo to free one hand, and with it he picked up the shotgun from the desk and pointed it at Larry Frank. The bullets fell to the floor again, followed by Henry's gun.

Mr. Landry pulled back as far as he could, until Ronaldo's face was turned up at the ceiling. Now he could push down and drive the plastic into the nose and mouth.

Mike slipped his hand out from beneath the plastic and squeezed Ronaldo to the chair between an arm and a shoulder. He wiped Ronaldo's snot from his hand on the carpet.

Ronaldo wouldn't die. Mr. Landry pushed down so hard that the bags began to stretch. His cheeks shook. Mike jumped up from the floor and plopped down onto Ronaldo's lap like a starlet. He bounced to pump the breath out of Ronaldo. Now Ronaldo's arms were free, but he had only enough brain left to flap them.

Mike wanted to get off.

"Five minutes makes sure," said Mr. Landry. His glasses had fallen off. The whole time, he looked through the plastic at Ronaldo's smothered face. He watched him die and didn't look away.

* * *

"This is awful," Larry Frank, "This is the most awful thing I've ever seen. Nobody deserves to *smother*."

Hines was sitting on the floor against the wall with his legs pulled up to his chest. He had taken off the yellow glasses.

Mr. Landry had left the plastic over Ronaldo's face. Henry hoped that hand or face would move. Neither did. He hoped that Ronaldo's ghost would haunt him, so Ronaldo would be less dead. It wouldn't.

Killing him had been more exercise than Mr. Landry was used to. He was sitting behind the desk, trying to catch his breath. "What's so awful, Larry."

"I thought you were to going to shoot him," Larry Frank said, "That's why I was loading Henry's gun, see?"

"Shut up, Larry."

"Okay."

Mike had settled back in the other chair, with an unreadable pig-face. Mr. Landry said, "I did it this way for two reasons. We got neighbors. And the second reason is to get us back in line. I am the motherfucking chicken, you chicken shits. Ian, no more drugs and worthless swag out of your house. From now on, you do nothing but work the phone to Sao Paolo."

Mr. Landry walked from behind the desk and stood over Henry. Henry could look up at him with just one eye. "Do you see that?" he said. He pointed at Ronaldo's body.

Henry nodded.

Mr. Landry spoke very slowly. He kicked a bullet away from Henry's nose. "Henry, think before you answer: What can you give me that I can't take?"

"I'll work for you," Henry said. He swallowed, "I'll work in the eye bank."

"Very good, Henry. Larry, let him up."

He felt a hand tugging at the cuffs, and then they were loose. His leg flopped to the floor. The cuffs had cut into his wrist and ankle. He still felt like he had them on.

"And Larry, I'm going to pretend that I didn't see that shit with the gun just now," Mr. Landry said.

Larry Frank started to speak.

"Spare me. Your lesson is that I am the rooster and you are the—I don't know. The rabbit. You turn on me, and I will serve you up. Ronaldo got greedy, and I am serving up his dead ass."

Henry didn't hear Larry Frank answer. He pushed himself up onto his feet. He scooped up his revolver from the floor. He didn't touch a single bullet; Mike watched for that. He put the gun in his pocket. He had thought it was only a trick of perspective from the floor, but standing he saw it also: Mr. Landry seemed to have grown a foot by killing Ronaldo. He could smother them all and be nine feet tall.

*　　　　*　　　　*

Hines gave them a ride back downtown. Larry Frank was dropped off at the police station for the review board. Before he got out, he said, "I wasn't going to do anything to Ed Landry with your gun, Henry." He did not look at them.

Once Larry Frank was gone, Hines said to Henry, "I don't think you should feel like this was your fault."

"I know it's not my fault," Henry snapped.

Hines had the yellow glasses on again. He had gone to the bathroom after the murder and arranged himself. "I think that Paolo's suicide was my fault," he said, "That kills me. The only thing that makes me feel better is putting together outfits. So I wish you would quit mocking me for that."

Henry thought of the Paolo in the pictures, and how all of this had started—with Paolo's money and Hines's acid. Hines had the acid back. He still didn't know where Paolo's money came from. He said, "Did Paolo sell drugs?"

"The only thing Paolo did wrong was have me for a father," Hines said.

Henry didn't tell him about the money he had found. As far as he knew, no one knew about the money except for him and Ronaldo. Now it was no one except for him.

24

If I act normal, I will be normal.

He rolled onto his back, and with the first breath felt like he was being shrink wrapped, like a toy in its package. Like Ronaldo's smothered face. Ten hours of dreamless sleep, and he was still tired.

The shower didn't wash away the coating he felt. He wasn't sad; he knew that. If he were sad he would cry. His brain evidently allowed him this coating so that he wouldn't feel anything, and that was fine with him.

I can live the rest of my life like this, he thought as he dried off, this isn't so bad.

Anatomy class would end two weeks after Thanksgiving. Each lab received a dot-matrix list to be taped to the blackboard. They hadn't seen dot-matrix in years. Mr. The Cadaver, the list read, had been a salesman, 67 years old. Also in Lab D were a homemaker, 74; retired policeman, 68; and physician (gastroenterologist), 77. Lab A: Catholic priest, 80; truck driver, 58; mining camp chef, 62; retired salesman, 84. Lab B: physician (general surgeon), 72; homemaker, 80; homemaker, 56; unknown, ? Lab C: attorney, 72; stock broker, 71; university professor (Spanish) 72; veteran (Korea), 63. Lab E: homemaker, 48; unknown, ?; physician (medical illustrator), 84; landscape architect, 80. Lab F: university professor (Economics), 81; dance instructor, 56; physician (pediatrician),71; graduate student, 25. Lab G: homemaker, 75; nurse's aide, 50; manager, 65; commercial fisherman, 61.

Causes of death were not listed. The annual cadaver memorial service would be held that day at lunch in the freshman auditorium, with refreshments afterward. Finger sandwiches would be served.

Earnest had the small intestine bunched up at Mr. The Cadaver's feet, holding the sharp scissors in his other hand. "I, like, so don't want to do this," he said. Since they had begun dating, he had been infected with Amanda's diction. She had made no mention to Henry of the message he had left when he was drunk; Earnest hadn't spoken to him for a few days.

Henry was sitting on the counter, staring at the floor. Amanda stood next to him, and facing the wall so that the others couldn't hear, she said to him, "Are you all right?"

His face had begun to feel puffy, but he was afraid to check it in the mirror. "I'm fine," he said, "Ready for Thanksgiving."

"Are you going to your parents' house?" she asked.

He had forgotten that they had sent him a ticket, and that he was supposed to leave that afternoon. In about four hours.

"Yes," he said.

"You don't look fine," she said.

Earnest was jealous that she was talking to him. "Who wants to do this?" he said more loudly, holding up the intestine and waving the scissors.

"There won't be stool except in the colon, if that's what you're worried about," Eric said with a sneer. He was sitting on a stool with his hands on one knee; he had been pouting since they had started the abdominal cavity; there was nothing complicated in there for him to dissect. He would be happy again when they started on the penis, after Thanksgiving.

Earnest snipped a hole in the intestine and checked. Satisfied, he cut windows into the duodenum, ileum, and jejunum.

"I know what's on your mind," Amanda said to Henry, still watching Earnest.

So she worked for Mr. Landry too, Henry thought. He wasn't surprised.

"You're bothered about your girlfriend," she said, "Eric told me. I feel so, so bad for you."

Oh yes–the teenage junkie joke. Henry said, "I would feel bad for me too."

Earnest held up the right colon, a gray sausage as big around as his forearm until its contents sludged away from his hand. "I'm not doing this," he said, "Henry, come do this."

He was joking, Henry knew, but Amanda had made him self-conscious. He hopped up from the counter, put on some gloves, and took the colon and scissors from him.

"Finally, he does something," Eric muttered.

"What am I supposed to do?" Henry said.

Earnest traced a line on the colon with his finger. "Slit it open here. You're supposed to pass a probe through the ileo-cecal valve."

He nicked the colon; it was tougher than it looked, and a little slimey to allow it to slip away from insult. He thought the inside was coated with green mucous. He pushed it away with his finger to find the valve, and when he pushed the slime away it separated in clumps. Mucus wouldn't separate like that. This was green shit, like a baby's. Baby shit that smelled like cadaver cologne: born to die. Born dead.

He stood up with a hand over his mouth; his throat bucked. Eric and Amanda and Earnest were all watching his face, concerned, but smiling. "Henry, do you feel okay?" Eric asked.

He ran to the toilet sink and retched. Gradually, applause and cheers came from the other students. No one had puked the whole semester.

When he stood up, Amanda said, "I want to see you change a diaper! You're going to be the cutest dad!"

* * *

His body carried his brain after the other students and sat it down to watch the memorial service. About half of his class attended; about ninety percent would be present for the refreshments afterward. The ceremony would consist of inspirational readings by students so inspired, followed by a procession of candle-holding first-years, one from each lab table. A folding table in the front of the room held rows of unlit candles, one for each cadaver. Each student lit one of the candles with his or her own. No one knew what this meant. At the last minute, the freshman Cadaver Ceremony Committee had asked the previous year's committee what they had done. So it had happened for years.

The course director welcomed them. Two students read from the Bible; Kahlil Gibran was sandwiched between them, read by that long-haired guy. A black woman student sang "Amazing Grace" while the candles filed past. A few female students cried.

Henry saw that Eric had changed to a shirt, tie, and blazer—one of a few so dressed. As Eric touched flame-to-wick, Henry thought through a fog, it's right for him to do it. He loved Mr. The Cadaver.

The reception was over. He held a tuna fish finger sandwich. Iago Pachary, that crazy guy from high school, walked by with friends. He handed Henry a bag of sour cream and onion Zapp's potato chips. "You want these?" he asked.

* * *

He was on his way home, on Canal Street, when he realized that he had forgotten the chips at school, most likely on a urinal in the bathroom. He ducked into Woolworth's to replace the chips. But he was looking over a bin of bandannas before he remembered why he was there.

He found the chips on a clip rack, and remembered the flavor. He held the bag in both hands.

What am I doing here, he thought, who cares about potato chips.

He didn't feel like he might cry, but he put one hand over his eyes and stood very still. When he lowered his hand, he saw one of the store clerks staring at him. He put the chips back under their clip and walked out of the store.

Hours later, he sat at his desk. Studying notes was out of the question; he read the same two lines over and over. He opened his Netter, and held his head in his hands, and did not allow himself to look up from the watercolors of flayed people.

If Ronaldo were a vampire who had been staked, and Henry were his hunchback, he would pull out the stake and offer his own throat to bring him back. If Ronaldo had donated a kidney, he would have accepted it and let it filter his own blood. Keeping just an organ alive would be better by far than this.

He wasn't yet sad, or even sure that he missed him. He just did not feel right. Coated. If Ronaldo were alive, he wouldn't have this coat. He flipped through the abdomen and leg again and again and again, watching the legs rot away and grow back, depending on which way the pages turned.

Perhaps he was worried that Larry Frank or Mr. Landry was going to kill him; that was likely part of it. He stacked some empty beer and Coke cans inside the door to the street. If the door opened, it would knock over the cans, and he would hear. And if he heard, he had to be able to do something about it. He unlocked the trunk and loaded his shotgun.

He went back to the Netter Atlas with the gun on his hip. It's weight made him feel better. He flipped to the section on the back and arm. Only three months ago, he had been studying this. He had studied this in Hines's house while Paolo was being buried. He had already forgotten the names of these muscles.

The phone rang. He let the answering machine get it. It was his father, calling from the Tampa airport, wondering why he wasn't there.

He managed to smile at that. "I knew I forgot something," he said aloud.

He decided that he might as well sleep. It was 7:40.

* * *

For two hours he lay in the dark, blinking at the ceiling now and again. He remembered an afternoon in high school. He and Ronaldo were in detention, for what he couldn't remember. They were to sit up straight and stare straight ahead for an hour. Movement would earn them another detention.

Ronaldo was sitting two desks ahead of him and to the left. Henry could move his eyes without drawing the attention of the disciplinarian. He noted that Ronaldo was the only one in detention with his shoes shined; he knew Ronaldo had done it on his own, without being told.

He sat up in bed. The apartment was so quiet that it might have been snowing outside.

He couldn't study, and he couldn't sleep. Acting normal would require one or the other. Tomorrow, his parents would call again, and he would have to make up an excuse for missing the flight. The thought made him unbearably tired. But he couldn't sleep.

How many times would he have to lie about this over the coming years. He could never be happy with a secret like this. He guessed that he hadn't been happy for some time, or he would have never gone looking for thrills selling LSD.

He sat at his desk: *Re: feel better: what to do*

Drink—it had worked when Catherine left him. But the thought of leaving the apartment to buy beer was just too tiresome.

Suicide

He looked at the word, still attached to the ball of the pen, and looked at the hand that had written it. His hand.

Why not. His closest friend was dead, and that friend hadn't been so close after all. And Catherine was off in Michigan.

Resolved: suicide.

Once it's written, no turning back.

*　　　　*　　　　*

He was sitting on the edge of the bed with the shotgun in his lap, belly up. He pumped out a shell—no reason, he just liked the sound—and it rolled under the bed. He reached for it; the crimping looked like Mr. The Cadaver's anus. He would not die by anus.

From the trunk he took his AR-15, the M16 twin. But the AR-15 had no tragedy to it. Stamped steel and plastic—it might as well be a stereo. And people see the magazine hanging from the middle and think "assault rifle."

"Better him than me," his landlord would think on finding his body. Anybody who didn't know guns would think only a nut on the brink of rampage would own a gun like that.

If I ever kill myself with a rifle, he thought, it will have to be a .30-aught that's brought down a deer every winter. The strap would be cowhide, tooled with an eagle. Now there's a tragic gun.

The Glock was in pieces in the Bayou St. John mud. That left his .38. He didn't feel like using his .38. He didn't feel like killing himself anymore, actually. Why? The answer came to him as quietly as the phantom snow outside.

Were Ronaldo a ghost, he'd have shown himself by now. He might be in heaven; Henry had no proof of heaven. But years ago, Ronaldo had sat in detention with his shoes shined. He knew that; he needed no proof.

Ronaldo was dead. Without oxygen his brain cells could not keep the extracellular calcium out, and out the cells went, billion by billion. But Ronaldo approximated life in Henry's memory. Years would pass, and he would forget Ronaldo's face like he was forgetting Catherine's. But he could give Ronaldo a few more years. A few beat none.

Ronaldo's heaven was Henry's hippocampus. The hippocampus in cross-section is shaped like a sea-horse. Paolo rode on Hines's. Wait—was it the hippocampus, the part of the brain that remembers? Neuroscience was next semester. If he blew out his brain, Ronaldo would die again.

Hines remembered Paolo as a good boy. Henry had a sack of drug money in his bathtub's side that said he had been a bad one. If Henry hadn't stolen the money, Hines would know that, and have a lesser lodge for Paolo in his head.

He unloaded the shotgun and locked it away. Tomorrow, Thanksgiving, he would work on Ronaldo's heaven.

25

Ronaldo's mother lived by a pumping station off of Power Boulevard. After a hard rain, a headache smell seeped up from the floor. That's the way she described it: "It smells like a head cold." Once, she complained to the Parish. Two men in street clothes held clipboards in her living room and sniffed. She never saw them again.

He had caught a cab out here; he was walking toward the front door, wondering if the living room would smell after all the recent rain. Today was clear, and cold enough that a deep breath hurt. A police car came up the street, slowing down as it went by.

It was a New Orleans police car, out here in Jefferson Parish. Larry Frank was driving, with his elbow out the window. He waved. There was another cop next to him, a black man, reading a magazine.

Henry waved back. He got the message: keep your mouth shut.

He never intended otherwise. He rang the doorbell. His finger was still on the button when Ronaldo's mother opened the door. "Where's Ronaldo," she said. She was angry, not worried.

"Hello, Ms. Pitero," Henry said. She didn't look as old as she had when he was seventeen; she wasn't much older than that when she had Ronaldo. Her hair looked better black, and short like this; she had a beauty mark by her mouth that he knew had not been there when he had last seen her.

"Hello, Henry," she sing-songed. She said, "Ronaldo's going to his paw-paw's today. Where is he." "Paw-paw" was Metairie talk for grandfather.

"I thought all his grandparents were dead," Henry said, "May I come in?"

She stepped aside for him. Orange-peel perfume came from her when she moved. "Those are my parents who's dead," she said.

The living room stunk—yes, like nasopharyngeal mucus. "We never got the smell fixed," she said, picking up a can of air-freshener printed with red flowers. The stuff looked like flour coming out of the can; it settled to the carpet and vanished. He sat on the sofa, made of faked red lacquer to look Japanese. The room was just as he remembered it, but the television had gotten bigger and turned black. The table lamp in the corner was on; she liked to keep the rest of the house dark.

She was wearing a floppy white turtleneck sweater and black leggings. It seemed a strangely shapely thing to wear for Thanksgiving dinner; her new boyfriend was likely invited. She sat across from him, crossed her legs, and caught the sweater when it rode up. When she was single, she moped around in a white bathrobe.

Even through his grief-coat, her legs were distracting him. She could be my mother, he thought; I need a girlfriend. Soon. But he was also glad that something had penetrated the coat.

"We're going to his daddy's daddy's house," she explained, "Mr. Pitero senior is a dear, dear friend of mine, especially since his wife passed." On the table next to her was an ashtray, nose-dived with her skinny cigarettes. Fresh lipstick marked the morning's butts. Smoking roughened most voices, but it seemed to have made hers even more shrill. She winked at him, "I sometimes think I married the wrong Pitero."

"Well, he's single now, right?" Henry said.

She turned an ear toward him—surely he hadn't said that.

"I mean," he said, blushing, "At least you still have the name."

She didn't think it was funny. He didn't think it was funny.

She stiffened and raised her chin. "Henry, I know that the only reason you're here is because Ronaldo sent you with an excuse. Just make me laugh. Sometimes he still comes up with good ones."

"He left the country with some girl," Henry said, "I don't think he's coming back."

She looked at him with heavy-lidded eyes, sighed, and pulled a pack of cigarettes out of the sofa. She placed it by the ashtray; she never smoked around non-smokers. "Was this girl pregnant?" she asked.

Henry looked at the gold cross she had dangling on a chain from the ledge of her turtleneck. "Yes," he said.

"The last girl he knocked up," she said, "I paid to get rid of it. I'm too young to be a grandma. I'm always going to be too young. If he's in jail, tell him to call his father. Again." She gave him a bored, smug smirk, "But if he's in jail, it was probably his daddy that put him there."

"She couldn't get an abortion," Henry said, "She's Brazilian. Real Catholic."

"When did that stop anybody?"

"South America's different."

"Ronaldo doesn't speak Spanish."

"They speak Portugese."

"Henry. Heart," she said it like there was another "h" in the middle of the word, "you're embarrassing yourself."

Henry crossed his legs and folded his arms. "He wanted to get rid of it," he said, "and she probably would have. But her family wouldn't have it."

She smiled at him, folded her arms and crossed her legs like his—she would play along, for now.

"He's really in love with her," he said, "he's so in love. They met at the casino."

"It won't last," she said.

"She was losing all this money and didn't care. That's how he noticed her. Her family's rich." He remembered a documentary Catherine had taken him to, about labor exploitation in Brazil. "They own liquid crystal mines. She's an undergraduate at Tulane."

He remembered an Italian film Catherine had made him see: "She missed her period and called her aunt in Rome. The family is so big that her aunt is only four years older, and they can talk. But the aunt wasn't old enough for this, and too Catholic. It got back to her father. He flew up here and wanted to meet Ronaldo. Ronaldo wanted me to go, so that he could have someone else with him who spoke English.

"Ms. Pitero, you should have seen this. He took us to dinner at the Windsor Court. He had his wife with him and two bodyguards. The bodyguards sat on either side of Ronaldo. The mother liked Ronaldo. He was dressed as well as the father. But she couldn't speak English. The father spoke perfect English, but the only thing he said was 'What year were you born?' to Ronaldo. The father bought a bottle of wine from that year.

"Nobody talked. When they did, they just spoke Portugese. Ronaldo wouldn't look up from his plate; they were big bodyguards. I just smiled as much as I could. Only the mom smiled back. The dad talked a little to his daughter. I was sitting next to her. She started to cry, but didn't get up. So Ronaldo said to me, 'What do I do, Hank?'

"I said, 'You're supposed to marry her.'

"So he said, 'Consuela, will you marry me?' The mother understood that. She started crying, she was so happy. The next day, they got Ronaldo a passport and a ticket."

Ms. Pitero's smile had fallen. "Is she pretty?" she asked.

"Beautiful," Henry said.

"And if she's at Tulane," she said, "she must be smart."

"Yes," he said, "She was pre-med. Now she's pre-mom."

She laughed. "So Ronaldo has a beautiful, smart, rich girl, whose dad will set him up, and he won't bring her to meet me? Even before all this happened? Henry, I don't believe a word of it."

This was the last stitch: he had to pull hard enough to tighten it all up; pull too hard and the story would fall apart. "Nicole," he said, "She's black."

She said, "How black."

"She's pretty dark."

Her fingers played with one another, trying to feel their way to a cigarette. She laughed again, but this time it sounded like a cough. "What do you call a black spic? Spigger?" she said, "Now there's going to be a black spic Italian."

She put a hand over her eyes. Her chin quivered. She stood up and hurried out of the room.

"Ms. Pitero?" Henry called.

She came back with a roll of toilet paper, dabbing furiously at her eyes. "I'm not crying because she's black," she said, standing over him, "That doesn't matter to me, if he's happy and in love. He should have known that. You should have told him."

Henry looked up at her. "I tried."

"You should have tried harder," she said, "I get none of that money? Who takes care of me? What a day to find out, too. I want you to get out."

He shot to his feet and opened the front door. She was right behind him, ready to slam it. Before she did, she said, "I hope you never have children. You'll be a terrible father."

*   *   *

She would guess the truth, after a time. But for that time, she would believe her son was alive.

Lying to her hadn't made him feel much better; not as much as he had hoped. But it had scrubbed away a layer of the numbness, enough that now he was annoyed at Ronaldo for being dead. And he found himself believing in God again, just for someone to smoulder at.

At home, he pulled the money out of the wall of his tub. I'm sick of taking care of you, Paolo, he thought, It's time you moved on.

He put on the coat and tie that had not yet arrived during orientation, and stuffed the breast pockets with $300 of Paolo's money. He walked up the middle of Canal Street, where the buses ran, and kept his eyes open for Larry Frank. He saw only a distant cop car. Almost everything was closed except for the casino, and behind it, the Windsor Court.

He had to wait hours for a table. He spent sixty dollars at the bar, sitting in a blue chair more comfortable than his bed. Horsemen jumped a fence on the far wall. Families, one running all the way down to a great-great grandchild, wanted pictures in front of the painting. He was happy to take the pictures for them. He imagined that they wondered why he was alone, or who he was waiting for. He pretended he was a cardiothoracic surgeon: no time for family when you're stitching up hearts.

Then the CT surgeon got a table and ate sturgeon bisque. He didn't care that this wasn't Thanksgiving food. Mushrooms, flash-fried spinach, a lobster. A burst pastry, spilling fruit. He wanted a bottle of white wine from his birth year, but it was too expensive. He got one from the year he finished high school.

He handed over Paolo's cash, swaying on his feet by the table. The waiter didn't snicker as he paid in ones. He imagined standing waist deep in a calm river, and shoving the bills off in stacks into the water. It was a Brazilian river. Ronaldo and his bride lived within a day's drive.

He didn't think money would really float like that. No one will ever know about the money, Paolo. I'll blow the rest and you'll be clean.

THE END

About the Author

Jacques S. Whitecloud was born and raised in New Orleans. He studied writing at Cornell University, and obtained an MFA from University of Montana. He graduated from Tulane Medical School in 1998.

Printed in the United States
31502LVS00002B/145

9 780595 175222

The Sin Eater

New Orleans: Henry Marrier's been good too long. A medical school geek, closet gun freak, and crime buff, he's tired of the books and toeing the line. Ronaldo is his best friend from high school. Ex drug dealer and current mortician's apprentice, he's got work for Henry: guard the houses of the dead while the funeral's going on. Don't steal from them yourself. Especially not drugs, drug money, and evidence of other sin. But Henry's been good too long, and being bad is much easier than he would ever dream—or want. Faked funerals. Corpse mutilation. Deadly strippers, a crop of eyeballs, and murder. How did he get here, again? More importantly, how can he get back?

www.iuniverse.com